D0807911

PRAISE FOR BRYAN SMITH:

"DEPRAVED lives up to its name in the most brutal and visceral way. Sort of like a roller-coaster ride... but with battery acid and razor blades on the handlebars. Smith's most effective and merciless work to date!" -- Ronald Kelly, author of *Fear*

"This is a classic tale of a small-town haunting." -- *Fangoria* on *Soultaker*

"Bryan Smith is a force to be reckoned with!" -- Douglas Clegg, author of *The Attraction*

"A superb mix of action, characterization, humor, multiple storylines, sex, violence and an unflagging pace. Impressive." -- Cemetery Dance Weekly on *House of Blood*

"A feast of good old-fashioned horror. Don't pass this one up!" -- Brain Keene, author of *The Rising*

"House of Blood is a unique and riveting excursion into modern horror. Here's an author exploding onto the genre!" -- Edward Lee, author of *House Infernal*

"The pacing is dead on and the horror is exceptional." -- *Dread Central* on *The Freakshow*

PRAISE FOR SAMANTHA KOLESNIK

"This is a novella that is worthy of attention, and cements Kolesnik's already well-earned reputation as a storyteller to watch." - Waylon Jordan, *iHorror.com*, on *Waif*

BELETH STATION

SAMANTHA KOLESNIK

BRYAN SMITH

Cover by Matthew Revert

matthewrevert.com

Troy, NY

CLASH Books

clashbooks.com

Publicity: Clashmediabooks@gmail.com

ISBN: 978-1955904834

To Lex Quinn and Michael Lombardo, whom I know would undoubtedly have my back if I ever landed in a town like Beleth Station. In so many ways, you both were with me the entire summer in which this book was written, encouraging me to take risks and letting me know that if I fell or broke, you'd be there to put me back together. Though I've crafted many characters in my lifetime of writing, I could never create anyone on the page with hearts as big as yours.

And so this one's for you, my dear friends.

Samantha Kolesnik

BELETH STATION: A NIGHT TO REMEMBER

SAMANTHA KOLESNIK

CHAPTER 1
THE NIGHT BEFORE

A MASKED, machete-wielding maniac chased a petite woman on the television set. It wasn't long before he caught up to his prey and hacked her to pieces with faintly sexual fervor. Blood sprayed everywhere, but it didn't bother Krista. She saw the gushing, spraying fluids as something else entirely.

Krista wasn't thinking about the film. She'd more or less put it on to have noise in the background, an excuse she could give Tom for how she was spending her time. If she had something audible upstairs—whether it was the treadmill or TV—he was less likely to bother her.

And she didn't want to be bothered—not tonight.

Her phone lit up and she immediately checked it. It was a furniture ad from a mailing list she'd unsubscribed from many times over.

The disappointment was crushing, and somehow also simultaneously exhilarating. She *wanted* to want. This ebb and flow of anticipation for messages from Nick sent her thoughts in bizarre, exciting directions. The longing, the waiting, the preoccupied thoughts—it all aroused her.

But, far more than anything she saw on the television set, her newfound energy terrified her—embarrassed her even. It was *possession*. Something deep inside of her had to be exorcized and Krista was apprehensive about what that would entail.

She slinked upstairs to her bedroom and pushed all of the hanging oversized sweaters to the side. Hanging in the back, pressed up against the wall, was a black silky negligee she hadn't worn in years. Tom and Krista's townhouse, which they'd shared for the past ten years of their marriage, held lots of little forgotten gems like that black silky negligee. Caches of Krista's life that she'd stored away forever—*or so she thought.*

Krista pulled the negligee off the hanger and held it up in front of her full-length mirror. This was her room, the one room she had all for herself, but still—she found her eyes wandering to the open door, and straining to hear if Tom was coming up the stairs. Even though they'd been married for ten years, the thought of him seeing her naked felt violatory. Sometimes it couldn't be avoided, and he always made remarks.

Tom and his remarks...

Krista eased the door shut and quietly turned the lock. She pulled down her black leggings and slid her sweater up over her head. Her naked reflection stared back at her in the full-length mirror, and she looked at it with a sense of voyeuristic wonder. This was one of her favorite games, and she hadn't played in so long. There were many nights, in fact, when Krista thought she'd never have that kind of voyeuristic buzz again. The curve of her narrow waist, the freckles beneath her collarbone, which decorated the slope of her breasts, the way her brown hair just lightly danced on the skin of her shoulders—she loved to look at all of it and wonder which parts Nick would like best. She imagined how his face might change expression when she disrobed for him later. How his facial muscles would slacken, unconsciously, as he drank in the same pieces of her that she was gazing at now. It made her *want* again.

There was one piece of her she wasn't sure Nick would like, though. Timidly—reverently, even—her fingers eased down to her inner right thigh. She turned her leg outward so that she could see the oblong burn mark in the mirror. Her little secret—an 'X' marks the spot in the soft, tender inner flesh of her thigh, high up enough that a mini dress would still cover it. The most recent burn had begun scarring over, but it was still red and raw. The skin felt kind of sandpapery beneath her fingers, like an old sunburn just beginning to heal. An outsider might assume it was a mistake.

It was no mistake. And she was itching to open the wound again.

She could hear Tom's footsteps coming up the stairs. She hurriedly threw her sweater back on, inside out, and unlocked the door as soon as she heard the handle rattling.

"Why was the door locked?"

She stared up at Tom, who blocked the doorway, and suddenly she felt all too aware of her small size. If she were bolder, maybe she would've just shoved past him and walked away, but instead she shrank backward into the center of her room, and tried to pull the sweater hem down to her thighs.

"Krista. You're not having one of your little daydreams again, are you?"

Before she could protest, Tom grabbed her, pinning her arms to her sides in one hold. With his other arm, he pried her legs apart to expose the burn mark on her thigh. Krista thought about trying to fight him off, but it was too hard emotionally, too reminiscent of her childhood. Her body went slack like a doll's, and her thoughts drifted somewhere else in the room, as if they were balled up in the corner of the ceiling looking down at Tom forcing her legs apart.

"Good," he whispered into her ear, satisfied that the burn was healing.

When he whispered, his lips grazed her earlobe and it was then, when she feared he might try to do more, that she finally said something.

"I told my mother I'd call her." This was a lie. Mostly, she wondered if Nick finally messaged her. Did he change his mind about picking her up later that evening, after Tom went to bed? She hoped not.

"Your mom can wait," Tom said, his hand moving up under her sweater.

"No."

Krista got one of her arms loose and moved it up under her sweater to grab his arm. There was tension as she tried to pull his hand out from under, but finally he yielded.

She didn't have to look at him to know he was angry. It was

there, floating in the air between them—the shared knowledge that their marriage would only improve inasmuch as Krista was willing to let him touch her. So long as she didn't let him do what he wanted with her body, it was clear they'd remain in a perpetual stalemate, and that she'd be subjected to his myriad unkindnesses.

There was a time, early in their marriage, when she could more easily summon the kind of mentally-distracted passivity required to endure her husband's advances, but she'd found that the more often she played dead, the more often she *felt* dead. Besides, Tom wasn't satisfied with Krista just laying there, an object at his disposal. He wanted her to perform to a level where he could believe she *wanted* to be his object. Krista certainly had practice in this kind of performance—and for other men before Tom, men she'd had more emotional invest-ment in pleasing—it could be fun, even. A guessing game of which buttons to push, a playful let's-try-and-see.

But with Tom, everything physical was degrading. Sharing her body with him felt like letting something she loved be broken repeatedly. The same parts of her that she had just looked at in the mirror so curiously could expediently be soiled by Tom's unwanted hands—and all of her newfound voyeuristic gazing would be gone in an instant.

And so their marriage, by and large, had become an endless game of advance and retreat, with Krista often being cornered in the end. When it got to the point where it was clear that she'd only have sex with him if physically forced to, Tom had begun controlling other aspects of her life. It was a slow, painful effort to wear her down until she would acquiesce.

And if she didn't acquiesce…

There was one place Tom couldn't touch, and it was far more intimate than anything between her legs—only Tom was too dim to understand that.

Krista's imagination was the piece of her, above all else, that she held most dear. It was the place that was all her own, which is why whenever she put words to her thoughts, she'd take a lighter to them and watch them slowly burn. No one would ever know the depths of her fantasies, or the limits of her mind.

The burn scar on her thigh was the only proof Krista's secret world existed at all.

The burn mark that Tom wanted to erase.

It was that secret, intimate place deep within her thoughts that she hid in now, as Tom had decided he wasn't going to yield after all.

The weight of his body on top of her was so heavy that it felt futile to resist, though some part of her knew she did. It was simply too hard to remember how long or hard she fought when this happened; the only proof was the bruises that would doubtlessly form on her wrists after, the painful ache between her legs, the perpetually invasive impression her body held of having been intruded.

His breath, hot and close to her face, got fast and shallow. She hoped this meant he was almost done. His humiliating endearments—whispered close to her ear—came into her mind and were quickly, embarrassingly compartmentalized to some inner chest only she held the key to. That's where much of Tom resided for Krista, locked away in a place too painful to share.

It wasn't the first time Tom had raped Krista.
But it would be the last.

CHAPTER 2
LITTLE CRITTERS

PRETTY GIRLS. He knew that much.

Not that it did much for him—the prettiness.

The one with the smaller tits was Jenny. She had those tiny ones—so small she didn't bother wearing a bra. The cool morning air in the Pennsylvania mountains made her nipples hard through her sweater, and he'd spent a few hours last night imagining what they'd look like in those sterile specimen jars the doctor made you piss in.

No need for a scalpel; Erel could bite them right off.

Suck on them like jawbreakers, and let them slowly melt in his mouth.

It was Jenny who saw him first that morning. He'd come around the back of their campsite, quiet as a mouse until he *wasn't*. Jenny's wide-eyed shock at seeing him behind her, and the way her skittish body shivered involuntarily—it was the first time Erel's dick had gotten hard in weeks. The way women's bodies shook like that when they were afraid reminded him of the reels his granddad used to watch in the garage.

Erel had never made a woman cum—what the fuck was the point—but he'd seen it plenty of times projected on the wall of that old garage. The way their thighs tensed and their eyes rolled back. Funny little critters.

What he didn't understand about other men was they didn't realize women did the same thing when afraid, only... *better.*

If Tom, Dick and Harry liked how a woman convulsed getting off, they were missing out. Because a woman's body did all sorts of fun things when it was getting cut open. There were so many unique ways you could make a bird's wings twitch. Erel knew. He wasn't no dummy, as his mom had liked to say.

No sooner was the blood flowing to his dick, though, than it stopped. Everything went soft again—soft as Jenny's face slipping from animal fear into dumb familiarity.

"You scared me!"

Her shrill, uncertain voice brought the other little thing out from the tent. *Carrie.* A bit stronger, that one. Red curls hanging around her shoulders. Her strength would make her harder to put down. It wasn't just her strength that had Erel take note, though. It was that the little thing had her hackles up around Erel all the time. If it was anything that convinced Erel he was meant to hunt, it was that.

That no matter where he went, those little bitties got their hairs on edge around him. If they weren't meant to be his prey, why the hell did they act like it?

"Didn't mean to scare you," Erel said.

He let his eyes drop just long enough to Jenny's tits so that she'd notice and have to react. Sure enough, she brought an arm up over them, squishing the small mounds of flesh underneath. So small. He could cut into the grain or against it.

Carrie took a few steps closer to her friend. They always thought they were safer in numbers. What little critters didn't understand was getting close like that, hip to hip, just made them easier to control in the end.

Erel let the silence hang in the air. He could taste their curiosity as it turned from mere question to suspicion, and when it was finally clear they were doubting he was there for any good reason, it was then that he deigned to speak—

"Just checking in on y'all, is all. I'd want someone to do the same for my daughters."

It was Carrie who responded. Without a single hint of a

smile, she gestured around to their tidy campsite, "I think we're good."

Jenny, emboldened by her friend and feeling safe in the crook of Carrie's arm, no doubt, repeated this in more polite, defensive words, "Yeah we appreciate it, but we have everything we need."

Erel nodded and tugged the brim of his hat down.

"Well, just be careful, is all. I'd hate to see anything happen."

He let the 'anything' float into the air where he was sure it would swirl around in the backs of their minds come nightfall, long after they'd thought they'd seen the last of him.

That uncertainty was a pleasure they could all enjoy, because Erel wasn't sure what he was going to do to those pretty little things just yet.

Deciding was half the fun.

CHAPTER 3
NOW OR NEVER

KRISTA LET THE HOT WATER—SO hot, it almost scalded—run over her body. She'd been crying, but she was trying her best to stop. What she craved right now, more than anything, was to hurt herself.

But Tom, who was now asleep downstairs on the couch, had taken all of her lighters weeks ago. She'd buy new ones and somehow, he'd always find them.

She just wanted to feel anything against her skin that was of her own volition, something to make her feel back in her body, a body she could pretend had never been taken from her. Right now she was so deeply detached in the dark recesses of a consciousness outside of herself, that she longed to be grounded in her own flesh again—to be *present*. She told herself it was over, that it would never happen again, but still her only coping mechanism persisted and wouldn't let her come back to feeling one with her own flesh. Krista knew it was this very thing—this splitting into a consciousness that disassociated from her body —that had kept her alive for so long, but at the same time, she hated it. She badly wanted to be able to look at herself, and feel herself, without having the shameful intrusions of things she didn't want enter her thoughts.

And behind the desire to feel pain, she had another thought which scared her more than the thought of slicing her thigh or burning a new mark.

It was a sad little desire that she didn't know what to make of.

Krista really wanted to be held. It was this embarrassing desire, to just be held and to be able to cry, that made her finally break down.

Because Krista realized, in all her history—childhood included—she had never been able to do that. To feel safe. To let go, and to know it was going to be ok.

To be truly vulnerable.

Someone always wanted something from her in the end.

What did Nick want? That question was at the forefront of her thoughts as she finally turned off the water and stepped out to dry herself. She dried off her body first and then wrapped the towel around her hair in a twist the way she'd learned to do back in grade school. Mercifully, the memory came back to her then, of a friend at summer camp showing her how to twist the towel around her long locks so that it would stay up in a comfortable poof. The thought of it made her relax—it had been one of those small rites of passages, a soft detail that girls shared with other girls to make their lives a little more comfortable.

It was a nice memory, and it brought a smile to Krista's face.

She took it as a sign that what she was doing wasn't so bad. Sure, she was running out on Tom, and she knew there'd be some form of hell to pay for it later, but Krista didn't fear what would come after.

As she slid black leggings over her freshly shaved legs, she grappled with the consideration that she might not come back at all. That she didn't *have* to come back ever.

There were so many things of hers throughout the house—possessions that had defined or consumed her life at various stages. None of it mattered now.

Because if it didn't work out with Nick, it was game over for Krista Mabry.

Krista packed light. She hadn't told Nick anything about her plans because she didn't want to burden him with undue pressure. That was so like Krista—to keep everything bottled up out of fear of being burdensome. As far as Nick knew, they were going away for a weekend to be together. They hadn't fucked yet, and she was sure, on some level, he was hoping this would be the weekend. It was her idea, after all, to pick out the cheapest cabin they could find in the shitty, has-been Poconos region. To get away to the remotest place that was still within a day or night's drive from both of them.

Most things between her and Nick were her idea. It wasn't that he wasn't receptive—he was *very* receptive. But he let her take the lead on how she chose to get close and when. He seemed to sense on some level that she was like a wounded animal, and so he more often than not held his hand out palm up, with little expectation.

She packed a small backpack full of the usual staples—her hairbrush, a change of clothes, a few pairs of socks, her cell phone charger, and a full bottle of sleeping pills. The pills rattled in the bag even after she zipped it up. They seemed to call to her, *Just In Case.*

It was cold outside this time of year in Pennsylvania, and she knew it would be even colder up in the mountains, but Krista didn't want to bother with a coat. She was wearing a slinky, black dress that felt great against her skin. It was soft and clung to her breasts in a swooping neckline that showed off her cleavage and all of the freckles that dotted her breasts. She felt comfortable in it. It was the sort of thing she never wore around Tom—a relic of Krista-of-old.

There was a pad of paper on the fridge that she and Tom used for shopping list reminders. She tore a sheet off and thought about what to write. With the pen in her hand, the fact that she was really leaving felt more immediate.

After contemplating niceties and flowery sentiments that would've felt disingenuous, Krista settled on:

"Tom,

I'm leaving you. Don't look for me.

Krista."

It felt woefully inadequate, and at the same time, it was all he deserved.

She looped one strap of her backpack around her arm, grabbed her purse, and tiptoed down the stairs to the front door.

Easing the door open without waking Tom, who was asleep on the couch in his office down the hall, exhilarated Krista. It was the last obstacle to freedom.

As she stepped out into the chilly Pennsylvania autumn air, a spider's web glinting in the porchlight above her, she let it sink in.

She was free.

At the turn of the road four houses down, she saw the blink of Nick's headlights.

It was now or never.

CHAPTER 4
SWEET NOTHINGS

THEIR SPECIAL NIGHT HAD ARRIVED. He was going to make those little girls feel out of control. Make their eyes roll back, and their insides wet. He tried not to think about it too hard because he needed to keep his head about him.

Needless to say, he was about to give them a ride *he* wouldn't forget.

Erel had his legs stretched out in front of him, and was propped back behind the treeline on one hand, with the other stroking his Buck 110. He liked to lock it in place and unlock it, so that he could see the glint of the metal in the moonlight.

There was a stirring inside of the tent. Ripples in the fabric. It had to be Jenny. She got up several times during the night to piss, something Erel had tried to get off on and failed. But he did love to watch her pale ass in the light of the moon.

She squatted like a dog about ten feet from the tent, and he could see that it was hard for her to relax enough to let it all out. But then, slowly—at first a trickle, and then a stream, little Jenny finally relaxed enough to relieve herself.

After she was finished, she shook her ass just above the grass until she thought she was dry enough to go join Carrie inside the tent. There was something canine-like about how she did it, and it had made Erel surprisingly hard the first night he saw her shake her ass dry. But it wasn't enough—just a fleeting rush of blood, a hint of what he *could* feel, if only he could get inside her warm, tight throat.

He liked seeing her act like a dog and he wanted to know what it was going to take to make her bark.

Maybe he'd keep Jenny for a little while. Teach her a trick or two, and make her beg for her dinner. Get her hungry enough and desperate enough that she'd do *anything* and wag her ass like she liked it.

Erel did have a liking for dogs. That much was something he was always sure of about himself, the one thin thread of identity he was satisfied enough with keeping.

As a kid, he'd slept with dogs plenty, and he could smell the scent of a bitch's sweat from a mile away. Granddad had put Erel in the kennel when he was a child, and it was fair to say he'd learned a lot from it. There was something about being forced to eat out of a dog bowl that had awoken something in him long ago. At first, it was humiliating—getting his nose shoved in his own shit—but then it rewired Erel into something else entirely.

He wasn't a dog anymore. He'd just been raised like one.

Wasn't exactly human, neither, as far as he could tell.

The Buck 110.

One of the few things Erel had kept from Granddad after the old bastard finally died. It was a short blade and it wasn't the sharpest. It required a lot of maintenance to keep its edge, but what Erel liked about it was the weight. It was small enough to easily conceal, and yet still had a good heft in his hand. It felt more solid than holding his dick, and turned him on twice as much.

Granddad had always called it a pussy blade, probably because Erel had taken such a liking to it, but Erel had to admit, he'd made the 3.75" blade live up to the insult. It *had* been inside a fair amount of pussy—had seen more pussy, in fact, than most men could ever dream of.

He was also aware that the blade he was holding was coveted. There were many men in blue and black, men with badges, and men with daughters of their own, who were seeking Erel's Buck 110, even as Erel watched the tent fabric in front of him come to a complete still. Jenny was probably back in her sleeping bag. He wondered if Carrie roused at all when Jenny had opened the tent flap, or if the redhead was out cold. It was easier to get a deep sleep in the chilly autumn air up in the mountains. Once the body got warm, sleep settled in like a heavy blanket all its own.

Erel would wait, but it wouldn't be much longer now. The night was ripening and it had been some time since he'd had his last release. There once was a time when Erel had envied other men, especially when Erel was in his teenage years. Neighborhood kids would share their fathers' magazines, pilfered from bathroom cabinets and top bedroom closet shelves, and they'd stare at the glossy fold-outs of soft, shaved cunts like they'd never seen anything so intoxicating. At that time, Erel did recall wanting to be excited by it like the other guys, but it did nothing for him. All he could do was mutter something in imitation.

Any time he saw something others found beautiful, the only way he could get excited by it at all was to picture it degraded.

Jenny had done Erel more favors than she probably realized. Her nighttime trips outside the tent made it certain that hearing the zipper on the entrance wouldn't immediately alarm the other half of the pair. If Jenny woke up first, Erel was positive he could easily overpower her. It wouldn't take much to render her slight form submissive. It wasn't just the shape of their bodies or muscle tone that mattered in this regard. Erel had been doing this long enough to know that attitude factored in more heavily. The way Jenny made herself smile and laugh when around him, even though Erel knew she was uncomfortable, told him everything he needed to know about how she'd be in a fight. Carrie, on the other hand, always looked him in the eye on the brief occasions he'd made himself known. She was more assertive, and therefore more of a liability. Carrie would have to be put down first. There was no question.

Erel very slowly unzipped the semi-circle flap to the girls' tent. His preference was to catch them by surprise when he was already inside rather than risk having them charge at him and potentially escape the tent's confines. He was large enough that once inside completely, he could block the entrance and there wouldn't be a way for the girls to easily escape.

It was hard to see inside the tent at first. There was a dark outline of their two forms both snugly trapped in respective sleeping bags. He let his eyes adjust, aware that time was not on his side for this initial assault. Fortunately, the moonlight came in through a mesh window and as Erel's eyes adjusted, he caught the sight of Carrie's red hair, fanned out around her head. Her mouth was slack with the relaxation of deep sleep, her hands daintily up by her chest, almost as if she were unconsciously in prayer.

Prayer. A funny concept, that.

Just as some fucks were hard and fast, the shortest possible route to getting off—and others were long and slow, more about discovery than the end result—such was Erel's approach to killing. He wasn't without his own sense of romance.

Carrie would be hard and fast.

Jenny—she would be slow, but not gentle—a special toy.

Carrie was a throwaway, and Jenny would be a memory.

As soon as Erel's boots were both firmly planted on the tent's vinyl floor, his back now fully within the interior, the categorization of the two mounds in front of him made perfect sense. It was clear as day now how the night would proceed, with all of its intricate games—so clear that Erel suspected he was *meant* to do this. Something had led him to this point, something that even he didn't understand.

Of course, just like anything else in life, the kill Erel planned was never quite the kill he got. They were always slightly more chaotic—messier—and more exhilarating than in his fantasies. It was the element of unpredictability that made the assault more vigorous and the arousal more potent. For example, as he climbed on top of Carrie, he would never have imagined that the first word out of her mouth would be, "Mom." The word, so soft and innocently spoken, muttered in the girl's dreamlike haze between deep sleep and consciousness, excited Erel.

It was not but five to ten seconds after the word escaped Carrie's sleep-dry lips, that the girl opened her eyes and saw what the weight on her stomach was. It was this moment that was everything for Erel. The horrified expression on Carrie's face—the way her eyes bulged out involuntarily—the hesitation before unhinging her jaw into a pointless scream—it was so private, so intimate.

So singular.

No man would ever make little Carrie scream quite like that. Not after Erel was through with her.

The Buck 110 went in so deeply, Erel's knuckles sank into the wet opening in her slender neck. A short blade, like the one he preferred, meant the cuts had to be more vigorous. He sliced along the side to ensure he'd cut through the big artery. That was key—to slice along the side, and at least two inches deep. Anything less than two inches like in the movies was a joke. You had to go handle-deep and really slice. There was friction just like cutting any other kind of meat. Everything had a grain to it, most especially women. Erel didn't care so much about the art of butchering, as he did about the pleasures it provided him.

The best part of killing, as far as Erel was concerned, was that the body would stay warm and loose enough for the next couple of hours. Plenty of time to get inside and be Carrie's last paramour.

Jenny, splashed with the blood of her redheaded friend, sat up and stared at Erel like she was looking at the devil himself. The terror on her face and the way Erel just knew she was hoping this wasn't real, made him laugh to the point that he almost wanted to thank her. It had been a long time since he'd found anything quite as funny as the shock and awe on her blood-spattered, delicate face. This close, he saw the way her nose turned up at the end and in his heightened state of arousal, with one warm and ready and Jenny on the back burner, he found it all awfully endearing. He'd nibble on it later, let Jenny feel him taking it off her face.

But time was of the essence.

He went to work on Carrie, but he assured Jenny in as sincere a way as he could muster.

"Don't worry, I'll have plenty left for you."

CHAPTER 5
ROAD GAMES

THERE WAS a feeling of youthful abandon in the air.

Krista rolled down the passenger side window even though it was cold out and had started to rain. Raindrops dotted the door panel and Krista extended her hand outside to catch a few in her palm while Nick accelerated down the main road leading out from her and Tom's townhouse neighborhood.

She didn't know yet how to interpret the tension between them. Two possibilities skipped along her thoughts—that it could be sexual tension alone, or that it was something bigger than that—two synergistic souls colliding at breakneck speed. There was an ominous feeling to the abandon, like Fate had other things planned for both of them and somehow they'd found a loophole by meeting up.

It was a feeling of being up to no good, of doing something that was just too damn pleasurable, and that overarching worry of someone else noticing, *seeing it all*. Krista wasn't a particularly religious person, even though her parents had brought her up to pray, but she did have a sense of foreboding whenever she got to liking something as much as she liked talking to Nick. Something good like that couldn't last, the way she figured it.

Her last moments with Tom lurked in the background of her thoughts, and the only small comfort she had was that if worse came to worse, the rattling pills in her backpack were a surefire exit.

"Did you tell him you were leaving? Did you do it like we talked about?"

Nick intermittently took his eyes off the road to glance at her. Krista knew he was checking for her reaction, trying to see if she'd had the guts to finally do what they'd discussed...

"Not exactly..."

"Krista."

"I left a note."

"A *note*?"

"Don't be angry."

Nick rolled her window up without asking and Krista immediately missed the chill air on her face. The car, filling fast with Nick's disappointment, began to feel claustrophobic. He couldn't understand what it was like for her to live with Tom—how Tom had a way of making every small decision feel insurmountable unless he approved it. There was no *telling* Tom she was done.

"*Are* you angry?" Krista asked again, her voice slipping into softness the way it always did when she felt anxious.

"I'm not angry. I'm worried."

"Well don't be. I don't want you to worry about him. I don't even want to think about him right now."

Krista leaned away from Nick and rested her head against the window. Her left hand anxiously twirled her hair.

Nick placed a hand on her thigh, his fingers close to the oval-shaped burn mark, hidden at the moment by her leggings. He gave her leg a squeeze that she was sure was meant to be comforting, though it caused a different sensation altogether. The proximity of his hand, the feeling of heat on her leg from his touch—it made her thoughts drift toward the night's possibilities.

"I'm sorry. Now that I think about it, maybe it's better you left a note. I'm just... honestly..."

Nick became distracted by another car turning in front of him, so Krista finished his sentence for him.

"Nervous?"

Nick laughed, and it cut through the awkward tension. "A little." His hand moved up her thigh incrementally—that subtle hint of a desire to explore. "Is this ok?"

She lightly danced her fingers atop his, and gently guided his hand further up her leg. It was her answer.

But they left it at that for a time—Nick's hand on her thigh, his grip tightening and softening intermittently as he drove. Sometimes he took his hand away, but it always quickly returned and Krista spent the next hour or so imagining what his fingers would feel like inside of her, even as they talked about books, movies, memories—anything and everything but the tension between them.

They'd been on 81 North for the bulk of the drive so far and the heavy traffic, coupled with Nick's penchant for tailgating, made Krista nervous. She found herself telling him to watch out several times during their conversation and finally, she asked if they could exit the highway altogether.

"Yeah, ok, we shouldn't be too far now anyway."

Even though he took the next exit off the highway, Krista could tell he wasn't exactly thrilled by the turn of events. Still, she felt much more at ease on the back mountain roads, even though they were poorly paved and some of the houses, illuminated only by porchlight, looked unsettling at this time of night.

The slower pace of the last leg of their ride before arriving at the cabin allowed Krista to broach a subject she'd wanted to bring up, but was unsure how.

"You know what's crazy?"

"What?"

Her lips twisted into an embarrassed, involuntary kind of smile. She bit her lip and wondered if she should say anything at all.

"What?" Nick asked again, this time sparing a few glances her way as he drove, a confused smile now on his face, too.

"It might sound weird if I tell you."

"I like weird."

She laughed at that. And then finally—she just let it all out— every self-conscious mouthful—

"Well, sometimes I get to wondering if certain bodies are made for other bodies."

"In what way?"

"Like... I've had sex with other men—and I know we haven't yet—but when I've had sex with other men, and I'm not even talking about Tom because I've told you it's always terrible with Tom—but when I've had sex with other men, I don't really feel much. But when I think about you…"

She paused mid-ramble, trying to come up with the right way to express the thought she'd flipped over in her mind so many times before this night when thinking about Nick.

"When I think about you, my body responds in this way that I think it craves you. It's weird, right?"

"It's not weird." Nick's voice had changed. He missed a turn on the GPS, but kept driving anyway. She didn't much care about the directions at the moment, either. Krista was too invested in finally getting across this idea she'd been trying for so long to articulate, first to herself and now to Nick.

"I feel like it's a little weird sometimes. Like, I'll just think of you—just the very image of you—or a memory of something you've said—the inflection of your voice—and my body gets, like…"

"Like?"

"I shouldn't say."

"No. Now you have to say."

They both laughed.

"Okay, like, I just get so ridiculously aroused by you. I get so wet that I get this idea, this philosophy kind of, that the mere thought of you sends my body into this readiness mode. Like it's preparing itself for you automatically, like it just *knows* what it wants, and what it wants is you inside of it."

Even in the dim light of the car interior, Krista could tell Nick's breathing had changed. She'd never spoken to him so explicitly before, and it felt both scary and exciting to finally describe the ways in which she thought about him. The thought of him getting turned on by her words emboldened her to express her thoughts on the topic even more.

"I kind of was thinking about it like I'm a soft-boiled egg… and I *hate* soft-boiled eggs, but hear me out."

Krista grabbed Nick's hand from the steering wheel and guided it to her leg. She moved it up and down her thigh. Then she hoisted herself up enough from the passenger seat to slide her leggings down. She wasn't wearing anything under them. She then put Nick's hand back on her leg. The feel of his skin against hers was an altogether new discovery—an outright revelation, as far as Krista was concerned.

"It's like when we were first talking, you were delicately cracking away at this hard shell and then as you gently cleared away all of my defenses, you got to softer and softer layers of me until finally, tonight, it's just…"

Krista unbuckled her seatbelt.

"What are you doing?"

She didn't respond verbally. They were on some dark and empty rural road, not a car in sight. Large swathes of rock wall and woods, with big unlit houses breaking up the scenery. Pushing back the passenger seat, Krista turned so that she was squarely facing Nick. She took his hand—the same one that had just been caressing her thigh—and ran her tongue along his middle finger.

He started to say something, but she shut him up by quickly enveloping his entire finger in the warmth of her mouth. She then guided his hand in between her legs. There was an electric anticipatory moment right before his fingers were fully inside of her—quickly followed by the feverish primal instinct for *more.*

Krista wanted to tell him how much more she wanted him, and in which ways. She was about to open her mouth when a loud noise—almost like the sound inside of a plane during take-off—overtook them. The car suddenly fishtailed to the side, bounced off the metal guard-rail and Krista slammed into the passenger side door.

Nick immediately asked if she was alright but Krista wasn't sure how to answer. There was a sense of delirious shock—had they hit a deer? Did Nick drive off the road? As the first initial moments passed after the car had come to a stop, the pain in Krista's side lit up. She had hit the car door with a lot of force.

"I think I'm okay, but my side hurts. My shoulder feels like it was hit with a hammer or something."

"Okay, one sec—"

Nick took his cell phone out, but as soon as he started dialing, blue and red lights flashed behind them.

"Thank fucking god. At least we'll be able to get out of here sooner." Nick seemed relieved.

Krista, however, was not relieved—not at all. Any lingering

arousal she'd had from their little road game was now as far as possible from the forefront of her thoughts. It hurt her shoulder to do so, but she reached down and quickly pulled up her leggings while watching in the rearview mirror as the cop car's driver-side door opened.

Krista wondered where the cop had been waiting, that he was able to get to them so quickly. Had he been watching them? She hadn't seen any lights—hadn't even seen a single car up here until just a few moments ago.

CHAPTER 6
WELCOME TO PARADISE

MISTY LEE WAS late for work again, though it was no fault of her own. Dad had stumbled home late from Nowhere Special, his clothes reeking of piss and booze. Even after she was out of the car and heading on foot toward the Paradise Inn office, Misty could still conjure up the smell of her father. It was a rancid odor she'd come to associate with her dad ever since the old Medallion Paper Mill had closed down when she was a child.

Dad wasn't the only casualty of Medallion's demise. There were plenty of other fathers, some now dead, others incarcerated, who had fallen by the wayside after Beleth Station's largest employer went under so many years ago.

The ripples of the old mill's bankruptcy kept flowing outward into every crevice of Beleth until Misty was sure there wasn't a soul alive in the town who hadn't felt the pain of losing Medallion. Men who once were able to afford mortgages and families now worked for minimum wage, or didn't work at all—or, as was more frequent than not in Beleth Station, decided to pound all their hopes and dreams into a line of crushed painkillers.

There was a common thread among all the kids Misty had grown up with, and that was the line, *"I'm going to get the fuck out of here."*

But... as Misty got older, dropped out of senior year, and

started working at the Paradise Inn full-time, she soon realized it was harder to leave home than any of them thought.

There was June, who was already pregnant with her second child, and Maggie, who had gone to harder drugs before disappearing, and then there was Noelle, Misty's closest friend from the neighborhood, who was a frequent visitor to the Paradise— a thought that Misty tried not to think about much.

The parking lot wasn't too full at this hour, but as the night went on, cars would cruise in—some of them regulars—and some, curious out-of-towners—for an hour or three at the Paradise. It was a dangerous job for a woman to work the night shift, but it paid a buck-fifty per hour differential, something Misty couldn't pass up in Beleth. Opportunities for legitimate work were scarce.

Hank, who worked second shift, was asleep in the motel's office chair. He stirred when Misty unlocked the door. As was habit, she immediately locked the door again after entering, and put her purse and valuables inside the filing cabinet, out of sight from anyone peering through the glass. The office was furnished as cheaply as possible so as not to tempt anyone's funny ideas.

Of course, the ladies inside the rooms had much more cash on hand than the office safe did, but out-of-towners didn't always know that, and there had been a robbery or two from time to time.

Not a wise idea. Not in Beleth, anyway.

"Thought you'd never get here."

"Yeah, neither did I."

Hank said "mmhmm" in his usual drawl. He wasn't much of a talker, but occasionally he'd open up to Misty about his ex-wife, Tina, and how she'd fucked him six ways to Monday over child support. "Y'know, she's banging that plumber up on Wisconsin Ave," he'd mumble around a cigarette, "And I'm paying their fucking mortgage."

Misty never had much to say on the subject. She didn't mind Hank, but she didn't exactly like him either. He was better than some of the other men who had worked second shift before, but he still had his fair share of eccentricities. He liked to leave a magazine or two under the room log binder. Strange magazines

—things Misty had never even thought might exist. Though, she had to admit to herself that there was an odd curiosity about them, and sometimes she suspected Hank left them there as a way to provoke her. He had to know she'd look.

She couldn't *not* look.

At least that's what she told herself. But the nights were long, and it was easy to glimpse at the images during dead hours, to fill herself with a mixture of revulsion and awe—the wonder of how and why someone might be aroused by *those things*, in particular.

Embarrassing things.

Nothing *she* would do.

At least, that's what she told herself.

"Well I gotta get on. Last call at Nowhere Special in, oh—" Hank checked his watch, "Thirty minutes. You have a good night, Miss Misty." That's what Hank called her—*Miss Misty*.

"Have a good night. Don't drink too much."

He laughed, turned the lock, and was gone.

Cigarette smoke lingered in the office. Misty went to empty the glass ashtray into the miniature trash can and sighed when she saw it was full. That was one thing she didn't do—empty the trash at night. She never left the office, not until it was light out the next day and her shift was over. It was hard sometimes to stay in there all night because the bathroom was outside. It was a separate single stall made of concrete with a lock and peeling red paint that said, "STAFF ONLY".

There were a few reasons Misty didn't leave the office at night, but the main one was what happened to Isabelle Daniels back in 1993. Isabelle Daniels worked the night shift at the Paradise from '91 to '93 while she was going to nursing school over in Topville. She was one of those young ladies who really shined in Beleth—someone people thought might be going places, a girl who actually stood a chance of getting out and doing something good with her life.

But on July 9th, 1993, when Isabelle was on her way to empty the trash around 4AM, she was hit over the back of the head with a brick, dragged behind the dumpsters, raped and either killed during the process or shortly thereafter. Sheriff Ray Hall, who had just gotten out of the police academy in '93, often liked to mention as a word of warning to young folks in Beleth, that Isabelle's head looked like congealed stew. She had been hit over fifty times with the brick, and apparently even though a skull could take a lot of damage, it couldn't take *that* much.

"Doesn't matter if you're nice. Nice girls die, too."

Misty always remembered that line from Sheriff Hall—the way his voice echoed throughout their small high school gymnasium before he showed them all a slide of safety tips, and finally a hazy senior picture of Isabelle Daniels, the short span of her life underneath. Two years too close together and separated by a hyphen that was supposed to somehow represent everything that girl had hoped and dreamed in between.

Misty had company.

It was a white Buick with a taped up side mirror. She'd seen it before. It was one of the regular crews that came around once or twice a month. They often hopped motels to avoid getting too locked into a routine.

Two men got out of the car, and Misty could see the women crammed into the backseat. These, she called nightlies. They were the crews that would buy a full night, set up in two rooms and see a rotating menagerie of guests until dawn broke. Then, they'd all pile back into the car and wouldn't be seen again for a few weeks, sometimes longer. Misty rarely got a good look at the girls—only their slender, scantily-clad forms as they walked in and out of the row of rooms at the Paradise. The women were never the ones to check in or out, and in a sad way, Misty felt like they were ghosts haunting motels up and down the Pennsylvania mountains.

One of the men approached the office while the other lingered near the Buick. Misty edged away from the slot in the glass—something learned from experience—as the man came closer. When he finally stepped into the light of the overhang, she saw that he wore one of those old pastel bowling shirts, partially unbuttoned. He tapped his fingertips on the edge of the desk which extended a few inches beyond the glass's slot opening, a space where customers could put their smokes or wallet while they settled up. Misty noted a darkly-etched tattoo of a skull on his forearm, a bulge of brain matter squeezing out from one of the eye sockets. When she looked up at the man's eyes, she could see that he had been following her gaze—had taken note of her looking at his ink.

There was an unexpected tension between them at this first bout of eye contact, though it wasn't the good kind. The man made Misty feel uneasy. The way he held her gaze, even after she looked away—and then looked again—gave her the sense of being *consumed*.

"How many rooms do you need and for how long?" She made her voice as flat and cold as she could when she asked, purposely omitting any small-talk.

"Two. I want those ones." The man pointed to the left, at some space Misty couldn't see from where she was standing within the office.

"Which ones?"

"The two on the very end if you got 'em."

"I can do that. How long?" Misty dug through the key bin while she waited for his answer. The Paradise still had old-fashioned turnkeys. It was too expensive to upgrade and besides, none of their patrons seemed to mind one way or the other. There was a single master key kept in a locked drawer, just in case a guest decided to overstay, or—as had happened on more than one occasion—a guest decided to end their own life at the Paradise, something Misty found incomprehensible.

"Just the night."

Misty opened the room log to the current page, which was bookmarked with a large paperclip, and penned in the room numbers and date. While doing so, she repeated back to him, "Two rooms, one night. Rooms eight and seven on the end— eighty-three dollars, cash. You gotta be out by ten or it's fifteen an hour after. No breakfast. Vending machines out back, but there's not much in 'em."

The man handed her the money through the slot. She watched him pull out the bills from a larger wad of cash and it was another moment of him taking note of her looking.

"You probably don't see money like this around these parts much, do you?"

Misty tried not to roll her eyes as she made change.

"I see enough."

"You get in with the right folks, you could make way more than you're making here."

Misty ignored him and pushed his change through the opening.

She thought he was going to say something else, but in the distance she saw the red and blue lights of Sheriff Hall's patrol car coming their way. It caught the man's attention at the same time it caught hers and he was suddenly much less interested in Misty. Leaving the room keys and without asking for his money back, the man jogged over to the Buick and left in a hurry. Misty watched the crew drive off at the same time as she saw Sheriff Hall pull in.

Strange.

Sheriff Hall usually didn't come around the Paradise, except in the case of a body. As the folks around town liked to say sometimes, you don't interfere with the local business.

CHAPTER 7
NOWHERE SPECIAL

EREL KNEW he shouldn't take souvenirs and he'd get rid of her as soon as he was able to, but what was left of Jenny remained in his trunk. There was something about the pieces of her leftovers that were very hard to part with immediately.

The tip of her nose was rubbery with a vague lick of salt to it —something that called him to gnaw on until he could mash it fully between his teeth. She hadn't liked that much—hadn't liked seeing part of her leave. There were things she had said in the height of the moment. Jenny had tried bargaining her way out of Erel's games with layers of both clever and desperate suggestions. That was the way with many of his more intelligent conquests—they could come up with all sorts of offers once they realized what they were in for. The first part leaves them and suddenly they're willing to do just about anything to save the parts that remain.

He'd never had a saltier lick than Jenny. That's why he supposed he took a few scraps to go, even though he knew he shouldn't have. It was better to leave the mess for someone else to clean up than to take the mess with you. Erel was mature enough, good enough at his craft, to know that. But he wanted to gnaw on part of her later. It was that salty undertone to her flesh, the rubbery chewy consistency that eked out juicy tidbits at just the right intervals, that made him hard-up to leave all of her at the campsite.

In the meantime, Erel meandered through the back mountain roads, pausing at each intersection to consider the importance of turning left or right. Erel had come to savor a type of game in his head. When he went on his drives, he knew that in equal part, turning right meant some woman not yet discovered was doomed, but that in the same breath, a very different woman, had he turned left instead, would be spared. In this way, Erel felt something of a godliness, though nothing nearly as holy—if he had to describe it, he would've admitted he viewed himself as a force of nature, his impulses dictating the forecast as much and as uncontrollably as moisture in the atmosphere. Erel didn't feel responsible for his actions; after all, he didn't create himself—he just was.

The game was fun to play, and as he viewed the pale green sign in front of him, straight ahead to Beleth Station, or right to Hancock, or left to Pittsville, he pictured three different abstract women. There was a sense of excitement in knowing that, depending on which way he chose to drive, the clock on a woman's life would begin running out. Which woman—he didn't know yet—but he would discover her soon enough.

Straight ahead was the way.

Beleth Station was a town on its way out—Erel felt as though he were witnessing a town's carcass as he drove past row after row of dreary, crumbling townhouses. There were a few women smoking or sitting out on their porches drinking, but they already looked so dead in the streetlight that Erel wouldn't have been able to have any fun with the chase.

He came to a stop at a red light, and noticed a slanted green neon sign hanging in the first floor window of a townhouse: "NOWHERE SPECIAL". He pulled the car a little to the right, closer to the building, and squinted in the dark at a cardboard notice next to the neon. Handwritten drink specials in black marker, a few of them crossed out. It was hard to see inside but the place appeared to be open.

Erel pulled around the corner and parked the car. Even though pieces of Jenny were in his trunk, he didn't bother locking it.

Fuck it.

It was a bit of a kick to do shit like that—especially when he knew just how much a few of the men in blue wanted to find him.

Nowhere Special lived up to its name. It was a muggy bar, far too rank with the scent of men to suit Erel, but he took a seat nonetheless. Erel didn't like to drink, but he ordered a beer all the same just to take a look around and to tuck into the vibe of the place. Most of the men, many still in work clothes, looked tired and worn out, maybe strung out on debt or worse. Erel only spotted two women—one cozied up to a balding man in the corner and another, maybe fifty or so, mascara dripping from her eyes, scouting around for someone, anyone.

Erel wasn't the guy for that, and he avoided looking at the wretch, for fear of giving her ideas.

A heavyset man with an easy smile walked through the door. The bell chime made Erel notice him. The bartender acknowledged the guy in a way that Erel could tell meant they'd known each other for some time.

"Hank! How's it going? Just get off at the Paradise?"

The man took a seat next to Erel, his larger build overshadowing Erel's lanky form.

"Thank the fuck I did," Hank said, and both he and the bartender shared an easy laugh.

"This'll take the edge off, huh."

The bartender pulled out a brown medicine-shaped bottle, an obviously-handmade label slapped on it. A grating sound pierced Erel's ears as Hank dragged the bottle across the uneven wooden bartop before finally picking it up and taking a drink.

Erel contemplated asking what was in the bottle, but then thought better of it. Hank seemed hellbent on drinking whatever it was as quickly as possible—taking large swigs like he was starving for the shit. When he was finished, he put the bottle back on the bartop with a hollow clang.

"Glenn. Another."

The bartender reached underneath and swapped out the empty bottle for another round of medicine.

Erel felt a bit skittish about the whole thing, and he hated feeling skittish. Hank's large, confident body and his easy mannerisms reminded Erel of Granddad. Drinking always reminded Erel of Granddad, but Hank most especially emanated something of the same ilk. Erel couldn't quite put his finger on it, but it was enough to set him off balance.

The taste of rubber filled Erel's mouth, and it wasn't the same kind of salty, pleasurable rubber as Jenny. For a moment, Erel recalled the time Granddad had made him lick his boot soles clean as punishment for shitting in the kennel. There were all sorts of clever punishments over the years—hard-won, at that—but this one in particular always rankled Erel. His granddad had insisted on wearing the boots when Erel cleaned them, and he'd gotten the sense that his grandfather had picked the dirtiest pair he owned. He wasn't allowed to use his hands, but instead had to lick and bite at the rubber from a position of all fours until every speck of dirt, gum, and shit had been cleaned from them.

The memory was enough to make Erel drink and in spite of himself, he realized he had finished an entire beer.

"You see that?"

Erel perked up at Hank's question, looking over his shoulder to make sure the man was actually speaking to him.

Hank pointed his thumb back at the woman who had just moments ago been cozying up to the balding man in the corner. She now was with another man, and Erel realized there was more going on than he had initially thought.

"She charges fifteen a fuck. Fifteen!" Hank laughed.

Erel didn't respond beyond a nod, but that didn't deter Hank, who was now looking a little red in the face.

"She's a regular ride around here. She's got a kid at home— Jackie—a little fucked in the head. You know what I mean?" Hank took another drink. "Who knows whose he is, she's fucked half of Beleth."

Erel pushed his empty beer can from one hand to the other. He suddenly wanted to be rid of Nowhere Special, to go back to his car and take himself and the bits of Jenny on to a new place. Somewhere quiet...

"A woman like that just isn't no fun, though. You know. Don't you?"

Hank put his hand on Erel's back a touch longer than a stranger should. Erel was keenly aware that even though he wasn't responding to Hank, that Hank seemed to be after something. Erel had cornered enough animals to know when he, himself, was being closed in on.

"Last call!" Glenn called out from the other end of the bar.

Erel could still feel the imprint from Hank's hand on his back. When he made eye contact with Hank, who loomed so large in the dim light of the hanging lamps, his suspicion was confirmed that the man, in turn, was staring directly back at him.

And Erel saw in Hank's eyes the same shade of sadistic glee he'd seen before—from Granddad, from Granddad's friends—most especially from the random men who'd had the urge and the money to satisfy it at young Erel's expense.

The taste of rubber filled Erel's mouth again and before he could stop himself, his throat muscles clenched uncontrollably and he gagged. He tried to catch himself midway which only made it worse. Bracing himself over the bartop with bowed arms, Erel swallowed back—with great force—the beer and bile that threatened to spill out from him.

Hank found the sight delightful and smacked Erel on the back again—this time more fraternally. Erel wished the man would stop touching him, but he couldn't find the appropriate words to say to make Hank back off.

Instead of speaking, Erel embraced a feeling he knew well, one that could subsume all of the unpleasantness boiling inside —it was a feeling of raw rage mixed with intense superiority.

The resolute solution to take a life, and watch it slip from another's body at the touch of his hands.

Determination settled Erel's stomach, and it was the cold knowledge of the unspeakable intimacies he'd experienced with over a dozen women in and out of Pennsylvania that made him say yes to Hank's strange invitation to come around and, as Hank put it, see something crazy.

When they left Nowhere Special, Hank reminded Erel for the third time, "This is just between me and you."

Erel knew just between me and you.

Jenny—what was left of her rotting in the trunk of his car—also knew.

CHAPTER 8
NOT QUITE ROMANTIC

WHEN THE SHERIFF had said he'd bring them to a hotel, Krista had something very different in mind than the unsightly strip of rooms called The Paradise Inn.

The sign, lit by a flickering fluorescent parking lot lamp, advertised an hourly rate and clean towels, but Krista was well-aware that nothing hourly was going to be *clean*. When the sheriff's car pulled into the parking lot, a few of the room curtains shifted—eyes peering out—before promptly closing again, perhaps tighter than they were before.

"Hey, uh—" Nick started to talk. Krista could see he was assessing the situation and trying to get his hands around it. For her sake, most likely. "Is there anything a little nicer around here?"

The silence that followed was thick.

Sheriff Hall, the officer who had picked them up after Nick's tire shredded, had been markedly talkative up until this point. In fact, there were moments during the drive along the back mountain roads—a strange route that Krista was sure had taken them down and up a fair amount of altitude due to her ears constantly adjusting—when Krista had wished the old man would just shut up already.

He struck Krista as the type of man who didn't need any reciprocation to keep a conversation going. As soon as they'd crossed over into "Beleth" as he called it, he'd gone on at length about some old paper mill, and about how the town used to be one of the main paper product suppliers in all of Pennsylvania.

Who fucking cares.

Still, Krista was aware she was sitting in the backseat of a police car and seeing as the sheriff hadn't given them any kind of citation, she was inclined to pretend to be interested in his idle history lessons.

Now, however, his sudden silence put Krista on edge and she found herself filling in the gaps with untruths.

"It's okay. This looks great for the night," she said, not at all surprised by the docile softness in her tone.

Nick spun his head around to look at her and she could see the question *'are you sure?'* written in the intensity of his gaze. He cared about her. It was the sense of it—of him actually giving a shit—that emboldened her to soothe the situation even more. She wanted to make it easier on Nick, even at the expense of her own comfort, and so she placed a hand on his leg and made a suggestion she didn't really believe, "It could be fun, even. A little adventure."

"Okay, I guess we're all set then. We appreciate you taking us all the way out here."

"Yes, thank you. We would've been stuck out there for awhile without you," Krista echoed Nick's sentiment.

They just needed the old man to finally get out of the car and let them leave.

But the sheriff didn't immediately respond. He had his index finger hooked inside his mouth, chipping away at something between his teeth. When he removed it, he finally spoke.

"A few things, while you're here." He turned around and set a hard gaze at both of them. "People here in Beleth have a way of knowing when you're of this place or not. Whether you're of the root, or traveled in on the wind. Sometimes, people and things that come in on the wind—especially pretty little things —" and here he directed his attention to Krista, "—have a habit of blowing away sometimes, never to be seen this way or that way, or any kind of way again." He twisted his lips to one side like he was chewing on something tucked away in his cheek.

"What the fuck is that supposed to mean?"

"Nick..."

"Ah, I don't mean to scare you. Just means, sometimes a small place like this, a little off-the-map dot like Beleth? Sometimes it can still surprise you, is all."

Nick and Krista exchanged concerned glances with each other while the sheriff unbuckled his belt and got out of the car. In a quick moment, Nick's door was open and they slid out. It was a noticeable relief to be outside of the vehicle, but as she looked toward the row of rooms, many with closed curtains and just vague shadows of humans behind them, her anxiety grew. As much as she wanted to be away from the sheriff, she also found the prospect of him leaving them to be equally dreadful.

"You get on, check in with Misty there—she's a nice girl, that one." The sheriff pointed at the exterior office where Krista could see a young woman staring out at them from behind glass. "I'll wait a moment longer, see that you get inside alright. Have a smoke while I wait."

Nick grabbed Krista's hand and they headed toward the little booth to check in. Krista turned around one last time and saw Sheriff Hall, still by his car, staring intently at the motel's dumpsters as he smoked his cigarette. She couldn't tell for sure in the dark, but she thought he looked a little sad—or, as she considered in the last moment peering at him before turning back around—he looked haunted.

While Nick handled the exchange of money and room keys, Krista stared up at the fluorescent overhang and watched the autumn moths swarm. *Beleth moths*, she thought.

Of the root.

CHAPTER 9
GAG REFLEX THEORY

"SAY. You ever think about what someone can take?"

Erel found Hank's line of questioning frustratingly vague. The looming man had been dancing around his surprise ever since they'd arrived at the farmhouse, and instead of getting to the point, Hank kept handing off beer after beer.

Like we're old friends, Erel thought.

"Take?"

"As I see it, there's two lines of thinking on this. Right?" Hank had a way of presenting ideas to himself as if he were reveling in his own philosophies, drunk off his own self-perceived brilliance. "You've got the limit of what someone can take in terms of pain, torture, withholding shit. All that. But then you've also got this other way of thinking about it."

Erel couldn't help but drink while the man talked. There was nothing else to do. Hank was too large—too loud—to permit interruptions.

"The other way," Hank continued, "is that you can change someone's whole idea of happiness. Simplify it for them, like." Hank's face slipped into a kind of secretive smile, like he really wanted to confess something but wouldn't just yet. He was dancing around it, seeing if Erel would flinch.

Erel wasn't going to flinch. In fact, the more Erel watched and listened to Hank, the more Erel started to drum up his own philosophy for the evening.

"You know. You can make someone you hurt terribly, do horrible nasty shit to—you can make them love you. Did you know that?"

Erel wasn't interested in any kind of love. He nodded to keep Hank talking.

Another beer.

"Because it's all relative, right? I call it my Gag Reflex Theory."

While Hank talked, Erel began taking a serious look around the farmhouse. Hank was intoxicated enough by this point that Erel didn't have to obviously direct his attention at him. The guy was on a roll—had been on a roll since the bar—had probably even decided then, Erel figured, that Erel was the one he was going to tell his big secret to.

Guys like Hank, Erel supposed, just had to tell *someone.*

"My ex wife, Tina. Take her, for example. We started out really sweet. You know how you have to do that at first? Pretend. But as with all broads, you can finally get them to that point, and then you reach a fork in the road."

Hank held out his beer-holding hand to the right, and his other hand to the left to illustrate. The more he drank, the more he moved his hands, and the more he spilled his beer. It gathered in tiny puddles all over the cheap linoleum.

"One way, which is how some guys figure it, is you go slow. Gentle. *Can I kiss you? Is this too hard? Are you ok?* That's the one way."

"Yeah. Fuck that."

It was the first thing Erel had said in a long time, and it was only uttered to rile Hank up more.

Hank finished off the beer in his hand and grabbed another. Erel marveled at how many the guy was putting away.

"Exactly. Fuck that. That's where gag reflex theory comes in. When I met Tina, she was just an itty bitty thing. We used to go riding in my dad's car after I'd get off my shift at Medallion. Dad had a real shitty used Ford Cortina and he used to leave trash in there all the time, so I was constantly shoveling out garbage so I could fit Tina and me in the back." Hank paused and let out a deep sigh, like he was hungry to relive the memory all over again.

"Anyway, we must've spent weeks making out in the back of that car. *Weeks*. Then finally, I got fed up with it and just stopped kissing her altogether. No more hair stroking, no more bullshit. Just stopped it all cold in its tracks. Got real sick of having to kiss her and tell her how much I loved her all night without getting my dick even looked at, let alone touched. And even though I really didn't plan on it being like this, once I backed off, suddenly Tina was *crazy* to get me to kiss her again. So I, you know—" Hank stopped there and chuckled. "I told her what would really make me happy was if she'd put my dick in her mouth. And at first she looked at me like I'd just suggested we go burn a house down or something. Yeah, she looked real freaked out. But then she started asking questions, telling me she'd never done that before, asking if I was sure I'd really like it, telling me she was worried she wouldn't do a good job."

Hank paused and laughed a bit harder.

"I said, oh, I think you'll do a really good job. The *best* job. And she really seemed to like hearing things like that. I don't know why, but she did. But she kept skirting the issue, saying she didn't know how to do it. Kept playing shy about the whole thing. And honestly, she was a bit shy. Real good girl. Not even sure she'd seen a man before me, that kind of innocent. Y'know? So I kinda..." Hank was amused so much by the thought in his head that he cut himself off with laughter.

"...I kinda fucked with her a little. It wasn't something I planned, ok? I'm not some fucking weirdo. So anyway, I talked her through that first time sticking my dick in her mouth because once it was out of my pants, she was looking at the thing stone-cold *terrified*. Gotta admit, her innocent terror did it for me. I got off on it a bit—not that she was scared because like I said, I'm no fucking weird guy. Just that she was so damn innocent. And so I talked her through that first time, how to make her lips, how to use her tongue, how she better at all cost keep her fucking teeth out of the way. So she finally lowers her head—finally puts her lips on my cock and moves maybe two-thirds down, and she's about to raise her head back up, right? Well I grabbed the back of her head, grabbed a fist-full of her hair in my hand and shoved her head down further so I was up in her throat. She struggled to move her head back up, too, but I made her take me in her throat for just long enough to get some tears on her cheeks, and to get her to really gag on it. She gagged so hard that by the time I let her up for air, she threw up all over her skirt."

Hank paused at that point to see if Erel was enjoying the story. Erel had never had a woman willingly put her mouth on his dick, and even if he had, he wasn't sure he would have enjoyed it. Erel didn't think there was anything particularly desirable about his dick—it was just a *thing* that served a purpose for him alone. Why would any woman want it? It wasn't the point whether they wanted it or not; he used women in service of it, in spite of their wants. But he did manage to fake a chuckle for Hank's benefit, nonetheless.

"So after she threw up, I really started laying into her. *How the fuck could you throw up, what kind of gross bitch are you. That's so disgusting. The smell. Jesus Christ. I should've known you were too immature for me.* And oh how she cried. Then I got on her ass about crying. And it was hilarious, man, because if she'd had any ounce of self-respect she would've jumped out of that car and high-tailed it to her Dad, y'know? But nope. She just started *begging* to let her try again. See, the way I laid into her, she suddenly felt like she had to prove herself, so then she started pleading with me to let her suck my cock one more time. *Just one more time, Hank. Please. I'll do better this time.* That's the kind of shit she said! And after that, it was a fucking beautiful relationship. That's gag reflex theory at work in the wild. *True love.*"

Hank, who'd been standing, pacing and gesticulating the entire time he'd told the story—which was far more of a thrill for himself than for his audience of one—finally slid a chair across the linoleum floor and sat. He looked a little tired, like the drunken high he'd been enjoying was finally starting to settle in his gut.

"You got any stories?" He smiled in a way that made Erel uneasy. "I bet you do. You probably got some good ones, *don't you.*"

CHAPTER 10
NOELLE, NOELLE

JACKIE WAS FUCKING PISSED.

He'd taken out his anger on his mother a few hours earlier, right before her whoring shift at the Paradise. Had given her a pinch so hard on her flabby upper arm that his nails sank into her skin and she bled a little.

It's not like he'd done it for a thrill. That wasn't to Jackie's taste. No, he'd done it because she was the only one, he felt, who might be able to tell him where the fuck on God's green earth Noelle had gone to.

Noelle, Noelle.

The name was like candy in his mouth, he'd said it so many times—quietly to himself, whispered in his head, and loudly while deep inside of her.

The first encounter had been paid. Jackie remembered marveling at how cheap it was. Noelle had rattled off three numbers like she'd been hawking her body on the regular for years, even though from what Jackie could tell, she was probably just shy of twenty-one.

"Twenty-thirty-fifty. Nothing in my ass."

Jackie hadn't really understood the tiered pricing and was too shy to ask, so he'd just handed over the fifty dollars and had hoped he was doing things right.

That first time had been a bust in more ways than one—an oddly erotic and confusing embarrassment that Jackie wished he could forget. Noelle touched his dick, already painfully hard, and had murmured something about him being ready for her. By the time she undid her jeans and guided his hand between her legs, he had unexpectedly jizzed in his pants, and was left standing in front of her, completely spent and ashamed to high hell. Here he had to pay to lose his virginity, and he'd still managed to fuck it up.

The times after that were better, though.

Different. Special.

Jackie let Noelle do anything and everything to him that she wanted. Things he wouldn't have even imagined wanting to try —somehow, she got him to say *yes, more, please* to whatever whim seemed to enter her pretty head. And he didn't pay her after that first time, either, which Jackie took a special pleasure in.

She didn't want the other men, but she wanted Jackie.

That's what he told himself, at least.

And more than anything right now, as he roamed the vacant halls of the old abandoned Medallion Paper Mill, Jackie wanted to hear her whisper in his ear that he'd done a good job, that he was her *good boy*.

Back in high school, when the thought of a woman wanting him was unthinkable at best, Jackie had only had the most rudimentary vanilla inklings of what sex might feel like, and in that way, he had realized now in hindsight that his imagination had been pretty mediocre in that regard. Or maybe he'd just found his own hand particularly uninspiring.

Noelle, however, woke up something deep inside of him—a feeling he couldn't particularly imagine himself having toward any other woman again. There was something about her—her cheaply dyed honey-blonde hair, the way she'd flash her upper thighs around town without a care in the world, the sound of her sing-songy voice when she told him what was going to happen to him if he was good—it turned him into a willing servant.

But the last time he'd seen her had been nine days ago and even though he'd gone around the Paradise multiple times trying to catch her after she worked over her regulars, he had been unable to track her down. Misty, who worked the night shift, had told him she hadn't seen Noelle for two weeks straight and when he'd pressed her about it, the bitch said, "What do you expect? You know what she's into." Misty always thought she was better than Noelle, though. Noelle had told Jackie all about Misty, how they used to hang around the neighborhood as kids together, how Misty was stuck up and thought she was too good for Beleth. And how Misty's father was a sad drunken husk of a man, a man Misty had to clean up after and make excuses for.

Serves her right, Jackie thought.

The old mill reeked of piss, sex and garbage. Jackie had already been here multiple times over the past nine days looking for Noelle, and he knew he'd keep returning. It was the place where they had last fucked.

The memory was especially vivid in Jackie's mind because he felt a mixture of shame, arousal and confusion when he thought of it.

Noelle had done something new that time—something awfully new. Something that caught Jackie completely off guard and he still wasn't sure how he felt about it, but in the moment he was just so hell-bent on making her happy that he'd gone along with it. It was afterwards that Jackie felt the shame and confusion, and it was the shame of it all that made him desperate to hear her approving words in his ear again.

Part of him worried he should have said *no*, that somehow he'd fucked up the good thing they had going by being just so damn... willing.

Noelle liked to be on top and when she was riding him, pressing his face into the grimy floor of the mill, Jackie had just assumed at the time that he'd finish inside of her, and that would be that, like usual. Like how it always was.

But that wasn't what happened—not that last time. Noelle rode him particularly aggressively that afternoon and he'd shot off inside of her even sooner than he'd expected. He'd started to relax and enjoy the post-sex endorphins when Noelle leaned down close to him, moved up off his dick and then placed her cunt, wet with his own cum and her fluids, right on his face.

"Clean up your mess."

He probably should have pushed her off, or gotten mad, but he hadn't done any of that.

No.

Jackie obeyed until his tongue had cleaned up every last drop.

It was after he was done, when she was satisfied that he'd finished the job, that Noelle had finally gotten off him and stroked his head adoringly, had told him how he was her good boy, how he'd *always* be her good boy. Those words—the way she said them—they made Jackie one hundred fucking percent sure he was in love.

But he'd blown it, obviously, because now she was gone, and no one—not even his blasted whore mother—could tell him where the hell Noelle was.

The longer Jackie walked the empty mill's graffitied halls, the angrier he became. Any remnants of his shame at the memory of their last fuck were washed away by searing resentment.

Maybe she did it to fuck with me. Maybe it was a joke.

She was probably off with one of her regulars, high as a kite, laughing about what she got some dumb dope to do for her.

It wouldn't be the first time someone had fucked with Jackie. That's all people in this shithole town ever did.

That's why, sometimes, Jackie liked to find old drunks and junkies in Medallion at night and rough them up. They rarely put up a fight, especially if they were deep in a nod.

It's not that it was a thrill. Violence wasn't to Jackie's taste.

He didn't enjoy it.

He just needed it sometimes.

A release.

He couldn't *always* be a good boy.

CHAPTER 11
PET PLAY

EREL HAD REVEALED JUST ENOUGH to get Hank to finally let him in on his secret.

Hank led Erel to a barn behind the farmhouse. The big man's gait was uneven—he'd had far too much to drink—and he waved his hands as he talked, but Erel couldn't make out the words since he stayed a few strides behind the entire time they walked. Erel knew from the moment he'd seen Hank enter the bar that he wanted to keep the man ahead of him, fully in his sights.

The barn was more isolated than the main farmhouse—situated further back on the lot—and surrounded on all sides by unkempt pasture, grasses tall enough to brush Erel's thighs as he walked. The structure was two stories tall with a crumbling foundation. Erel had remembered seeing many barns like it in the countryside of his youth, and the thought of barn rats entered his head. They could get up to a foot long, tail not included, and often came in during the colder months. They used to come into the kennel where Erel slept as a child, and they would wriggle their bodies through the bars of Erel's crate. They carried with them fleas, ticks, and all sorts of other pests. Mostly, Erel thought of this because he knew, judging by the structure's condition, that whatever Hank was hiding inside couldn't be dead. It just wouldn't keep in a place like this. The wildlife could get in easily and ravage it. Even in the Pennsylvania autumn, a body still decayed quickly.

So whatever it was—it was likely alive.

"Watch your step," Hank said, as he just barely caught himself from stumbling.

Erel looked down to see what had thrown Hank off balance —the barn steps had a hole in them patched with another plank of wood. If he wasn't careful, Erel likely would've caught his foot on it as well.

Hank opened the barn door and Erel was surprised that there wasn't any kind of lock or barrier to entry. The door swung open with a simple push of Hank's hand, and the resulting creak echoed throughout the vast interior. Two hanging light bulbs, held to the first floor's vaulted ceiling by cobwebbed metal chains, illuminated a poor man's ghastly treasure trove. It was hard to see too much past Hank, who still lingered close to the entrance, but Erel could make out piles of clutter. Old antiques, heaps of empty boxes, spoiled hay, a rusted bicycle with a missing wheel... the place was littered with useless stuff.

"You never know when you might need something, huh." Hank slurred the last few words. He was either getting sloppy, or was equally drunk on the high of finally showing someone whatever it was he had kept inside this place.

Hanging in the air above the scent of the mud, rust and barn mildew was the unmistakable scent of piss and shit, a rank odor that made Erel both repulsed and at the same time, animalistically curious.

Hank stumbled forward along a thin path in the piled clutter and Erel followed, a few paces behind. As the sound of their steps echoed throughout the barn, Erel heard a soft whimpering which got increasingly jagged and louder the more they walked. It was definitely a human woman's cries—it sounded like she'd been wounded, probably not mortally if Erel had to take a guess based on sound alone.

Hank took a left turn and led Erel behind a few rotting barn pillars. There, in a darkened corner, sitting atop layers of soiled towels was a four-foot-tall dog crate. A stained flannel blanket was draped across the top and front, but Erel could see a woman's filth-encrusted feet poking out from the side.

"Just between you and me now," Hank said again, this time with a bit more of a warning tone in his voice. He held up a finger lazily at Erel and then withdrew the flannel from the top of the crate with the flair of a magician showing off a prized trick.

And there she was, Hank's big secret. His little pet.

The woman couldn't have been that old—probably somewhere in her twenties—though he did note a world-weariness in her eyes that seemed more deeply-set than what was likely recent trauma. She had curled her legs up to her chest and was cowering in the far left corner of the crate. The towels beneath the crate's center looked deeply stained with a mixture of blood, piss and probably other fluids if Erel had to take a guess. The woman was occupying the least soiled section of her cage in a way that reminded Erel of his time in the kennel during his youth. Humans weren't too different from dogs in that way—many didn't want to lay in their own shit. Only a few ragtag breeds reveled in soiling themselves, and humans were no different, especially such youthful little critters like the one Hank had locked up.

Hank inserted his hand into the top bars of the crate and the woman instinctively cowered from his touch. "My Noelle," Hank said, and then he turned to Erel with the smug expression of a braggart, and asked, "What do you think of her?"

Erel took a few steps closer. His eyes were adjusting to the darkness of this corner of the barn. Noelle was pretty banged up. Fluids and blood matted her blonde hair, which hung down to her shoulders. There was a jagged edge to one spot of her hair where Erel surmised Hank had either ripped part of it out, or a chunk had been cut off. Her lips were swollen and busted, with fresh cuts around the outline of her mouth. She looked up at Erel through the bars of her cage and it was easy to see she was terrified, but that there was a faint flicker of hope in her brown eyes—hope at seeing someone different than the large man who had put her in this four-foot wide hell.

"Peehs," she rasped at Erel and he was confused for a moment, thinking she was referencing having to take a piss. On second thought, though, as she whimpered the same distorted word to him again, he saw that her front teeth had been knocked out. She was trying very hard to articulate the word "Please" but without those front teeth, it came out altered. Hank had removed her ability to say certain letters of the alphabet. Erel found this idea intriguing in spite of himself, the idea of someone taking years and years to teach this woman how to speak only to have a man like Hank remove that ability with blunt physical force. When had Noelle learned the letter "l", Erel wondered, and could she learn it again? What other sounds would Hank take from this little critter?

"Pees," Hank said back to her in a mocking tone that was much more forceful than Noelle could muster. "Pees?" He asked her again, feigning incredulity. Hank unzipped his pants and took out his dick—an ugly, veiny appendage that Erel would have rather not seen—and proceeded to lean over the crate, pissing into it. Noelle tried to reduce her size and folded in on herself, her hands up, covering her face and some of her hair as Hank's piss splashed all over her. Erel knew it was likely stinging the cuts on her face—getting into her nostrils, soaking into her hair, and seeping between her busted lips despite her best efforts to protect herself. Erel knew, because Granddad had done the same to him on more than one occasion. Had made him do worse. There was a particular taste to a man's piss, and it was hard to forget once experienced.

Noelle whimpered, in what was her own brutalized dialect. The sounds that were missing from her words were, in their own way, a record of all of the bad things Hank had done to her. Hank had permanently altered Noelle, Erel thought, in the same way a man might pick up a piece of furniture, strip it and make it his own.

As the stream of piss weakened until finally coming to an end in intermittent conclusive spurts, Hank gave his dick a little shake, let out a revolting groan and put it back in his pants.

Hank zipped up and turned to Erel again with a look of smug satisfaction. He was showing off.

"She tried to bite me the first time, so I took care of her front teeth. Makes fucking her face easier anyway," Hank said, as cut-and-dry as if he were reading from an instruction manual. "The only problem is, as I see it, is that she's wearing out faster than I thought."

Erel smiled then, because he finally saw Hank for what he was—a dumb dog that couldn't catch his own tail. For all of Hank's size and overbearing talk, the man had sensed he was maybe in a bit over his head. He had Noelle, sure, but the way he was laying into her, Hank was right—she wouldn't last much longer. And then what for the big, bad man? Erel found himself laughing—he must have been chuckling for a few moments before even realizing it, himself, because Hank was staring at him, bewildered and off-balance. Noelle's whimpering had ceased and she remained crouched in the corner, her bruised arms up around her head in a shield position.

"You're gonna need a replacement model, you keep on like you are."

"So you *do* know?" Hank asked, and the sudden tender curiosity he expressed in his face made Erel uncomfortable. Erel didn't need anyone and he didn't want to be around anyone who felt like they needed him.

"Oh I know," Erel said, and he decided that he'd finally tell Hank a little more. He'd reached that conclusion because he felt confident he was going to kill Hank. He'd never taken a man's life before but the revulsion he felt at Hank's mediocrity had to be sated.

"You uh… you ever…," Hank chuckled a little, nervous. "You ever do anything like this? This kinda thing?"

"Well, big guy. Let me put it to you in a way you can understand." Erel kept his tone friendly, controlled. He didn't want to get into a brawl with Hank—Erel would likely lose if the guy saw it coming first. He took out his Buck 110 in a non-aggressive way, the blade still folded. "You see this tool? Imagine it's a paintbrush."

Hank rubbed his eyes—he was tired, drunk, and sloppy. And he'd made the weak human mistake of needing to share. Erel didn't need to share with others. Like a freak turn in the weather, Erel killed at random, snuffing out souls in a private, intimate way that loved ones of his whims would try to mull over in their nightmares, wondering… *did she suffer?*

They always suffered.

Erel extended the blade. "Let's imagine this little unassuming knife is a paintbrush. Or like it. And you have painters who can take a paintbrush and they paint the most beautiful pictures with them. C'mon, even you must've seen a picture like that once or twice, right, big guy?" Erel took a step closer to Hank.

"Yeah. I guess so."

"Right. So you think of the prettiest painting you've ever seen. And you think of the guy who painted that. And then you think of that guy looking at a child's crayon scribble. That's how I feel looking at your Noelle. Like I'm looking at the work of an amateur."

Hank laughed uneasily. "Amateur? Fuck off."

"Yeah. Real jackleg shit."

"Jack what?"

"Talentless. You don't got it. You don't got what it takes to do it right. You're a dime-a-dozen. You probably got her by surprise, on dumb luck. And you don't want to get rid of her, do you? You want to keep her. She's your fucktoy. But you're wearing her out and soon enough you'll be in search of a new toy, only you're so fucking ham-fisted, you'll screw it up and end up in prison before you can even get your dick wet in the new toy's cunt. This—your Noelle—this bitch is all you got and you fucked it up. Fucked it up for her, too, because when she's found, she won't be art. She won't be a mystery. She won't be remembered. She'll just be a sad one-liner in the daily crime beat. You're a hack, Hank."

"Hey why don't you back the fuck off, huh." Hank took a step closer to Erel to close the distance between them by half. He towered over Erel, in both breadth and height, but Erel wasn't scared. On the contrary, Erel was encouraged by this aggression. He was getting to Hank and that's what he wanted.

"All I'm saying is, why don't you let her out of the crate and I'll show you a thing or two. She ain't gonna run, right? You at least got that part right."

"Yeah. She's not gonna run. You wanna fuck her? Maybe we both fuck her?"

Noelle let out a cry at hearing those words from Hank. Once she started crying again, she couldn't seem to stop.

"I don't want to fuck her, Hank. I don't want to put my dick inside of her. I want to take her insides *out*."

And Erel did want that. He wanted to see what other sounds he could strip away from Noelle. He wanted to see exactly what she could be reduced to.

For Hank's part, he seemed fired up at the prospect of having what he viewed as a partner. "What're you gonna do to her?" he asked, and Erel couldn't help but compare Hank's excitement to that of a child's on Christmas Eve.

Erel was going to reduce Noelle to parts that were greater than her sum—leave the remnants of her scattered about like detritus after a storm. Create barn rat food out of the bits of her face. Cut off little slivers one at a time and dice them, throw them in the spoiled hay for the rodents to snack on. And he'd keep a part of her, too, though he hadn't decided which yet. Maybe a part of that busted lip, above the removed front teeth. He could rub it on his dick after he killed Hank later, or eat it like jerky.

It'd be soft and rubbery—parts like that always kept well.

CHAPTER 12
REGRETS, MAYBE

KRISTA TOOK in their room for the evening—nicotine-stained walls, squashed bugs, ill-fitted sheets, and an unplugged box television set. The nightstand had the drawers kicked out, a few of its screws scattered on the nearby carpet. She wondered what the bathroom looked like.

Nick beat her to it and she waited near the door for his report. He'd taken on a nervous energy since they'd arrived at the Paradise Inn—a self-conscious anxiety which burdened Krista with reassuring him.

He took a long moment in the bathroom before finally poking his head out from the doorway. With a look of embarrassment—as if the room's condition were his own fault—he said, "It's pretty bad in here. Just want to give you a heads up."

Krista sat on the very edge of the bed, which seemed a touch smaller than standard hotel fare, and assured Nick that she was fine. It was a lie, but she wanted to share in the burden and responsibility for their immediate surroundings differing so much from what they'd envisioned for the weekend.

"I've stayed in worse places," she said.

"Have you?"

"Actually, no."

They both laughed as they looked around at the miscellany of stains, grime, and dust.

Nick, after a moment of apparent hesitation, moved over

to sit next to Krista. The physical tension between them returned and despite everything, the thought of him kissing her passed through her mind. She felt self-conscious at her recollection of the boldness she'd demonstrated in the car earlier—perhaps a byproduct of her self-destructive, impulsive inclinations—and now she was overcome with shy anxiety. It was one thing to grab Nick's hand and to slide her leggings off while in the dark distracted environment of a moving car. It was another thing entirely to be seen or touched in the harsh, full light of a hotel room. In the full exposure of that room, Krista couldn't be anyone but herself and she felt vulnerable in a way that both scared and intrigued her.

"I'm really sorry about all this, you know." Krista could tell by the tone of his voice that Nick meant every word.

"It's okay."

"It's not. I should've made that cop take us somewhere else. You know, it really pissed me off that he took us here, knowing you're with me."

Nick moved Krista's hair off her shoulder.

"Yeah. Somewhere else would've been nice, I have to admit. But tomorrow we'll get out of here, and this will be some funny story we can remember later."

"How's your shoulder?"

"I think it's going to bruise, probably, but it's okay. Just kinda sore."

Nick held her gaze until Krista couldn't take it any longer, and she looked away. As she flicked her eyes back to see if he was still staring at her, he began to move the neckline of her dress off her shoulder. He gently ran his fingers over the red mark that was already blossoming from where her shoulder had slammed into the car door earlier. "Yeah, that definitely looks like it's going to bruise. I hate that I hurt you."

"You didn't hurt me."

"I was driving, Krista."

"Still, it's not your fault."

"If I hadn't been distracted, I wouldn't have hit whatever I hit."

"You don't know that you hit anything, though. The tire

might've just..." She gestured vaguely, searching for the right words.

"What? Spontaneously combusted?"

They both smiled at that suggestion and Krista let the eye contact between them last long enough that Nick accepted her invitation. The kiss was far more intimate than what had transpired earlier between them. The first was long, gentle, and seeking. The second was more aggressive and she felt her breath catch when he slipped his tongue inside her mouth. It felt good and it was the subsequent arousal that made Krista's body apprehensively tense up.

She wasn't supposed to feel good.

There was an urgent temptation to let her thoughts drift away, to become something dead again, but Krista didn't want that with Nick. She wanted to be present. But being present was hard for Krista because of her past. Even though she desperately wanted to relax and enjoy the moment with Nick, there was a disorienting, painful slew of emotions she felt whenever a man touched her, especially if it felt good. Most of all, she struggled with the memories it brought up and all of the ensuing shame—two things that were easier to lock away in her mind than to process.

Nick intuitively felt Krista's demeanor change, and he paused. There was a question in his gaze and Krista sensed that he genuinely cared how she was feeling. This small gesture—which she was shamefully aware should be commonplace—was novel for her, and the novelty of it suddenly made her teary-eyed.

He immediately noticed the tears, his expression one of confused concern. "Hey now...what's going on?" He asked this question gently, and used his thumb to softly wipe away the falling tears from her face.

"It's not you." Krista didn't know how to explain her feelings to him. A self-conscious, overwhelming anxiety came over her. "I'm really sorry," she said, not knowing what else to say.

"You have nothing to be sorry about."

"We can continue if you want. I'm fine." Krista tried to stop the flow of tears—tried to will her thoughts to numb the shameful anxiety lighting her skin on fire. She wished she could just slip out of her flesh, or that she'd never had a body at all, because then she wouldn't have to remember the things people had done to it.

"Hey, Krista… Krista. Look at me."

Krista looked into Nick's eyes.

"You don't have to say you're fine if you're not fine. And if you don't want to tell me what's going on, that's okay, too. But I'm here to listen if you want to tell me. I hate seeing you sad."

"I'm sorry," she said again. She always felt apologetic for crying. Crying was something she was supposed to do when alone, when no one else had to deal with it.

"For what? What on earth could you be sorry for?"

"For crying. For ruining this whole evening."

"Okay, first of all, you never have to apologize for crying. Not to me, not to anyone. And secondly, I'm not sure if you've looked around this place, or remember the weird cop who bored us to tears talking about this stupid town's golden years, but I'm pretty sure it's not you who ruined this evening."

Krista laughed, even while she continued to cry, and Nick pulled her close to him and wrapped his arms around her.

"I love you, you know."

"I know," she said, and she realized that she did know, and that it was the awareness of that love that made this all the more high stakes for her, emotionally. "I'm really scared that if I tell you certain things about my past, things that happened to me, you're just going to think I'm gross and not want to be with me anymore."

"That's just not going to happen, Krista. There's nothing you could tell me that would change my feelings for you."

"You promise?"

"Yeah. I do."

Krista let Nick hold her for a while longer and with time, her body finally relaxed and she was able to stop crying. There was a surprising sense of safety to being in his arms—a feeling that caught Krista off guard, given their surroundings —but it was the feeling, in her gut, that Nick wasn't going to hurt her.

For the first time since she was a child, Krista considered the possibility that she might finally be able to enjoy physical touch with another person—that, maybe, with Nick, she could at long last feel safe in her body.

Krista had already fallen asleep when the screaming began.

She stirred awake, and saw that Nick was already standing up, about to look out the front blinds. It was hard for her to determine how long she'd been asleep, or what time it was.

"Turn the lights off first," Krista said.

"Oh—hey..." He half-turned around to look at her, but quickly returned his attention to the blinds, his hand about to part two slats when Krista repeated herself.

"Turn the lights off before you look outside. So you can see better."

Nick obeyed her request and flicked off the lights.

The screaming, which had stopped for a few moments, then began in earnest again. It was a man's screams—loud, deep and alarming. Krista had never heard anything like it before in her life.

Nick opened two slats in the blinds and peered out between them. Krista sat up in bed, staring at him expectantly.

"What do you see?"

He didn't answer.

"Nick. What do you see? I'm scared."

There was a loud crash from the room next door—at least it sounded like the room next door. Krista couldn't exactly pinpoint where the screaming was coming from.

"I can't see anything. I think it's coming from inside one of the rooms."

"I think we should call the police."

"Let's call the front desk first. Maybe they've already called the cops."

"There's no hotel phone, Nick... let's just call the police. Please."

Something—or someone—slammed into the wall of their room from the other side with such force that the box television set moved and the dresser drawers rattled.

"Jesus Christ," Nick said.

There was another noise this time, the sound of the door from the next room opening.

Krista couldn't stand not being able to know what was happening. She got out of bed and instinctively put on her shoes in case they'd have to leave in a hurry. Nick did not follow suit. He was still staring out between the blinds.

"What do you see?"

"There's a guy. He looks pretty hurt."

Krista got close to the window but before she could look outside, Nick stopped her with his arm. His grip was firm on her shoulder and she winced from the tenderness, but didn't think he'd noticed in the darkly lit room.

"Why don't you go in the bathroom and wait there." It wasn't really a question. Krista could tell he was on edge.

"Nick. What's going on? What do you see?"

"Just—"

The door to their room shook before he could finish his statement. Someone began banging loudly on it. It wasn't the measured knocking of hotel staff, but the desperate, urgent force of someone trying to break in.

"Krista, will you just fucking go in the bathroom and wait there," Nick whispered. Then, before she could say anything, he apologized in a softer whisper, "Hey, sorry. Just—just do it, okay?"

Krista had misgivings about leaving Nick, but her own instinct for survival kicked in and the best option at the moment was to hide. The only way out of the room was through the front door, so she went into the bathroom like Nick had asked. She kept the light off, closed the door, and slid down into a seated position with her knees up against her chest, her back against the door. There was neither a lock nor a window, and Krista was terrified that it would be all too easy for someone to break through the room's cheaply constructed entrance and then come into the bathroom and find her. Krista didn't know how to fight. She didn't know if Nick knew how to fight either —hadn't ever asked him. He didn't seem like much of a fighter.

The banging and screaming could still be heard through the closed bathroom door, though the sounds were a little more muffled. It was hard to make out exactly what was going on, and she wanted to call out Nick's name just to hear his voice...to know he was okay, but at the same time, she knew the best thing she could do right now would be to be completely quiet and still.

To play dead. She was good at that.

There was a moment of quiet and then Krista heard the glass break.

The window.

It was the first time she had heard Nick scream.

CHAPTER 13
NEVER LEAVE THE OFFICE AT NIGHT

MISTY HEARD the commotion from across the parking lot. She'd been leafing through one of Hank's magazines when she first heard the screaming. It sounded like it was coming from one of the rooms at the far end of the strip, close to where she'd put that sorry-looking couple Sheriff Hall had brought in earlier. Those folks—she could tell they weren't from around Beleth Station.

The woman had looked delicate, and the guy—more the college type than like anyone from around Beleth. An easy mark in these parts—a guy her own father would probably call weak, not that Misty much cared what her father thought about anyone anymore. The woman *had* been pretty, though.

Misty couldn't deny that she had found her alluring. *Krista*, the man had called her, just before they'd walked off to their room. Krista.

Misty whispered the name aloud, waiting to see if the screaming would continue. Screams weren't uncommon around the Paradise Inn, and if Misty was lucky, they would stop for good soon. Sometimes visitors got a little carried away with the girls and had to be put in their place. Misty figured that's what had happened.

She turned her thoughts again to Krista and tried to recall the woman's appearance. She had brown hair and soft features. There was a fragility to her demeanor, the way she almost hid behind the man she'd been traveling with. Misty remembered seeing the woman stare up at the moths that gathered around the overhead light. There was an innocence about her, and yet also something very troubled in her eyes—Misty didn't know why, but she felt the woman was going through something rough. That she was in pain. It was just a hunch Misty had. She'd seen a lot of pain over the years while living in Beleth Station, and she could spot it on a woman's face.

Misty hadn't been with a woman in a long time. It was something she didn't feel free to do in Beleth Station, but she would get out of this town one day and when she did, she considered that maybe she would be with a woman like Krista.

Misty had known another woman who'd had pain like that —who carried it in her eyes, locked away. Her childhood friend, Noelle. The briefest memories of the two of them kissing in her bedroom back in high school. The way Noelle had looked askance at her afterward, and had asked to try again to make sure she hadn't felt anything. The way Misty had lied and said she didn't feel anything, either. How both of them had laughed at the time, saying they were sure they weren't into women, but how later on, Misty had felt guilty for lying, knowing that wasn't true.

Misty felt embarrassed for looking at Hank's magazines during her shift—and she felt even more embarrassed by the things she saw depicted on the glossy pages—the things men were doing to women in Hank's magazines—Misty would never want to do. But she did like looking at the women's figures and letting her thoughts drift to how it might feel to touch them.

One day, she'd get out of this shithole town—maybe after her father finally died—and then, she'd be able to finally live the life she wanted. Or maybe she'd leave before her father died. What had he ever done for her? Maybe she'd steal away in the night and go to Philadelphia, or New York, or west to Pittsburgh. Anywhere but Beleth Station.

The plan wasn't that far-fetched either. The night shift differential she'd been earning working at the Paradise Inn was starting to add up, and she'd been saving enough to conceivably put down a deposit and first month's rent somewhere.

The screaming started up again. It was louder this time, and more constant. Misty craned her head as close to the glass front of the office booth as she could to try to get a look at the far end of the strip. A door opened. It was the room next to where she'd put Krista and her boyfriend for the night. The man who stumbled out into the parking lot was covered in blood. It was hard to discern his features in the dark, but it looked like someone had taken something heavy to his face more than once.

Misty marveled that the man could even walk at all, seeing how beaten up he was, and she supposed it had to be adrenaline keeping him upright. Whatever he had done to one of the girls, it had really pissed someone off.

Misty grabbed the phone to dial Sheriff Hall, but stopped mid-dial when she saw the man turn his attention to the room where Krista and her boyfriend were staying. He was beating on the door heavily, screaming for them to open up.

It was just a few more numbers on the keypad to get Sheriff Hall on the line—and Misty would complete the call in a moment—but she couldn't take her eyes off the bloodied, bludgeoned man. She needed to see if he was going to get into Krista's room.

He better not hurt her.

Just as Misty finished dialing and heard the ring on the other end, the beaten man broke the glass window and crawled into Krista's room. Misty put the phone receiver on the desk, Sheriff Hall's voice calling out from it.

Two more men—both of whom Misty recognized from around town, both carrying crowbars, climbed through the smashed window after the beaten man. Male screaming, accentuated by the crashing of furniture, rang out from the gaping smashed window and echoed across the parking lot.

Misty knew she should pick up the phone, but she was transfixed by what was unfolding in front of her. She didn't want to take her face from the glass. She feared that if she diverted her attention for even a moment, that she'd miss something crucial. There was something paralytic about witnessing violence. In theory, Misty knew she should help, but she wasn't sure how she could. She wasn't supposed to leave the office at night.

Sheriff Hall's voice still rang out from the receiver, like a record skipping over and over, and Misty was too lazy to set it right. It was Krista she was concerned for—Krista whom she was watching out for, her face pressed close against the glass, eyes unblinking.

As the screams died down, the two men carrying crowbars exited the room—through the door this time—dragging behind them what looked like Nick, but much worse for wear. They dragged him by his hands as his body slid across the parking lot concrete, scratching up his back something fierce. He wasn't fighting back; he barely looked conscious, blood running down one side of his face.

The other man—the one who had seemingly started it all by smashing the window—was nowhere to be seen from where Misty was standing. The two crowbar-toting men hoisted Nick's unconscious body into the trunk of their car. One of them spun his head around to where Misty was in the illuminated office booth and she immediately crouched down out of sight.

Oh God don't let them come over here.

The door to the office was locked, as always, but she didn't know how well it would stand up to repeated forceful attempts to get in, if they really wanted to get inside. But her fears were lessened when she heard what could only be the engine of a car, and screeching tires. Trepidatiously, Misty arose from her crouched position and could see that the car was no longer in the parking lot.

She finally picked up the receiver, but Sheriff Hall was no longer on the line. She presumed he was already on his way since he knew she wouldn't call unless it were something serious.

Misty now faced a difficult decision. She could either leave the office, which she swore never to do, to check on Krista and the other man who had looked pretty badly hurt, or she could stay in the booth and wait for the sheriff to arrive.

The recollection of Krista's pretty brunette hair, her intelligent eyes roving around the Paradise Motel like she'd never seen anything like it before...

Misty decided to take a chance. She took the Paradise master room key from the desk drawer and unlocked the office entrance. The darkness of the night felt especially foreboding as she left the booth's safety. Thoughts of Isabelle Daniels, and how Sheriff Hall had warned that her head had looked like putty after she was murdered, ravaged any sense of confidence Misty might've otherwise had.

Still, there were people who might be hurt and it was Misty's responsibility to go see about that. Shamefully, she knew this was something she hadn't always done. There were plenty of times in the past where working girls had been beaten or worse, and Misty had often turned a blind eye to those incidents. The fear of retribution for interfering with Beleth Station's industry was deeply ingrained in her, and it was just easier to look away and to try to forget.

But Krista was different. She was an out-of-towner and had nothing to do with the income of this place. Sheriff Hall should've never taken her and Nick to the Paradise. The couple was too soft for it—they should've been driven far away from this hellhole, as far as Misty was concerned. For fuck's sake, Misty, herself, wanted to get as far away from Beleth Station as she possibly could. She knew what this town did to people—how it sucked them dry and used their carcasses for firewood. The town was full of lifeless meat sacks—people who once had souls and had lost them to the town somewhere along the way. Old mill rats who regaled the youth with the town's heyday, a peak that seemed so far gone, it felt like fiction. Like a legend to soothe the pain of everyday life.

A refrain of 'we once were great' while everything disintegrated into shit and sank the history further and further into the background, now so dim that it could barely be seen behind all the boarded up windows, the skulking drunks, and the women who'd been about the life a little too long to feel anything anymore.

Misty thought of it all as she walked toward the far end of the Paradise, and every ounce of history she'd ever known about the town came flooding back to her, like a life flashing before her eyes, as she saw Krista Mabry stumble out of the room, wild-eyed and terrified.

"They took him!"

Krista lurched toward Misty with fear writ large across her

face. She turned her gaze every which way, as if expecting to be attacked from every direction. Misty approached the traumatized woman, hoping to calm her down and guide her back to the office where they could both lock themselves inside.

To Misty's horror, though, Krista held out a defensive hand as Misty approached.

"Don't come any closer." The terror in Krista's eyes turned to determination, and Misty felt sure the woman meant to defend herself from any perceived threat—of which Misty could only conclude she was one.

"Hey, I'm not going to hurt you… your adrenaline must be in high gear."

"Not going to hurt me? Not going to hurt me! They took Nick. You knew they would, didn't you? Gave us that room on purpose? Think this is some sick game?"

The door to another occupied room swung open and two women stuck their heads out, staring.

Krista yelled at them, too, "You see what's happening here! She's trying to kill me. They took my boyfriend. His name is Nick Rawlison."

One of the women bystanders laughed, and Misty could hear her murmur, "High as fuck." They waved their hands at Krista in a go-on motion and soon ducked back inside the room. Misty heard the door lock. What didn't concern the residents of Paradise directly, tended to not concern them at all. Most in Beleth didn't see anything, and didn't say anything, no matter the crime.

Misty tried again to persuade Krista. "Okay, I won't come near you, but why don't you follow me back to the office. It has a lock, and we can stay there until the sheriff arrives. Does that sound good?"

"No, fuck that. I'm not going anywhere with you. I don't trust *you*."

Misty sighed. This was going nowhere fast.

"Fine. Stay here, then. I'm going to go back to the office and call the Sheriff's office again. Make sure he's on his way."

Krista loosened up at that; Misty could see the tension visibly leave Krista's body and she started to tremble lightly, as if the adrenaline and fear were subsiding.

"I'll wait here," Krista said, much less aggressively.

Misty nodded, and turned on her heel to hurry back to the booth at the other end of the parking lot.

As Misty walked closer to the booth, she saw something unexpected. Hank's car was parked by the dumpsters, but there wasn't anyone in it. She opened the office door and looked around from within the doorway, but didn't see him. She wondered if he'd forgotten something and came back to pick it up.

Her body stiffened as something cold and sharp met the soft skin of her neck. The pressure was just enough to stop Misty from breathing, for fear of being cut.

"You must be Miss Misty," an unfamiliar voice said. "Now don't say anything, and do as I say, and we won't hurt you. Understood? Raise your right hand if you understand. Misty slowly raised her right hand to show she understood what the man had told her.

She wondered if this was one of the same men who had taken Nick, but she didn't have a chance to ask. The man kept the blade to her throat as he held her close, his other hand firmly gripped on her left arm. He guided her back out of the office doorway and much to her shock, over to Hank's car by the dumpsters.

As she got closer, Hank appeared from behind one of the dumpsters, popped open his trunk, and grabbed Misty by the feet while the other man hoisted up her shoulders.

"See, I told you she'd be easy."

It was the last thing she heard from Hank before the trunk slammed shut.

In the trunk's darkness, the images in Hank's magazines drifted through her mind. She had a very good idea of what he intended to do to her, and the knowledge made her wish she were already dead.

CHAPTER 14
STORED BELOW GROUND

THE SKIN on Jackie's knuckles was missing in long strips and it felt like a hammer had been taken to both of his wrists. As the fight's adrenaline faded and the pain settled in, Jackie worried he'd broken some small bones in his hands, a consequence of rage-fueled recklessness.

Looking at the homeless man's battered face and its mess of unnatural bumps and blood-spattered bruises, it wasn't readily evident to Jackie if he'd committed murder or mere assault. He didn't want to get close enough to feel a pulse.

In fact, Jackie wanted to get as far away from the bloodied man as possible. He could scarcely remember throwing the first punch, though he knew it had caught the addict by surprise.

Usually he'd use a piece of pipe or a brick found around the mill for these kinds of exploits, but today Jackie had felt compelled to use his hands. There was some extra release—some fleeting sensation of power and ensuing illusory ego—in using his fists to pound another man's flesh. To watch a face change in front of his eyes, and to keep hammering away until he felt like he was spent.

It was weird, Jackie thought, taking a bloodied knuckle to his lips, that he didn't get aggressive like that during sex. No, if anything, he was docile with Noelle—compliant, meek, and approval-seeking.

He considered bitterly that maybe he should have been

more aggressive with her. It was one of the theories circulating in his tormented mind after she disappeared—that he should've done to her what his mom's many boyfriends had done over the years—alternated sweetness with violence. And Jackie knew he had violence in him. Proof of it was crumpled on the cement in front of him, possibly dead, and further evidence radiated pain from his own scarred, injured hands. Violence had swelled in Jackie from a young age. It had seemed to seep into his growing bones from childhood onward, a byproduct of Beleth Station's poverty and cruelty. Jackie's mom had been a town favor since he was a boy, and there was no shortage of jokes that the other kids had cracked at his expense.

Jackie couldn't say exactly when the first thought of violence had entered his mind, but once the fantasies had begun, they never stopped. He'd stare dead-faced at the other kids and let their jokes run off him like water, while in his mind he imagined all sorts of things. Tearing their eyes out and pissing in the sockets. Shoving scissors through their nostrils into their brains, giving them foul lobotomies. These fantasies, he would store away in a private collection so interior that only he knew about them. The issue had been, and always was, that Jackie was essentially a coward. Instead of confronting the boys who harassed him, he took out his anger on weaker, unsuspecting subjects—and fortunately, Beleth Station had its fill of forgettable people. But it was never arousing for Jackie. Being in the throes of sex was akin to beating a man, in that Jackie did often lose his awareness of the world around him in the adrenaline-high midst of the act, but it was ultimately a different sort of thrill. Bludgeoning flesh until it caved and flattened like putty lit up a different compartment of Jackie's brain. It was like taking out his private collection of violent urges for a special audience. And on the other hand, in many ways, it was also akin to taking a shit. At the end of it all, it was a private release and not one he cared to spend much time thinking about once it was finished.

With Noelle, things were different. There had been a time when Jackie tried to mix it up with Noelle. He'd gotten the funny idea that he was an aberrant man for letting her dominate him. It was a pervasive sensation that he still couldn't shake fully, a self-accusation of being a sexual defect. When other guys talked about sex, none of their stories matched Jackie's own experience, nor did their tales particularly excite him. While he knew that some of what the other guys said was exaggerated, it unnerved him how his time with Noelle varied so much from everything he'd ever known about what was expected of him as a man.

There had been an afternoon when he'd met up with Noelle midday, had slid into the same room she was renting out at the Paradise, and had laid with her a while. They talked at first—that was something Jackie liked about Noelle—that she'd listen to him talk about his mom, his childhood, his love of comic books and seventies action films. Nothing was off limits with her and she seemed to genuinely be interested in what he had to say, which was more than he could say for just about anyone else in Beleth Station.

But then the afternoon had taken its usual turn. Noelle pressed a finger to his lips after she'd had her fill of conversation. She'd propped herself up on her elbows, her legs spread, and looked at Jackie expectantly. This was a usual progression for the two of them and though Jackie had begun his relationship with Noelle as an awkward amateur, over time she had taught him the exact tempo, motion, and pressure required to please her. There were whole afternoons spent where Noelle barely touched Jackie at all—it was left up to her whims whether or not he would get off, and it was that thrilling uncertainty that encouraged his efforts when his head was between her legs. He didn't immediately comply that one afternoon, though.

No, he had looked away, shyly considering how he might try to be more dominant with her, how he could be more like a 'man' like the other guys he knew. Jackie felt a flush of embarrassment at the recollection of it while he stood in the mill, his fists throbbing, thinking back to how stupid he'd been when he'd grabbed a handful of Noelle's hair and had tried to force her head down on his cock. It had been severely misguided—an awkward, overly-forceful display that wouldn't have been of much use, anyway, as his dick had gone limp from the anxiety of it all.

"What the fuck are you doing?" She had been efficient in twisting her body and wedging a foot up to kick his chest, even while his fingers still grappled for control. Jackie surmised she was practiced at getting guys off of her because he wasn't expecting the swiftness with which she freed herself from his grasp. It was only when he'd noticed the clump of hair in his fist that he realized how hard he'd been holding onto her hair, and a deep, intractable shame swept through him.

"That's not like you," Noelle had said, massaging her head and running her fingers through her hair. He'd watched her pull out the tangles with her hands while he fought back tears. And even though he'd just hurt her, she let him lay his head in her lap, the two of them not talking—just existing for a time.

But what the fuck did she know, anyway, Jackie thought, his head still reeling from the beat-down he'd given the homeless squatter.

The refrain *she's just some whore* ran through his head like a ticker tape, but it never made him feel an ounce better. Because, he knew, she wasn't *just* anything to him—he loved her. He had loved her with all of his heart, and now she was gone. She'd left him in this decrepit shithole town with only his blasted mother to talk to.

A weepy-eyed dog appeared in the doorway of the vacant mill workroom. It wasn't terribly unusual to see animals in the old mill—Jackie had seen plenty of rats, at least—but this dog was a particularly strange sight. The poor mutt looked like it didn't have an easy life; its coat was matted, overgrown and from the looks of a few open sores, likely bug-infested. He was a big mutt—hard to tell exactly from this distance, but Jackie estimated the dog stood at about hip level.

The mutt shook its head in an unnatural rhythm, froth-like drool dripping from its open mouth. Jackie considered the dog might be rabies-infected, possibly from one of the mill rats or another animal, but the mutt didn't seem aggressive in the slightest. It also didn't approach Jackie at first. Two yellow canine eyes, weepy with black and brown build-up, stared at him, and Jackie stared back, though after a time he wished he could look away.

The dog made Jackie's skin crawl; there was a presence to its yellow eyes that seemed to compel. Jackie was under the strange impression that perhaps the mutt wasn't actually a dog at all.

That's crazy. Of course it's just a dog.

The homeless man stirred and Jackie was filled with relief. At least the man was breathing—a conclusion Jackie wasn't sure of just moments ago. The dog looked at the homeless man and then back again at Jackie, a surreal sense of acknowledgment in its eyes. It then walked over to a closed door to Jackie's right, pausing to turn its head. Graffiti and damp moss adorned the door, as well as a few old nails where it looked like maybe a sign had been hung in better days.

The dog pawed at the door and looked at Jackie again, frothy spit dripping from its muzzle.

Jackie hadn't gone through that door before—in fact, Jackie, like most of Beleth Station's youth, had only explored a small percentage of the old Medallion Paper Mill's rooms. It was largely considered dangerous to go too deep into the mill. Even though it'd been declared a superfund site so many years ago, it was long-believed that Medallion had hidden most of its pollu- tants, or improperly disposed of them in such a way that the EPA wouldn't be able to decipher head from tail. It was never exactly determined what truthfully happened as the mill had folded before the investigation could begin in earnest, but there were enough cancer clusters, enough malformed pups and kittens around Beleth Station, to give credence to the rumors about Medallion.

Jackie took a few steps closer to the dog. He was hesitant to approach as he knew wild dogs could be unpredictable, even violent, but he bent down to the dog's eye level and held out a hand. The mutt licked at Jackie's bleeding knuckles and the wetness of the saliva both soothed and stung at the same time.

"Egh...hey now." Jackie retracted his hand. Up close, he could see the dog's gooped-up eyes more clearly. Big ovals of yellow ringed with gunk that looked like it might ooze off at any moment. The sores on the dog's missing fur patches lent a strange polka-dot pattern to its otherwise matted coat. A sorry sight.

The dog pawed again at the door and looked at Jackie. Its

lips curled back from its teeth and Jackie had the bizarre expectation that the mutt might say something to him.

It was a preposterous expectation, Jackie knew, and yet at the same time, he could swear it looked like the animal was about to speak. A chill went down his spine as he imagined, conjured up from old comics he probably had long since read and forgotten, that perhaps the dog was a demon.

He shook off the thought, reminding himself that the demon had just lapped at his bleeding knuckles, which didn't seem that scary at all.

Finally working up the nerve, Jackie decided to pull on the door where the dog was pawing. Maybe the dog sensed food was in there, or maybe it was another mill exit that Jackie wasn't even aware of. The Medallion was large, having been the town's primary employer for so long, and had undergone multiple expansions in its heyday, under different contractors. Back in the day, Jackie had heard from Beleth's older residents, the Medallion was sometimes said to have been three mills in one, and its oldest workers were the only ones who truly knew the full layout, having been there since the building's humble beginnings. Those workers, the originals, were all dead now, of course.

What was left of the Medallion were sprawling vacant factory grounds, with nooks, vaults, workrooms, wings and storage facilities left poorly documented and completely untended to. The above-ground, with its shifty light that came in through the frosted windows, felt relatively safe, and was the preferred playground of teens, junkies, and unremarkables alike.

But what faced Jackie was a staircase leading down. Jackie never went below ground. In fact, he was downright superstitious about it due to all of the rumors about Medallion's unsavory activities.

Yet, as the dog limped downstairs, its sore-crusted hind legs bobbing with each miniature step, Jackie found himself following. As the light faded from the open door above, Jackie was surprised to see a hazy fluorescent glow as he took the first turn on the descending staircase. He kept a hand on the wall while he walked down the stairs and soon his fingers were slick with dampness. Briefly, he worried about mold but his attention was promptly fixed again on not losing his balance as he descended further and further, his own steps echoing behind the dog's clacking claws.

"Hey boy, slow now..."

Jackie only spoke because he wanted to hear anyone's voice as he went lower and lower into the mill, even if it was his own. Somehow hearing his own voice was a comfort. He wondered how and why the fluorescent lights were on? Was this area being worked on? Rehabbed? He couldn't imagine that would be so. The Medallion had long since been abandoned with no future repurposing in mind due to the superfund controversies.

"Where you taking me, boy?"

The dog didn't stop to look back at Jackie and instead kept limping along, its body descending in a slow, rhythmic gallop down the cement stairs. Jackie followed. He was far enough along the descent that to go back by himself at this point almost felt scarier than to continue to follow the dog. At least the dog was another breathing creature, and it seemed to be taking him somewhere. And besides, there was light, so maybe there were people nearby.

He started to panic that maybe the homeless man he'd beaten up in the room above would stir awake, and if there were people below ground, maybe they would find out what he'd done to the poor man. Jackie could get in a lot of trouble. At the very least, they'd probably ask him what happened to his hands.

After what seemed like an eternity—far too many sets of stairs to count—the steps finally ended, and opened up into a fluorescent-lit room full of large sealed canisters. The lights overhead flickered and gave Jackie the creeps.

The dog looked back at Jackie and gave the same impression as it had upstairs, that it wanted to speak, or at least had some recognition of conscious communication.

"Where you taking me, boy?" Jackie asked again, though this time his voice was quieter. He could hear rustling in the room, and human laughter.

He cautiously followed the mutt through an aisle of canisters until he came upon what he could only presume were the dog's owners. A group of four people sat around a card table. There was a man in a dirty blue jumper, a young attractive woman, a teenage boy in an old band t-shirt, and a middle-aged man with deep scars along his forearms. They all stared at Jackie, cards in their hands.

"Well we'll have to reshuffle now," the man in the jumper said.

"Oh let's finish this hand, can't we?" That was the young beautiful woman who asked. Jackie noted that her eyes looked terribly sad, and he wondered why she was down here, or why any of them were down here. It was an odd place to be playing cards.

The light seemed to grow dimmer, the flicker more aggressive. The dog sat next to the man with scars on his forearms and peeled back its lips, froth gathering around bared teeth until it dripped onto the cement floor. Shadows cast by the large canisters, which were stacked three high, grew darker and fell over the card players' faces. In the darkness, Jackie began to see things—hallucinations, he was sure—but it looked like the young woman's head was gaping, bleeding, and bashed in. It was a brief vision and then it dissipated as she got up from the table and disappeared into a canister aisle for a moment.

"You ever play Pass the Time?" the man in the jumper asked. He wasn't looking at Jackie, but somehow Jackie knew the question was directed at him.

"No, I'm not much of a card player."

The young woman came out from the canister aisle, a folding chair scraping along the cement behind her.

"Well, have a seat 'n we'll teach ya," the scarred man said. The young woman pulled up the empty chair to the table, positioned it between where she was sitting and where the man in the dirty jumper sat.

"I don't think I have time for a card game."

"You can't leave until you play a hand," Jumper said.

"Just one hand," the young woman said, and she patted the chair next to her. There was something uncanny about her—like he'd seen her face somewhere, but he couldn't place it. "Did you go to Beleth High by chance?" He cringed after he asked because the scarred man chuckled, no doubt laughing at Jackie. Men always laughed at Jackie.

"I did!" Her sad eyes belied the excitement in her voice.

"There was a brief time where it was called Medallion High," Jumper said.

"Mmhmm," the scarred man agreed.

"Are we going to play this hand or what?" It was the first time the teenager had spoken and he sounded either pissed off or tired, Jackie couldn't tell. Jackie wondered whether the teenager and the young woman were these two men's relatives. Maybe one of them was the groundskeeper? But he was pretty sure Medallion Paper Mill no longer had any employees.

"Sit down, won't ya?" the scarred man said, a little more firmly than the others.

Jackie decided to sit down, though he wasn't positive it was his decision at all. He felt somehow lured here, into this strange underground storage room.

The woman gathered the cards into the center of the table and sloshed them around.

"That's not how ya shuffle for Chrissake," the scarred man complained.

"It's how I shuffle," she said.

"Well it ain't right. Didn't anyone ever teach ya?"

"Let her be," Jumper said, and the woman continued to slosh the cards around until she had finally gathered them again in a neat stack. She dealt them counterclockwise until the entire deck was distributed.

"Uh, what are we playing again?" Jackie knew very few card games, and they were only childish ones he'd learned as a kid, like War and Go Fish.

"Pass the Time," the woman said.

"I don't know that one."

"It's easy. I put a card down first, face up. Then you put a card down, face up. And so forth. Until all of our cards are in the center of the table."

"And then what?"

"And then, once they are all in the center of the table, I pick one up. And then you pick one up. And so forth. Until they're all in our hands again."

"So what's the point?"

"Pass the time."

"Yeah but like, who wins?"

"There are no winners."

"Can we play already? I'm getting bored," the teenager said.

The woman put a card down in the center. A two of diamonds. "I don't like diamonds, so I always put them down first and pick them up last," she said, and she laughed a small, sad laugh. It had an edge of insanity to it.

It was Jackie's turn, but he didn't immediately put down a card. He hadn't even looked at his hand yet. The discomfort of the situation was settling in and he started to regret following the dog down here. These people weren't right—there was something uncanny about each of them. He looked closely at Jumper, and saw that on the man's coverall, there was a Medallion Paper Mill emblem.

Strange.

And the woman—where had he seen her before?

"What's your name?" He blurted it out.

"Isabelle."

"Isabelle Daniels?"

"Who's asking, anyway?" She smiled sweetly at him and the shadows edged in around her face. On the half where the light didn't touch, Jackie saw a pulverized, gaping wound, bits of carnage dangling from man-made openings. And then, the light expanded again to full illumination and Isabelle was restored, her beauty made tragic by the agony in her eyes.

"You can't be Isabelle Daniels. She—"

"Play a fucking card, won't ya." It wasn't a request coming from the scarred man this time. It was a command.

Jackie put a card down; he didn't even look at it until it was in the center of the table.

"Queen of hearts. I'll be grabbing that on the next pick up for sure," Jumper said.

Jackie started to get up, but the sound of the chair on the concrete stirred the mutt, who snarled at Jackie.

"Oh you can't leave once a hand has started," Isabelle said.

"Well how does a hand end?"

"When the time passes."

"How much time?"

"No sense of it really. Not here. Not below ground."

"Why am I here?"

"You *shouldn't* have come here."

It was Jackie's turn again. He played another card. They went round and round like that, until he grew dizzy. Sometimes he saw them as people, and other times, he swore he was playing cards with corpses. There was a fruity, sour scent in the air, and the canisters cast such long, looming shadows over the table. Jackie could've sworn, as the card game wore on, that the shadows grew more ominous, deeper, and stranger, as if they, themselves, were growing limbs and branches. He felt like he was fighting for light, and air.

It was hard to breathe this deep in the mill. It was hard to see.

But there was a scent in the air, of fruit and decay, of pulp and rot.

The mutt shook its head feverishly, snot dripping from its eyes, and Jackie felt like he could hear the dog speaking to him, a strange mind to mind connection.

It told him to keep playing. Just one more hand, and then he could leave. But keep playing for now, the mutt intoned. Beleth needed him, needed his bones.

They were the foundation.

Had to pass the time down here, like all good corpses and poisons do, pass the time below ground for the living. Pass the time in the stench of ripe decay.

Jackie played another card, then another, unsure if he was breathing any longer, or if he was the dying thought of a corpse in a canister, an imagined life after death that was in reality perhaps the last neuron fired before suffocation.

But the time passed.

Every town was built on the backs of those who came previously, the bones of those stored below.

CHAPTER 15
ONLY PRODUCT

KRISTA KNEW she had to get help, and get the hell out of Beleth Station, fast. She wasn't sure that the town's one sheriff would be equipped to deal with everything that had transpired that evening.

Her thoughts raced, alternating between fearing for her own safety and fearing for the safety of Nick. She could still remember the traumatizing sounds of his screams while she had held her knees to her chest in the bathroom, her breath so still that she thought she might die if she had to hold it any longer.

Now she ran through the streets of Beleth Station, knocking on doors and seeing if anyone might answer. At the same time, she felt terrified that someone might answer because what if it was the wrong someone? Was anyone in this town normal? She felt like she might be better served just running straight out of the town's limits and trying her luck on an adjacent highway, but that was a tough thing to do given Beleth Station's location. She would've had to run on dark mountain roads in the chill autumn, and already her legs were starting to give out. She needed someone in the town to help her.

Dragging her down was the weight of her backpack, which still rattled with the many pills she had inside, her little safety cache in case things with Nick had gone sour. It now seemed foolish, somehow, even laughable, that she had those pills, considering all her mind was fixated on at the moment was the primal need to survive. Perhaps she'd had everything wrong because in that moment, as she panted for air stumbling down Beleth Station's downtown thoroughfare, she wanted nothing more than to make it through this ordeal, to be alive and to get one more chance with Nick. One more time in his arms, and one more time hearing him tell her everything was going to be okay.

And then there was the opposing train of thought in her head, the one laced with shame and guilt. The one that made her feel like she was responsible for everything that had happened that night because she had agreed to the trip in the first place. If she had stayed behind with Tom, if she could've somehow found a way to have been content with that life, then none of this would have happened. Nick could be dead right now, for all she knew, and the weight of that hit her like a ton of bricks.

Finally, she came across a neon sign that said, "Nowhere Special" and peered inside the window. It didn't look like anyone was in there, but she saw a light on in the back. Lights usually meant people. Krista wondered if some of the staff there, or maybe the owner, had stayed behind after hours. Maybe a server or the like was still cleaning up. Someone who could help her at this time of night.

She knocked on the door, but after waiting a few moments, no one answered. Krista looked up and down the street from where she was standing outside the establishment. On a utility pole, in the dim glow of the changing street light at the intersection, Krista caught the text "HAVE YOU SEEN NOELLE ADAMS" on a black-and-white flyer featuring a young girl's face. Krista could easily imagine Nick's face and name there in place of Noelle's. Who was Noelle, she wondered, before quickly snapping her attention back to the door of Nowhere Special. Krista knocked again, this time louder. She worried about drawing too much attention to herself, and at the same time wanted anyone at all to notice her, to see her. She had a simultaneous desperation for help, coupled with an intense paranoia that whoever had taken Nick, whoever had killed that other man, and whoever had shoved that poor motel clerk into the trunk of their car, would somehow track Krista down, too.

When no one answered the door, Krista took her chances and pushed. Much to her surprise and relief, the door swung open without much effort and Krista was soon inside a bar that smelled like piss, sweat, and stale smoke. The overwhelming stench set a foul roil in her stomach, but she kept on toward the light in the back. As she walked closer, well past the bar and the few tables that were scattered about, she could see that the light was coming from a back room—shining through a rectangular window in the door. She looked in and saw Sheriff Hall, as well as a few other men. Seeing the Sheriff provided Krista with instant relief, and she shoved the back room's door open, stumbling inside with such relieved exhaustion that she thought she might collapse on the spot.

Sheriff Hall turned to face her, as did the other men. They all looked at her with alarm and suspicion, which didn't surprise Krista since she was sure she made for quite an unusual sight, especially at this hour.

"What's she doing here?" One of the men asked.

"Should we pack her up, too?" That came from another direction.

Krista suddenly felt ill with another surge of adrenaline, and she started to take in her surroundings. On the opposite side of the room were several large sacks with quarter-sized holes punched in them. The bulges in the sacks looked like human figures, and one of them stirred, limbs thrashing out and making the thick fabric bulge in fist shapes, and foot shapes. Sounds emanated from a few of the sacks, doubtlessly spurred on by the sound of Krista's voice—cries for help, as well as gurgles, and screams. One of the men took a metal poker and stabbed at the sacks indiscriminately. That put an end to the screaming, but it caused a new problem—blood. Blood seeped out from one of the sacks and pooled on the ground.

"If you ruined one of our products, you're going to have to replace it with new inventory, Glenn," Sheriff Hall warned.

Krista backed up slowly, but Sheriff Hall was on her before she could dart out of the room. He put his hand over her shoulder and shut the door behind her. He pulled a key out of his pocket and locked the deadbolt.

"Afraid you can't leave now, Ms. Mabry," he said.

"Is Nick in one of those?" Krista asked. She wasn't sure if she wanted to know the answer.

"These?" The man called Glenn said. "These aren't Nick, Bob, or Joe. No men in those sacks. Only product."

The other men chuckled in agreement, and Krista watched as one of them brought a cup of something thick and black, like asphalt sludge, to his lips. The sight of it unnerved Krista, as she couldn't make out what it was.

"You want some?" The sheriff asked. He must've seen her gazing at the tarry substance. "It's medicine. Helps keep the benzene poison low."

Krista shook her head. She didn't want to drink anything these men gave her. Her eyes kept shooting back to the sacks on the other side of the room. She stared at the human bulges through the fabric and tried to determine which one was Nick. He had to be in one of those sacks. She hoped it wasn't the one that had been stabbed with the poker and bleeding. The thought of him in one of those claustrophobic sacks, hearing her voice in the same room as him, brought tears to her eyes.

"Now you say this Nick is missing, yeah? That the man you came with? The one who couldn't even drive a car straight?" The other men laughed a little at the sheriff's words, but Krista got the sense they were laughing more to boost the sheriff's ego than out of actual amusement.

Krista nodded. Her mouth felt dry, like it would take every ounce of effort for her to speak right then.

"Well why don't you come with me? We'll leave these boys to their business, and I'll take you down to the station. Ask you a few questions and see if we can't figure out where this Nick fellow is."

Krista didn't trust the sheriff, but she had no choice. He grabbed her upper arm firmly, twisted the key in the deadbolt and soon she was walking by his side, her arm held fast in his. His patrol car was close by, parallel parked near the bar. The sheriff shoved her in the back, and it felt uncanny to be there again, but this time without Nick. She remembered how Nick had looked at her with concern when they'd pulled up to the Paradise Inn. If only she had insisted they'd gone somewhere else. If only she had admitted that the place had scared her. Instead, her god-forsaken people pleasing tendencies had landed them both in a boatload of trouble.

"You're not going to hurt him, right? Like, you'll let him go?"

Even if he was going to hurt Nick, Krista somehow hoped the sheriff would lie to her and tell her everything was going to be okay. She felt barely able to absorb the reality of the situation, or the grim condition she found herself in.

Sheriff Hall started the engine and began nosing the car along the main street of Beleth Station. He was taking his time about things, turning his gaze this way and that, even though the streets were mostly empty. It looked like a ghost town.

He ignored Krista's question completely, and instead started a new train of conversation, one that made no sense to Krista.

"You ever been married?" He asked. He flicked his gaze back at her in the rearview mirror. She looked away.

"I am married. Technically."

"Hm. To that fellow, Nick?"

"No."

Krista didn't know why she was being honest. She could have lied. Maybe she *should* have lied. But something about the despair she felt, and the fact that Nick was nowhere to be found, made lying seem preposterous right now. It felt like if there was ever a time she could be truthful, even about things that made her feel ashamed, it was now. Perhaps that feeling was brought about by the sensation that she might not make it through the night alive. She didn't trust Sheriff Hall, and didn't know what he might do to her, or where he was truly taking her.

"I was married once," Sheriff Hall continued. She got that sense again, like she'd had earlier when he'd brought Nick and her to the Paradise, that he didn't need much prompting to continue talking. It felt like once he started, he was his own conversational propeller, stuck on telling his full story regardless of the interest on the other end.

"Martha was her name. Beautiful gal, wholesome on the

outside, but not so much in the bedroom. Not for me. With me, she was a right whore. But *only* for me." He then looked at her in the rearview mirror again. "You ever a whore for one man, Ms. Mabry?" A slimy smile spread across his face.

Krista leaned against the door. She wanted to shrink away from his gaze.

"I don't know what you mean," she said quietly.

"Oh come on. You must have been a little slut for *someone*. For that Nick fellow, maybe? Anyway, Martha was a slut for me. Couldn't get enough of me. I'd come home to her begging for my cock. And it was like that for years. But then one year, over five years into our marriage I'm talking, she tells me she has a fantasy. But then she tells me she doesn't want to share what it is because she thinks I'll think she's weird." Sheriff Hall laughed at his own recollection. "And I said 'Martha, you've let me fuck you in the ass while you eat from a dog bowl, what could be weirder than that?' Well fuck. Let me tell you. She had this old fantasy, from the time she was a young woman, to pretend to be dead and have a guy fuck her."

Krista really didn't want to hear anymore, but Sheriff Hall continued on anyway, even as they came to a stop outside of an end unit in a row of townhouses. It didn't look like any kind of police station.

"And I said, okay. We can try that. I'd seen enough dead bodies in my line of work that I figured why not. And I'll tell ya, Ms. Mabry, sometimes those dead bodies are lookers, too. I see all kinds. Sometimes, you do kinda wonder if that pussy is still warm enough to get inside it a little."

Sheriff Hall paused his story to turn the car off.

"Where are we?"

He didn't answer. He got out of the car and opened her door. Krista briefly considered trying to flee, but the sight of the gun in his holster resolved her to follow his orders for now. Maybe there would be a time soon when she could get him distracted enough so that she could get away. For now, she had to focus on surviving. Every tired nerve in her brain was fixated on surviving the next moment, and once that moment had come and gone, and she was still alive, she then trained them all toward figuring out how to survive the subsequent moment.

There was no thought of a future anymore—only how to get through the present time and still be breathing when it passed.

The sheriff led her up the walkway to the townhouse, his hand firmly gripped around her upper arm. His hold on her was so forceful that she was sure her arm would bruise soon.

The townhouse opened up into a darkly-lit living room, with dated decor and old furniture. Framed photos lined an upright piano, and a cheaply upholstered couch sat across from a box television set. On the opposite side of the couch was a blanket-covered recliner that looked like it also served as a catch-all for laundry. The house smelled vaguely musty, like it didn't get much air circulation.

"You can have a seat," he said.

Krista chose the farthest end of the couch from the sheriff to sit, but it didn't matter as he ended up cozying up right next to her, so close that she could smell the rot and alcohol on his breath. He placed a hand on her thigh and smiled when she didn't brush it off. She wanted to, but she also sensed that maybe her best chance for survival would be to comply for now.

"So as I was saying, Martha wanted me to fuck her like she was a dead woman. At first, our attempts were pretty funny. She'd lay still and try to hold her breath, or I'd wrap my fingers around her throat and try to bring her to the brink of asphyxiation, but just the brink. You know? And then—then, we got a system down where she'd lay in a tub of ice until she was a bit blue and wow did we both like that. The coldness and the coloring were a real turn on, but the trembling could be off putting, so sometimes she'd agree to be sedated, or other times I'd try to tie her up or restrain her so her body would stay still. It was a challenge."

Sheriff Hall moved his hand further up Krista's thigh and she tried to shrink farther away from him on the couch. His fingers seemed to creep closer and closer to the space between her legs as he talked.

"Still, though, even with our games, I began to fantasize about the real thing. You know what I mean?"

Krista looked away. She did not know what he meant.

"But it was good while it lasted. The fun stuff. And I can say that the real thing was good, too, but not as good. The thing about doing it the real way, is you only can get a few more times in before the body is just no good anymore. Too stiff, too settled. It's a brief period of euphoria after death, a very short period of fucking, where she can't say no, can't tell you no to anything. I mean, you can do *anything* to a corpse. Shit she didn't want to do while she was alive, oh well. She's gonna do it now." He laughed and slid his hand fully in between Krista's legs, feeling her crotch through her leggings. A tear rolled down her cheek.

"Oh hey, now why are you crying? Is it about that Nick fellow?"

Sheriff Hall retracted his hand and got up, looking down at her with curiosity.

"It's best if you forget about him. Best you realize that what once had a name attached to it, that had meaning to you, is now like an item on a shelf. It'll go to the highest bidder. Nothing named 'Nick' really exists anymore. Not in the sense you're thinking of, at least."

Krista had been trying to hold back the flood of tears welling inside of her, but now she finally let them loose and they poured out of her eyes, sobs coming out of her throat and belaboring her breath.

"You do realize whose house you're in, right? I don't mean to brag, but you could do a lot worse. I'm a pretty big deal around these parts. And ever since I saw you on that mountain road, I thought, that's the one. That's the one who's going to be my next wife."

Krista stared up at the sheriff, completely shell-shocked.

"But first, we got to take your little body for a test drive. You know what I mean? Can't buy the car if it doesn't ride well." Sheriff Hall chuckled to himself.

He yanked her up by the arm and dragged her toward the kitchen where a freezer chest hummed along one side of the wall.

"Undo that latch and take a look inside."

Krista undid the metal latches and hoisted the freezer lid up until it leaned against the wall. Cold air hit her face and evaporated some of her tears. The entire freezer was full of ice bags.

"Take them one by one into the tub there, untie them, and

dump them in. I'll be watching you so don't do anything stupid."

Krista took one bag like she was told—it felt like it was maybe ten pounds, and carried it in both arms over to the bathroom, where a tub was waiting half full of water. She untied the ice bag and poured it in, watching the ice splash and float around in the water. Then she returned to the freezer chest for another bag. She must have carried at least ten bags before the tub looked full of ice, cold mist coming off the surface.

"Now get undressed."

Krista backed up into the bathroom, a cornered animal, while Sheriff Hall stood in the doorway, watching her. "Please don't make me do that."

"If you don't, I'll have to cut the clothes off you, and I don't think you'll like that much."

Krista understood quickly by the look in his eyes, which had hardened considerably. She slid off her leggings and tried to take her mind elsewhere, like she used to do back with Tom. Tom. It was funny how she had once thought Tom was as bad as men got. But she was wrong. It seemed like no matter how low a man went, there was always a man willing to go lower. When she pulled her dress and bra off, she immediately covered her breasts with her arms.

"Now get in the tub. Even if you start to feel like you might lose consciousness, or you start turning blue, just stay there. I'll come for you when I'm ready. I want you cold."

Krista got in the bathtub. The shocking cold of the ice sent painful shivers across her body. It was hard to not leap out of the tub, but she couldn't with the sheriff watching her from the doorway. The way he was leering at her, his eyes scanning across her every curve as she sank into the icy water, made her wish for a quick death. She had to think fast.

As the sheriff turned to leave, Krista called out, "My backpack."

"What about it?"

"It's in your car. It has my medicine in it. I need it or I get really sick."

"Sick? What's wrong with you?" He seemed suspicious.

"I have diabetes," she lied. She had no idea if he knew much about diabetes; she sure didn't, but it was the first thing that came to her mind. He nodded and left, closing the door behind him. Krista prayed he'd return with her backpack.

It was her only hope.

CHAPTER 16
PUT IT ON ICE

IT HAD BEEN two hours since Sheriff Hall had left pretty Krista Mabry on ice. The thought of getting to feel her cold flesh and to stick his fingers inside of her, to feel the contrast of her inner warmth with her outer pasty iciness… it all aroused him to no end. He couldn't help but contemplate whether or not he should leave her in just a little too long, risk her dying or not. But if she died, he knew he wouldn't get to have as much fun with her as he wanted.

Memories of Martha ran through his mind. It had been a long time since he'd had the affection of a woman like that. She used to tell him that when he fucked her 'dead' body, it felt like he'd never leave her, like they'd be together for eternity. They'd lie together in bed while she warmed up in his arms, and she'd ask him if he'd continue to fuck her after she really died.

"I can't bear the thought of you fucking someone else after I go. Maybe you can keep my corpse forever," she'd say, and even though she'd laugh a little as she said it, he could tell by the tears streaming down her face that she was also serious. She was a morbid one, that Martha.

"How the fuck would I keep your corpse around that long, Martha?" He'd ask, and just him asking would send her into another hysteric fit of sobs. She really wanted to be assured that he'd keep fucking her after she died, that he'd never fuck another woman after her. And her pretending to be dead, her getting on the ice as they called it—it soothed her. It made her feel like it was viable, after all, for them to keep on loving each other after death.

"Well what happens when I finally croak?" He asked.

"Then we spirit-fuck," she said, and he thought that was the stupidest goddamned thing he'd ever heard.

But there was also something charming about Martha's crazy ideas. It made him feel good that the woman wanted his dick so badly she hoped his ghost would be fucking her ghost one day. No one had ever liked his dick that much, not even him.

The thoughts and memories of Martha—bless her rotten, long-gone soul—were turning him on. He felt it was finally time to go get Krista off the ice and to give her a whirl. He wondered how she'd stack up against his late wife, and if she'd come around to loving it just like Martha had. Krista was younger, with a supple body. There was something even more of a turn on about fucking a more youthful body that had been on ice like that. Something more power-giving about it, like the woman was letting him take her youth away, letting him pretend to kill her over and over.

He opened the bathroom door, expecting to see her blue-tinged curves in the melted ice bath, but instead his future wife lay in her own vomit on the tile floor, unconscious, with an empty pill canister under the pedestal sink.

Goddamnit.

He felt for a pulse but it was so weak that he was sure she'd be dead within a few hours. Well, he wouldn't be getting many fun times out of this one, after all. He'd let her pulse die out and then he'd have to do with her what he could, but she'd stiffen up right soon, and that would be that.

What a fucking waste.

The phone rang from the kitchen and he went to go pick it up.

Glenn's voice was on the other end.

He listened for a while and then told Glenn he'd see what he could do, but that it'd better be quick. After he hung up the receiver, he took one last look at the crumpled Krista on the bathroom floor, and decided he'd have to roll the dice.

Hopefully her body would be supple enough for one last fuck by the time he got back to the house.

One last fuck before the grave.

CHAPTER 17
CHANGE OF PLANS

EREL AND HANK had had some fun with Misty back at Erel's house, but as Erel had informed Hank, killing Misty in the same place where they'd chopped up Noelle was not a wise bet. They had to diversify. They'd carried the girl back out to the trunk, though this time she was a lot less spritely. Tied up and bleeding, and didn't even put up a fight or a mere wriggle. Erel was a bit put off by the lack of spirit in her, but at the same time, he felt like he'd shown Hank how to break a woman in record time. And Hank did seem impressed by the whole progression of the night, though his newfound admiration for Erel was off-putting. It felt like Hank would've done anything for Erel at this point, and only because Erel was capable of far fouler things than Hank, things Hank wouldn't be able to do on his own, but was able to carry out only with the bolstering of another.

That was always the problem with people like Hank. They weren't independent spirits. They became liabilities in the end, because as easily as Hank could be swayed by Erel, he could just as easily be swayed by someone else. He could turn against Erel if he thought there was a risk to him.

Erel closed the trunk, though he was sad he was soon going to see the last of Misty's face. It had been a pretty face when they'd brought her to the barn, but they'd changed that. Pretty wasn't the right word to describe her any longer. She was something else now. Erel mulled over in his mind which word might be fitting for Misty now, but he couldn't come up with anything to match the new cigarette burns on her tongue, or the thin razor cuts up and down her breasts, so fine and repetitive they looked like sketched window blinds. Like maybe if you turned her nipples, they'd pop right open. Erel laughed at the thought. Hank looked at him, "What's so funny?"

Erel waved him off, and they both got into the front seats, Erel riding passenger.

"Out of town limits is best— somewhere remote. We dump her there."

"Alive?"

Erel gave Hank a look, and the look was all the answer Hank needed.

"You know, I could get used to this. Taking what I need like that."

Hank's ego had been building over the last twenty-four hours or so, built on the bones of young women. Erel didn't need that kind of ego stroke. Ego was for the weak. Erel just was. Being was enough. A cyclone never cared that it was a cyclone. A hurricane wasn't mindful of its own force. Some things simply were, and they passed through other people and towns like Nature intended.

They drove for a while, and Erel began to contemplate how and when he should dispose of Hank. He had to admit, it was a bit fun having a pupil, having someone to admire him for a change, and not in the way that his victims, the pretty little things, admired him. That was different. That was under threat of death. With Hank, it felt like an amateur craftsman in awe of a master, and there was something that gave Erel a sense of accomplishment over it. But Erel also knew that this sense of accomplishment was a weakness, and that he should dispense with the sentiment as quickly as it formed.

They started driving down the mountain and out of Beleth Station, when the sirens of a cop car sounded. They were being pulled over.

Erel turned to Hank. They'd have to do the cop first, and then Erel would take care of Hank and the girl.

CHAPTER 18
BEGINNING OR END

KRISTA SLOWLY CAME TO. Her stomach felt like it had been hit with a ton of cement. Everything—from her insides to her extremities—felt heavy and almost impossible to move. Bit by bit, she managed to pull herself up into a sitting position. She noticed that her entire front was covered in puke. She didn't know how many pills she had swallowed; she hadn't expected to live. There was both the disappointment that she was alive and now had used her only way out of this disaster, coupled with the blissful relief that she *was* still alive. The two feelings were dueling contradictions inside of her, and finally settled on one goal—get the fuck out of Beleth Station.

Krista saw her clothes crumpled in a far corner, partially covered with vomit. She didn't care. She would've worn a potato sack if it meant covering up. She felt cold and achy in a way she'd never experienced before. She felt cold to the point of physical pain. It made it hard for her to move and to coordinate simple actions like putting on her dress. Her brain struggled to get her limbs to follow directions and it was making her anxious as she didn't know if Sheriff Hall was still in the house. At any moment, he might come back into the bathroom.

Once she had her dress on, she stood up and opened the door. She didn't bother to put on her leggings. She would've appreciated the warmth, but she was in a hurry to get out. She didn't hear anyone in the house, and didn't see anyone across

the hall in the kitchen. Slowly, Krista walked out of the bathroom and toward the living room. Her movements felt like
clumsy lurches. Still no sign of Sheriff Hall.

She looked at the couch where they'd been sitting when he
assaulted her, and felt a renewed sense of fear and anxiety.

Slowly walking toward the front door, Krista finally got it
open and stumbled out onto the front walkway, her entire body
trembling. She went behind the townhouse row and started to
stumble in the opposite direction of Nowhere Special.

It was early morning and the sun was just starting to come
up over the horizon. There wasn't anyone out on the road, and
it again felt like Beleth Station was a ghost town.

Finally, she saw a sedan drive by with a man in the front
seat. Tall, lanky, non-threatening. She flagged the driver down,
stumbling toward the road. Krista prayed he'd see her and stop.

At first, the car sped past her at record speed and for a
moment, her body crumbled. But then, miraculously, it stopped
and went in reverse.

Oh thank God, there is a God, and He is good.

Krista internally swore to herself she'd live a life of altruism
if she could just get out of this wretched town alive.

The car eased back in reverse toward her and Krista cursed
the driver for reversing so slowly. She was terrified the sheriff
would come back and see her, would somehow accost her and
the driver, and that there'd be no escape.

But the car finally stopped at her side, and the tall man in
the driver's seat peered out at her. He looked a little worse for
wear, and he had something on his hands that looked strange—
rust-colored like dried blood.

"Where are you headed?" She asked.

"Out," he said with a strange smile.

Krista looked up and down the ghostly street, the memory
of Sheriff Hall's hand between her legs haunting her common
sense. She thought of Nick and wondered if he was still alive.

"You getting in?" the driver asked.

Krista didn't even answer. She just slid into the passenger
seat and pressed the door lock. Once she heard the click of the
lock and the driver put the car back in drive, her body
flooded with relief. She was going to be okay. And once she

got out of there, she'd somehow find a way to go back and help Nick.

"What's your name?" The man asked.

"Krista. Krista Mabry." It felt good to say her name aloud again. Life-affirming.

She looked over at the man, her eyes dropping again to the rust-flecked stains on his hands.

"What's yours?"

"Erel. It was supposed to be Earl, but my mom fucked up the birth certificate."

Erel drove fast, but not as fast as Krista would have liked. As they approached the town limits, she noticed something fluttering about inside the car. The winged insect settled on Krista's hand, and she recognized it as one of the Beleth moths. She rolled down the window and watched it fly back in the direction of the town just as they crested over the town limit on the mountain's descent.

She didn't know where they were going, or whether this would be the beginning or end, but Krista felt safer being out of that town. It felt like something dark had settled in Beleth Station long ago, something carried in on the wind that had taken root and never let up.

Erel turned the knob on the car's old AM/FM radio. The further they got from Beleth Station, the clearer the music became as the static cleared out. An old doo-wop song came on and Erel sang along, like he knew the lyrics well.

Pretty little thing. All the things I do for you. You make my heart sing...

... you pretty little thing.

BELETH STATION: THE GAUNTLET

BRYAN SMITH

ONE

A MASKED, machete-wielding maniac chased a petite woman down Main St. in Beleth Station. The hour wasn't late yet, maybe somewhere slightly north of nine in the evening, but the street was otherwise empty, and Krista Mabry felt like she was alone in the world, except for the madman trailing after her. The street before this one had also been empty. As far as she could tell, there wasn't another living soul remaining in this dying, blighted spot in the middle of nowhere.

She knew that wasn't true. There were signs of habitation. What looked like functional cars parked here and there. And working street lamps, glowing orbs that sat atop black poles lining the sidewalks. A faint sound of music was audible from somewhere nearby, though she was having trouble pinpointing the location. There were people here, but where the hell were they?

Surely they could hear her sounds of distress.

The screaming. The desperate cries for help.

Ringing out sharp and clear, explosively loud.

But all the shop doors up and down Main Street remained firmly shut, no fearful faces peeking out windows or from behind closed curtains or shutters, at least none she could see.

She glanced back to confirm he was still there, this absurd villain who looked and behaved like a refugee from some ancient slasher movie, complete with a cloth sack draped over his head, one with cut-out mouth and eye slits. She knew he was there. Deranged men intent on murder don't just give up the chase, especially with no one around to intervene. She shouldn't look back. It'd only slow her down. She needed to focus on forward movement only.

But primal instinct was a powerful force, her desire to *see* overriding cold pragmatism, sweeping it away like it was nothing.

And he was still there.

Of course he was.

Her heart swelled in her chest when she saw how much closer he was now. The gap between them was half what it was when she'd turned at the corner and started racing up Main. At this rate, he'd be upon her soon, looming over her from behind because he was tall, almost like a giant, raising that machete again, the blade now stained with the blood of her lover, the metal glinting once again in the soft, warm glow of the street lamps.

She screamed again.

Then she stumbled and nearly fell, her feet sliding away beneath her as the sole of one of her boots skidded over the studded lid of a manhole cover. For a moment, she saw fate rising up to meet her in the form of cracked and fading asphalt. In her head, she saw her face smashing against it, mashing her lips and shattering her teeth, an image so vivid it felt real, like a flash-forward glimpse of her immediate future. One more step forward without getting her feet solidly beneath her and it would have happened. She would have been on the cold ground with doom descending from above, immobilized by the pain and utterly powerless to stop it.

Then something happened inside her, something she didn't fully understand, a force rising up from within, driven by a will to survive so strong it stunned her. A force that brought her right leg forward more swiftly and surely than she ever would have dreamed possible.

She regained her footing and started running again.

Faster than she'd ever run in her life.

The maniac's heavy boots thumped harder on the pavement, his breathing louder now as he labored to keep up.

An alley was coming up on the right. The passage was a dark one, the light from the street lamps touching the space only slightly, but as she neared it the music became perceptibly louder, but muffled still, as if emerging from behind a closed door. Despite the surge of adrenaline and resurgent survival instinct, she could feel her body straining, nearing its limits. It was only a matter of time before she stumbled again, the speed of her flight causing her to miss some small obstruction in the road. There was still no one else out here in the street, but there was a small chance the alley could lead her to the source of that music and maybe, just maybe, someone would save her.

She ducked down the alley and kept running hard, barely breaking stride as she bumped into an overflowing trash can and knocked it over, kicking her way through the scattered debris as she continued rushing forward. The heavy tread of the maniac's booted feet echoed in the alley. He scraped the edge of his machete blade against the wall of the alley, a calculated move meant to unnerve Krista.

It worked.

She yelped and glanced back again.

He was no more than twenty feet away.

She slammed into the corner of a dumpster and shrieked in pain and surprise, tottering for a moment that would have proved fatal had it endured even another second, but she was able to spin about and get moving in the right direction again. Still running hard. Still straining. The light beyond the end of the alley growing brighter with every stride.

Then she was out of the alley and streaking across a street that was half the width of Main but not as well-lit. On the opposite side of the street was a bar called Nowhere Special, as a neon sign directly above the door told her. The music was coming from the other side of that door.

The madman still had not given up the chase.

He was so close, his breathing sounded like thunder in her ears.

Crying out again, she reached the sidewalk and hurled herself forward with everything she had left and crashed through the door.

TWO

Earlier

AT THE START of the trip, Nick felt a giddy-verging-on-delirious enthusiasm for the adventure he and Krista were undertaking along with a sense of transgression that was simultaneously exciting and terrifying. Though many would feel sympathy for Krista if they knew the details of what she'd been through over the course of her long, loveless marriage, more judgmental types–and there was never any shortage of those people–would say they were doing a bad thing here. That he was doing a bad thing.

Maybe the judgmental ones were right about that, technically, but only up to a point. The woman riding in the passenger seat of his Nissan Sentra was married to another man, one who wouldn't find out his wife had run off with someone else until he returned from a business trip in a few days, at which point ninety-nine varieties of flaming shit would most assuredly hit the fan. The guy would blow a gasket, maybe even call the police, despite the note Krista left clearly explaining she had left of her own volition. Tom Mabry was a volatile man. Nick had seen proof enough of that.

They lived on the same street. Sometimes he saw Tom

outside yelling at people. Once he saw the guy charge out of his townhouse clad in a blue bathrobe and sandals, his face a twisted visage of seething rage as he started screaming at an elderly lady out walking her little chihuahua. At the same time, Nick just happened to be taking his trash out two houses up the street. He didn't normally like to get in the middle of disagreements between neighbors, not even the bitter ones, but on this occasion he felt compelled to intervene.

The asshole towered over the frail old lady, who was cringing away from him and shaking. Her tiny dog was barking nonstop and straining to get at him. As far as Nick could tell, neither the woman nor the dog had done anything wrong at all, much less something worthy of generating this much frothing invective. Perhaps the outburst was over some past perceived offense, such as the dog pooping in his yard, but that didn't matter. The man was using his size and vastly superior strength to intimidate and frighten someone incapable of fighting back.

No one else was around to get between them, so it fell upon Nick to do the right thing, even though he'd much prefer to be back inside having his morning coffee. He dropped his bag of trash and trotted over, raising his voice to override the blistering volume Tom was generating. A lot of shouting back and forth at each other ensued. Tom was of the opinion that Nick should mind his own goddamn business, while Nick suggested any further unwillingness to back off and leave the woman alone might lead to consequences he wasn't prepared to handle.

More macho posturing ensued, with Tom issuing threats and Nick feeling obligated to respond in kind. He supposed he did a credible enough job of projecting an image of toughness, but in truth he was immensely relieved when Tom blinked first, turning away from him to go storming back into his townhouse. His heart was pounding as he watched the asshole's door slam shut.

What happened in the days after that was so unexpected he still had moments of being unable to fully wrap his head around it. It was no exaggeration to say it was the single most surprising thing to happen to him in the last several years.

Krista Mabry had observed the entire encounter from a second-storey room of the townhouse. Later, after Tom had gone to work for the day, she found one of Nick's social media accounts and sent him a message. The message was all about how grateful she was that he'd stood up to Tom, because hardly anyone ever did. At first he was hesitant about replying, seeing a potential for danger even then, how it could be like lighting the fuse on a powder keg.

Eventually, though, he did respond, and it was the beginning of weeks of messages going back and forth, progressing in a fashion that soon felt invested with a sense of inevitability.

And now here they were, running off together.

It was crazy. Wasn't it?

They wouldn't be able to stay in their rented cabin in the Poconos forever. Sooner or later real life would intrude again, make its usual tedious demands of them. Pre-existing obligations, financial and otherwise, wouldn't just go away. Eventually they would have to return to the street where they lived, and what might happen at that point was hard to even imagine. Their lives were there, everything they owned. Perhaps Krista would move in with him as a short-term solution, if it looked like things might work out between them, but even if that happened, staying there for very long wouldn't be viable. Just the thought of another screaming confrontation with Tom made him uptight. He'd prefer to avoid the possibility altogether, but that didn't seem likely.

But that was the future.

Right now it seemed far away, like something that one day might theoretically occur along an entirely different timeline, because they had more immediate things to worry about at the moment. After hours of driving deep into the heart of rural Pennsylvania, they'd decided to get off the highway and drive into a little town called Beleth Station. The Sentra was low on gas and the GPS was indicating the next town of any significant size was almost two hours distant. Down to perhaps an eighth of a tank, any attempt to get that far before refueling would be doomed to failure.

Now, however, they were faced with another dilemma.

Beleth Station was looking like a ghost town.

Or at least that was the impression one received upon entering the town, where street after street was entirely devoid of people. The first dilapidated buildings they saw were all dark and empty, like hulking ancient beasts rearing up out of the darkness. Before long, however, they encountered evidence of habitation in the form of the charmingly named Ruin Street. The working street lamps here at least confirmed the town was still attached to the power grid. There were also cars parked in front of buildings that didn't look quite as decrepit as the first ones they'd encountered. The vehicles weren't derelict husks either. Driving past a row of townhouses, they spied a few lighted windows here and there. All this suggested there must be a place somewhere within the blighted town where one could buy gas or even get a bite to eat, but they still weren't seeing any people out and about anywhere.

It was really fucking weird and creepy.

Then they arrived at a four-way stop where a sign indicated the cross street was called Ransom Avenue.

At that point Nick glanced at Krista and said, "Ruin and Ransom. How quaintly charming. Did the fucking Manson family build this town?"

Krista squinted at the street sign. "Hmm, I don't know. It's actually kind of funny, isn't it? Like whoever's in charge has a dark sense of humor. Maybe the next street will be the Boulevard of Broken Dreams."

Nick frowned. "Hmm, yeah, maybe you're right. About the sense of humor, I mean. I just hope the next street up isn't called Massacre Lane or Murder Strangers Avenue."

He craned his head around, scanning the immediate area in hopes of spotting a convenience store or even just a regular old-fashioned gas station, the kind that still existed in some places way out in the sticks, with analog number dials on the pumps instead of digital displays. Up on the left on the other side of the intersection was a place called Old Jim's General Store, but it appeared to be closed for the evening.

Because of course it was.

Nothing could just be easy or convenient, not in this forlorn place.

"Goddammit, there's got to be a gas station somewhere."

Nick took a left turn into the intersection, a random choice. The GPS knew nothing of the streets of Beleth Station, which was odd. He'd been on several lengthy road trips in recent years, including some that had taken him into some remote corners of the midwest and the south. All were mapped extensively on GPS. Why this weird little obscure burg in the middle of nowhere should be the one exception to that rule was one hell of a mystery. He'd love to hear an explanation for it and maybe he'd ask somebody wherever they eventually stopped for fuel. Assuming, of course, that they would be able to do that before the Sentra's tank ran dry.

Two more blocks up on Ransom, they at long last found the thing they were seeking, a little gas station with just two pumps out front. It even looked like it was open. The lights were on inside and out and someone was seated behind the sales counter. There were fist pumps and loud exclamations of relief from each of them. Things were looking up.

Finally.

Nick parked in front of one of the gas pumps. They got out and stretched. Nick grinned when he saw that the pumps were exactly the sort he'd envisioned, with rotary number dials. He got out his phone and encouraged Krista to pose sexily next to one of the pumps for a picture. She was happy to oblige and was in the process of perfecting her pose when the masked man with the machete emerged from the shadows and came rushing at them.

Or, rather, came rushing straight at Krista.

Nick didn't even think about it.

He dropped his phone and moved immediately to put himself between Krista and the hulking stranger who looked like he'd emerged fully formed from a nightmare fueled by faintly recalled memories of late night slasher movies.

Krista screamed.

The blade rose and fell, biting into his flesh and igniting a hot flash of searing pain unlike anything in his experience. Krista screamed again as he grappled with the masked man and tried to wrest the machete from his grasp, but the effort proved futile. The maniac was too strong and too big, taller than him by more than a foot. He was shoved away and then the blade flashed again, the steel biting into his yielding flesh a second time.

And then another time after that.

Then he was falling, hitting the ground hard like a dead weight.

Krista called out his name, deep anguish in her voice, and after that she was gone, running away down the street as the madman gave chase. Nick whimpered in pain and struggled to clear his suddenly blurry vision as he turned his head and watched the woman he loved run for her life.

He sniffled as his vision turned blurry again. "Run, baby, run."

At some point he became aware of someone else standing above him. Maybe more than one person, it was hard to tell. He was still staring off down the street, in the direction of where he'd last glimpsed Krista, only now she'd disappeared from view.

Strong hands grabbed hold of his ankles and dragged him away from the gas pumps.

THREE

THE OLD VAGRANT sprawled out in the midst of a pile of industrial debris looked dead. Smelled like it, too, a thick layer of oily-looking grime covering every visible inch of his flesh, his raggedy clothes imbued with a landfill stench no amount of detergent or machine washing could ever mitigate. There were clumps of dirt in his hair and an empty bottle of bottom shelf rotgut hooch on the floor near his outstretched hand.

These were merely the things Sean Crane deduced as he observed the man inside the rotting husk of the Medallion Paper Mill. He harbored no judgment against this particular pitiful wretch nor any of the others like him in Beleth Station. He did not begrudge them whatever escape or solace they were able to find inside a bottle or from a needle. For all he knew, what he was seeing here was a glimpse of his own future if somehow he was never able to escape the dying town his family had called home for generations.

He took a swig of his own cheap hooch and approached the man's unmoving form, giving his midsection a nudge with the toe of his boot. "Hey, man. Are you fucking dead?"

The man snorted in surprise and glanced blearily up at Sean after his eyes fluttered. "Not yet, goddammit. Hopefully soon."

His eyes closed and he was silently asleep again within seconds.

Sean moved away from him as he made his way across what

was once the production floor of the former paper mill, which once upon a time–just about a generation ago–was the town's primary employer. His father and uncles worked here when they were young. Now his father and two of his uncles were dead, legacy victims of the benzene poisoning that forced the mill's closure all those years ago. The one uncle who somehow avoided becoming part of the cancer cluster that claimed his siblings became Sean's guardian. Garret Crane did his best for a long while and then he shot himself shortly after Sean's eighteenth birthday. He didn't leave a note behind. Not that a note was necessary. The rationale behind the act was obvious.

A hole in the building's roof admitted pale moonlight, making it just possible to navigate this part of the mill's interior without constantly knocking into decrepit and non-functional pieces of industrial machinery. Sometimes, when a group of his peers were partying in here, they'd fill a steel barrel with debris and get a fire going. He came here tonight in hopes of finding just such a gathering, but he heard no telltale crackling of flames, caught nary a whiff of smoke.

Too bad.

He felt in desperate need of someone to talk to tonight. Someone he could look in the eye and confess something to without fear of being snitched out to the Elders. The old creeps who ran Beleth Station now did not allow its limited supply of young people to leave, because every fresh departure brought the town closer to actual death and to them, that simply was not acceptable. Draconian measures were in place to maintain their iron grip on the youth and the populace at large. There was no public internet access in Beleth Station, for one thing, and cell phones were considered contraband. Anyone caught with one was severely punished. All the routes in and out of town were continually monitored, making escape virtually impossible.

Sean wanted out. The desperation growing within him was on the verge of turning malignant, of devouring him, and he simply couldn't take it much longer.

He'd been hoping to find Emma here. She was the one he trusted the most, the one who most yearned the same way he did, and the one who made him believe a better future might actually be possible. If only they were brave enough and determined enough, if only he could convince her to try with him, maybe, just maybe, they could accomplish the rare feat of escaping without being tracked down and forcefully returned to the town.

Because that was the risk.

The Elders stopped at nothing to recapture those who fled, and the punishments the captured suffered upon return were always harsh. Visible scarring marked them all. The intent of it wasn't merely punishment, but to serve as a warning. It was a highly effective intimidation tool.

After making his way across the production floor, he entered a darker space, a hallway the moonlight spilling in through the hole in the roof could not quite reach. He capped his pint bottle of Jim Beam and shoved it into an inner pocket of his jacket. Then he dug a disposable lighter out of the hip pocket of his jeans and flicked it to life, allowing the thin column of flickering flame to guide him the rest of the way. The hallway was the first link in a maze-like chain of similar passages, stretches of which were lined with open doors to spaces that once functioned as offices or supply rooms, but which were now crash pads for vagrants and delinquents. Sounds of fucking often emanated from these spaces, but there were no such noises tonight.

Odd.

Emma and her friends usually stayed out there on the production floor, but the cafeteria was the next most likely place to find her. He didn't know what he'd do if she wasn't here tonight. Going to her house wasn't an option, as he didn't much care for having a shotgun shoved in his face by her perpetually raging drunk father.

Spying artificial lighting of some kind from within as he neared the cafeteria's double doors, he doused the lighter flame and felt despair give way to tentative excitement. There was a good chance she was in there, perhaps sitting in a circle with her friends around a portable camping lantern. He peeked through the glass window of one of the doors and there she was.

Standing naked and blood-spattered over the headless corpse of an unknown man.

A machete clutched in her trembling hand.

FOUR

THE DOOR YIELDED as she threw herself against it, negating any need to waste precious seconds by fumbling with the door knob. She tumbled into the bar and the door swung shut behind her as she pitched forward, her knees hitting the threadbare carpet covering the establishment's cement floor.

She looked up and saw a thin, balding man in a cheap suit staring at her from a tiny stage across the room. A black microphone was gripped in his right hand and in front of him was a teleprompter. He ceased singing "Hotel California" the instant she burst through the door, but the music from the karaoke machine continued to play. The look on his face suggested he was more annoyed than startled by the intrusion.

Craning her head around, she saw two older men nursing whiskey drinks at the bar. They glanced at her briefly and seemed to mentally shrug before returning their attention to the apparently far more compelling contents of the glasses in front of them. Standing behind the bar was a man in late middle age with a full head of salt-and-pepper hair. He glanced her way and she saw a flicker of what might have been actual concern for her well-being cross his features before his face went slack. The only other patron inside Nowhere Special was a heavyset woman with curly red hair sitting at one of a handful of small tables in front of the karaoke stage. The woman never even looked her way. There were two pool tables and a rack of cue sticks mounted on a wall to her right, but no one was playing billiards here tonight.

The man on the stage resumed singing "Hotel California".

Krista Mabry scrambled to her feet and raced over to the rack of cue sticks, ripping one loose and gripping the thinner, tapered end in both hands before spinning back toward the door. She was in the process of swinging the fat end of the stick around with the intent of clobbering the murdering maniac upside his sack-covered head when she saw that the door was still shut.

The madman had not followed her into the bar.

Breathing heavily and feeling like her heart was on the verge of catapulting itself through her chest wall, she stood where she was a while longer, maintaining a tight grip on the stick and waiting for the killer to make a belated appearance.

It didn't happen.

She glanced over at the bar and saw that the older men on stools were still sitting with their backs turned to her. Mounted on the wall behind the bar was an old-fashioned non-HD television, currently turned to a Flyers game. The men watched it while sipping from their glasses and digging peanuts out of a bowl. It was as if a woman in distress crashing into the place in dramatic fashion was the most humdrum thing in the world, something that happened every day, and maybe it did.

This was a strange town.

She wished Nick had never pulled off the highway, or that they'd turned around and left after beginning to perceive the oddness of the place. That the low fuel situation made this an irrational desire didn't matter. Winding up stranded on the highway for hours while waiting for someone from AAA to bring them gas would have been so much better than this, but of course she only knew that in retrospect. There'd been no reason to suspect they were entering a town like something out of a gothic fever dream.

Still clutching the pool cue stick with one hand, she stalked over to the bar and slapped its surface to get the bartender's attention. "You need to call the fucking police." She slapped the bar harder when the man didn't even glance her way. "Hey! Asshole! I'm talking to you. Some psycho attacked my boyfriend with a goddamned machete, and you need to call the fucking police right fucking now."

The man finally looked at her and held her gaze for a moment.

The maddening old song playing from the karaoke machine was finally winding down as the barkeep turned away from her and went to a phone sitting on a shelf behind the bar. He lifted the receiver off the cradle, punching in a number with an index finger as he put it to his ear. His gaze went to the television screen for a moment as he listened to the line ring, wincing as a winger for the New York Islanders sniped a top-shelf goal against the Flyers. Krista only just managed to resist an urge to lunge across the bar and slap the irritatingly nonchalant expression off the man's face.

Like, seriously, what the hell was wrong with these people?

The man mumbled something indistinct into the receiver, nodded as he listened again, and returned receiver to cradle without another word.

He looked at Krista and said, "Sheriff will be over directly. Can I get you a drink?'

Krista scowled.

"What the fuck, dude? Like, did you seriously not hear a single word I said? Did none of that penetrate your thick fucking skull in the slightest?" Her voice was rising as she bit off each bitter word, and she knew that to these people she probably sounded like a shrill, hysterical bitch, but by this point she did not give a single fuck what any of them thought about her. "My boyfriend was violently attacked in the streets of your nowhere little shitstain of a town, maybe even killed, and you're offering me a drink? That's the best you can do?"

The bartender shrugged.

Despite her protestations, he cracked open a bottle of Yuengling and set it on the bar in front of her anyway. She stared at it in seething disbelief for a moment before thinking, fuck it. Snatching the bottle off the bar, she chugged half its contents down within seconds.

The bar fell eerily silent and stayed that way for the next few minutes. No one spoke. The balding man in the suit stepped down from the little stage and joined the heavyset woman with red curls at her table. They glanced at each other, but said nothing. No one else got up on the stage to try their hand at warbling off-key versions of hits from yesteryear. The old men at the bar continued watching the Flyers game, but did not ask the bartender to turn up the volume. In the absence of conversation and music, every sound that did occur–every cough, every creak of a chair–felt uncomfortably amplified, like whispers inside a fundamentalist church in the last moments before the start of a Sunday sermon.

It was unnerving as hell.

Krista finished her beer and another one appeared in front of her within seconds, like magic. She grabbed it and again gulped down several ounces in rapid fashion. The fast drinking was symptomatic of her strained nerves as well as the urge to scream and cry she was only barely managing to contain. She didn't even like beer much, being more of a wine person.

She flinched when the door at the front of the bar began to creak open, her heart beating faster as she gripped the stick tighter. A fresh surge of terror had her on the verge of running again, this time in search of a rear exit from this den of detached and emotionless weirdos, but she relaxed as the door opened further and revealed a man wearing the tan uniform of a small town lawman.

The door swung shut behind him as he entered the establishment and approached the bar. The man's gaze went first to the bartender, who acknowledged his arrival with a silent nod. He scanned the bar's interior briefly before his gaze settled on Krista.

As he veered toward her, a warm, easy smile came to his face, and for a fleeting instant she felt a small flicker of hope and reassurance. Here at last, perhaps, was someone who might listen to her tale of violent assault and take it seriously.

He eyed the cue stick with a look of mild curiosity as he introduced himself. "Evening, ma'am. I'm Ray Hall, the one and only officer of the law in our friendly little town." He directed a tilt of his head at the bartender. "Glenn here tells me you ran into a spot of trouble here tonight. Is that right?"

Krista spent a moment shaking and trying to rein in her emotions before responding.

The man's words rankled.

Friendly little town? Is that a fucking joke?

She swallowed a lump in her throat and forced herself to take a deep, calming breath. Then, in as even a tone as she could manage, she told the cop all about the encounter with the masked maniac. She resisted the almost overwhelming impulse to rush through it, taking care to say everything she needed to say in as clear a manner as possible, so there could be no chance she was misunderstood about anything.

Hall made a contemplative sound as she finished her account of the harrowing events. "Wait right here just a minute."

He turned away from her and returned to the bar's front door, pulling it open and poking his head outside, pointedly taking a long look around at the area just outside Nowhere Special. This took maybe ten seconds. Then he closed the door again and came back to where she was standing.

The look on his face this time conveyed skepticism. "Good news. I see no signs of any masked marauders in the vicinity."

The bartender, Glenn, cleared his throat and broke his silence. "Probably just a misunderstanding. Some dumb kid playing a prank, maybe."

Krista directed a look of wide-eyed disbelief at each of them in turn before saying, "Are you both stupid, or are you just mocking me? There was no misunderstanding. And what does it matter if the fucking psycho isn't lurking right outside? I told you, my boyfriend was violently attacked. He needs medical attention. You need to stop standing around with your thumbs up your asses and get him some help."

Hall leaned uncomfortably close and sniffed at her breath. "Ma'am, have you been drinking?"

Krista made a sound of scoffing disbelief. "None of what I've told you has anything to do with the beer and a half this man practically shoved down my throat." Her eyes flicked briefly toward Glenn. "I'm stone sober and in full possession of all my senses, and fuck you if you're implying otherwise. Now, are you going to continue being absolutely useless, or are you going to actually do your job and help me?"

The lawman's expression turned colder for a moment, but

then the big, warm smile returned. The falseness of it was easier to discern this time, though. "I apologize for any perceived callousness on my part, miss. I truly didn't mean to offend or upset you. It's just that what you described is so unusual. This is a quiet, peaceful town. Might even be fair to call it boring, because if you look at the official record, you won't find recorded evidence of a murder occurring here for almost twenty years. What you described just sounds impossible to those of us who've lived here all our lives. It sounds more like something out of one of those old hack 'n' slash movies from the 80's."

"Friday the 13th Part 2," one of the old men at the bar chimed in. "The one where the big fella killin' all the teenagers wore a sack over his head."

Hall glanced at the man, whose gaze remained riveted to the television screen above the bar. "I'll take your word for it, Ralph." He looked at Krista. "But you're right, it's my job to investigate these things, regardless of how unlikely they sound. I'll go fetch my cruiser, and you and I can take a ride up to that gas station you mentioned, see what's what. How's that sound?"

Krista sighed. "It's better than the big fat nothing that's been done so far. So, okay. But you should call an ambulance to the scene, too, while you're at it."

The lawman smiled again as he took a backward step. "Consider it done."

Then he was gone.

Krista shivered in quasi-relief. She was far from convinced the cop was doing everything in his power to help, but some form of response was better than nothing.

In the lawman's absence, the eerie silence from before reasserted itself. Paranoid thoughts crept into her head as she grabbed the second beer and struggled to reassure herself as she resumed drinking it. Beleth Station was indeed a strange place, no doubt, but surely it wasn't a malignantly sinister one.

Or so she hoped.

FIVE

NICK SLIPPED in and out of consciousness after he was dragged away from the gas pumps. At times he only grayed out for a few seconds, experiencing flickering fragments of micro dreams before awareness of the real flesh and blood world returned, a phenomenon that invested everything with a quality of the surreal while making time feel like it was skipping ahead.

One moment he was being dragged across parking lot asphalt, then things went gray and for a handful of seconds he was inside a micro dream of being in a ferris wheel car at the top of the wheel's rotation, a cool summer breeze ruffling his hair in that last moment before the car's descent. Then reality returned and he was flat on his back in front of the gas station, no longer being dragged as the sound of a truck engine became audible. Next came another retreat into a gray, fuzzy dreamland, followed by conscious awareness of being lifted off the ground and deposited onto the bed of a battered old blue pickup. He heard the engine rev and stared up at the star-filled sky as the truck drove away from the gas station. As he listened to the throaty rumble of the vehicle's engine, vague but troubling thoughts of Krista and the danger she must be in intruded.

After that came a more protracted period of unconsciousness, a deeper spiral into dream territory, but this time, the dreams were imbued with a nightmarish tinge. He wandered alone through a strange and frightening hellscape with screams and howling winds reverberating all around. At one point during the disturbing dream, he saw Krista's severed head go flying through the crimson-tinged sky overhead, borne aloft by large, leathery wings. He screamed at the horrific sight and was still screaming in the moments after he woke up again.

This time when he woke, he was clearer-headed than before, cognizant enough to sense he'd been out cold for a while. He was also in an enormous amount of physical pain, far greater than the pain he'd experienced when the blade of the machete bit repeatedly into his flesh.

He was in a dimly lit and dank-smelling small room. His clothes had been removed and he was stretched out flat on his back on an elevated surface that bore some semblance to an operating table in a hospital, only far less comfortable. The table was not padded. Every physical ache felt amplified. His arms had been pulled backward, drawn tight behind his head and secured with what felt like leather restraints. His legs were secured in similar fashion, with leather straps cinched tight around his ankles. Perhaps most disturbing was the sight of an IV needle and tube inserted in a vein in the crook of his right elbow. The tube was attached to a heavy drip bag filled with a crimson fluid hanging from a pole. The drip pole was heavily rust-flecked and looked like an ancient relic extracted from the ruins of a Civil War era hospital.

Not exactly reassuring.

Then again, none of this was.

He lifted his head off the table and took a look around, spying no one else in the room with him. A door six feet directly opposite the foot of the table opened a small crack, admitting a vertical sliver of light. Voices conferring in muffled, indistinct whispers could be heard from the other side of the door. He considered crying out for help, but multiple layers of uncertainty made him refrain. This was a vaguely hospital-like setup, which allowed him to hold out some small measure of hope he'd been brought to this place by compassionate people interested only in helping him, but if that was the case, why the restraints? And why wasn't he being doped up with anesthetics to reduce the pain caused by his still-throbbing open wounds?

The bottom line was that this place could be anything from an ultra-crude backwoods medical clinic to some psycho's torture chamber.

The door opened and in walked two people clad in blood-spattered blue surgical gowns. A man and a woman. They wore nothing beneath the gowns. Nick wasn't a medical professional, but he was pretty sure that was not standard operational procedure at any legitimate medical facility. The woman wore surgical gloves on her upraised hands. She had long blonde hair pulled back in a ponytail. The man entered behind her, wheeling in an adjustable surgical tray on a stand. The tray was shinier and much newer-looking than the ancient drip pole. Arrayed on its surface was a variety of sharp instruments and spools of what looked like cheap suturing thread.

Oh, shit.

Nick shivered as dread consumed him, and he at last mustered the strength and will to speak. "What the hell's going on here? Where am I?"

The woman spent some moments inspecting the drip bag and the needle insertion in his vein, nodding and making a vague sound of approval. She stood over him now, looking straight down into his eyes as she said, "You've suffered an attack."

Nick sighed. "I know that, but what am I doing in this place instead of a real hospital? Nothing looks right." He sniffled and glanced at the drip pole. "What's in that bag?"

The woman smiled. "Pig blood."

Nick gaped at her, rendered momentarily incapable of intelligent response.

The woman's gloved hands descended to his face. She tugged at his lower and upper eyelids, checking for who fucking knew what. After that she pried open his mouth and pulled his lips away from his gums, sliding the tip of a latex-covered finger over them. "You've lost a dangerous amount of blood, so you're getting a transfusion. Pig DNA is the closest available to human DNA. The species share a ninety-eight percent genetic similarity. Did you know that?"

Nick frowned. "That may be, but I still don't think this is medically–"

The woman put a hand over his mouth and pinched his nostrils shut with the thumb and forefinger of her other hand. His eyes widened as he tried twisting free of her suffocating grip. Her face remained an impassive mask as she stared into his eyes and said, "Let that be the last time you question my expertise in medical matters. If you can agree to that, I'll let you breathe again."

Nick made a muffled noise of squealing distress meant to signal agreement, and the woman's hands came away from his face. He sucked in multiple deep gasps of air, tears temporarily blurring his vision as he shuddered in relief. Just as his vision began to clear, he felt a sharp stab of pain. He lifted his head and saw the woman driving a needle into his flesh, beginning the process of suturing a slash wound that arced diagonally across his chest.

The sharp jab of pain was the first of many as she worked with the practiced, deft skill that can only come from having performed a thing countless times, drawing the flaps of flesh together in a way that looked almost seamless[1] . The exhibition of skill, however, was far from reassuring, given her odd behavior and everything else about the setting. As she worked, the man who'd entered the room breathed heavily behind his surgical mask and laughed in a softly idiotic way every time he glanced at Nick's pain-contorted face. If he was fulfilling any practical purpose here, it wasn't an obvious one.

After she finished stitching up the chest wound, she immediately went to work on another wound, this one another slash straight across the meaty underside of his right forearm. That one was incurred when he'd held up his arms in a futile defensive gesture. Once again, no painkillers were administered despite his constant pleas for some form of relief. They were constant, that is, until the woman held a scalpel above his face and threatened to cut out one of his eyes if he didn't settle down and be quiet. He whimpered in abject misery but managed to hold back words of desperate supplication. It seemed clear the woman had received some type of formal medical training at some point in her life, but Nick was pretty sure the sadistic intimidation tactics she was utilizing here had not been part of that training.

Once she'd finished sewing up all the wounds, she again checked the drip bag and the needle insertion. She made vague noises of affirmation, as if pleased with all aspects of his care and treatment so far. But that was a laugh, seeing as all of this felt more like torture than anything resembling proper medical care. She checked his pulse and repeated the odd inspection of the undersides of his eyelids, which once again was highly uncomfortable. He wanted to ask her what the hell that was all about but his fear of being sadistically reprimanded made him refrain.

She pulled off her used surgical gloves and handed them to the man who was either her assistant or just some weird little freak who liked to watch her inflict pain on people. He tugged down the surgical mask, stuck out a stubby tongue, and began a meticulous process of slurping every drop of blood he could from the latex. When he was done, he repeated the process with the other glove. The woman went out of the room while the man enjoyed his bloody treat, returning some ten minutes later sans surgical gown and clad now only in black panties and bra.

Opening a hand, she showed him a solitary white pill cupped in her palm. Held in her other hand was a juice box with a straw. "Open wide, it's time to take your medicine."

Sighing in relief even as he continued to shiver from the pain, Nick opened his mouth wide and allowed her to feed him the pill. He felt it touch his dry, parched tongue and adhere to it. She positioned the juice box close to his mouth and pushed the slender straw between his lips. He closed his mouth and greedily sucked down as much of the citrusy beverage as he could manage, swallowing as he felt the pill slide down his gullet.

He sniffled and eyed the woman with pitiful gratitude. "Thank you. Was that morphine?"

She giggled. "Oh, no. No, no, no. We need you awake and alert for the Gauntlet later tonight. That was a rather strong dose of Dexedrine. You should feel your heart beginning to gallop within minutes. Don't be alarmed. It'll settle into a more manageable rhythm soon enough."

Nick gaped at her in disbelief.

Don't be alarmed? What the fuck is the Gauntlet?

He whimpered again, already feeling his heart speed up uncomfortably. "Are you insane? Why would you do this?"

She giggled again. "Insane? Possibly. I have been diagnosed with a colorful range of personality disorders. And I enjoy each of them immensely."

A louder whine escaped Nick's lips.

Fuuuuuuuuuck.

The woman laughed. The man laughed.

The room filled for several moments with the sound of their unhinged frivolity.

Nick's tone turned desperately beseeching as he said, "Please let me go. Please."

The demented pair ceased laughing and mocked him.

"*Oh, please.*"

"*Please, please, please.*"

The woman slapped her useless assistant hard enough to knock him to the floor, where he flopped around in a manic fashion and mimicked the sounds of a baby wailing in distress. By this point Nick was wishing he'd been left to bleed out and die in that gas station parking lot. He felt trapped in some carnival un-funhouse version of a nineteenth century insane asylum.

He closed his eyes tight and tried to will all the madness away.

He was not successful.

SIX

THERE WERE others in the cafeteria with Emma, but unlike her they were not nude. The bright glow of multiple portable lanterns lit the macabre scene as Sean pressed his face closer to the door window. Clad in baggy dark clothing that obscured distinctive body shapes and genders, the others stood in a loose semi-circle around her and the headless man on the floor.

Each of the mysterious observers wore hooded jackets. The hoods were up and cinched tight beneath their chins. What he assumed were bandanas covered the lower portions of their faces.

A wave of intense despair swept over Sean, because he knew at once what he was seeing. This was an initiation cere-mony. By beheading this man tonight, Emma was being inducted into the ranks of the Night Wolves, an independent gang of feared enforcers. Though they were not directly affili-ated with the council of Elders, the gang served their interests in various ways. The main thing they were known for was the ruthless pursuit and recapture of citizens who tried to escape the town. The livid scars marking the flesh of the recaptured were inflicted by Night Wolves during prolonged and intense torture sessions.

Becoming one of them wasn't something that happened overnight. This ceremony was the final step in a series of rituals, lasting over a period of months. Until tonight, he'd never personally witnessed an induction ceremony, but the lore of the Night Wolves, by design, was well-known in Beleth Station. There was no chance he was misinterpreting anything.

Emma was one of them now.

He'd never be able to trust her again.

As if sensing the presence of an additional, uninvited observer, she lifted her head, shifting her gaze from the dead man at her feet to the cafeteria doors. The hidden faces of the others turned in the same direction. While they might be able to discern an indistinct form lurking on the other side of the closed double doors, Sean doubted his face was visible in the darkness of the hallway. This was fortunate, because the identities of those belonging to the Night Wolves were a fiercely guarded secret. He didn't know precisely what might happen to him if they got their hands on him, but he knew for damn sure it wouldn't be pleasant.

They began moving toward the door.

Sean backed away fast and began running blindly back down the dark hallway, barreling straight ahead without regard to any unseen objects that might be in the way. As he ran, he heard the squeal of the cafeteria doors opening followed by some strident shouts.

Then came the sound of pounding footsteps.

The chase was on.

He ran toward the faint glimmer of pale moonlight just barely visible beyond the end of the corridor. Only by following that light would he stand any chance of surviving the next few minutes. Behind him, as they gave chase, the Night Wolves growled and howled in mimicry of the wild creatures for which they were named, sounds that sent a chill rippling through Sean's body and made his heart race faster.

The glimmer of moonlight grew incrementally brighter second by second, and soon he was able to discern the dark outlines of ruined and rotting pieces of industrial machinery standing out there on the production floor. A spark of hope ignited inside him as he began to believe he might have a real shot at outpacing and eluding his numerous pursuers, who continued to fill the hallway with their echoing cries and growls. He was about two-thirds of the way to the end of the passage, however, when someone stepped out of one of the former offices to stand directly in front of him.

That this was not an intentional intercept became clear in the final second before Sean collided with the man, who was another of the putrid-smelling alkie bums who lived in the ruins of the old mill. He turned toward Sean in that moment, the death-stench of his body and the stale foulness of his breath washing over him like poison gas, causing his eyes to water and making him gag. Hitting the man's stationary body at full speed was like running into a brick wall, albeit a rotten one that crumbled and fell beneath him. Through some miracle, he was able to remain on his feet as he stumbled forward and kept going, bouncing off one wall and then the opposite one in a zigzag pattern.

He was nearly to the end of the hallway by the time he was finally able to start running in a straight line again. By then the howls of the Night Wolves were louder and more frenzied than ever. The gap between them had closed considerably in the aftermath of the collision, and in his mind he saw them baring their fangs and extending their claws in preparation of pouncing. Only that was his fevered, frightened imagination, because they were just people, not real wolves on the verge of tearing him to bloody pieces after riding him to the ground.

The fingers of an outstretched hand brushed the collar of his leather jacket as he finally emerged from the hallway. He cut hard left a couple seconds later, dodging one of the broken old machines. The person immediately behind him hit the machine at full force, shrieking in sudden pain as he was impaled upon a protruding metal rod. Someone else screamed and there were fearsome cries of rage from others as Sean continued to weave his way across the trashed and debris-strewn production floor, a landscape as familiar to him as the back of his hand from years of hanging out here with all the other delinquents.

The hole in the roof was directly above him when he sensed the fastest among his pursuers closing in again. The growls of the Night Wolves grew throatier, meaner, and hungrier. Real wolves they might not be, but he found it too easy to imagine one or more tearing his throat open with their teeth anyway, driven to temporary madness by the chase, reveling in the lust for blood it had awakened.

They spread out behind him as he moved into the open area in the middle of the floor, and he feared he would soon find himself flanked and cornered, caught in a circle of furious predators slowly closing in around him. He became certain he was seconds away from being captured or killed when an unexpected thing happened.

All at once he realized the sounds of pursuit had ceased. There were no more pounding footsteps, no more frenzied howling and growling. All he heard now were his own gasping breaths. The sudden dead silence so startled him he felt compelled to slow his pace and glance backward. What he saw made him frown, because the Night Wolves were still there, but they were hanging back at the edge of the brighter pool of moonlight [1] [2] illuminating the middle part of the production floor. His sense was that they'd been closer than this, but had now retreated slightly for reasons he at first did not understand.

They seemed hesitant and uncertain, afraid of something.

But of what?

Sean was no longer running by that point. A part of him was alarmed by this, screaming at the rest of him that it was a waste to spend any time pondering the meaning of this unanticipated development. Survival instinct still dictated a need for relentless forward movement. Curiosity, however, overwhelmed the impulse to err on the side of caution.

He came to a complete stop and turned fully toward them. Distance, coupled with the hoods pulled up around their faces, made it impossible to see the eyes of the Night Wolves, but he saw the tension in the set of their bodies, the way they all swayed slightly, still in the grip of an interrupted adrenaline rush. He saw hands held stiffly at the sides of some of them, clenching and unclenching, restless from unspent violent energy.

Stopping to observe this initially unfathomable drastic shift still felt crazy and dangerous, yet he couldn't help himself because it was so bizarre and inexplicable. Even crazier was the impulse to shout out a question to them. They were the predators and he was their prey. So what the fuck?

He was opening his mouth with the intention of doing just that when he heard soft footsteps somewhere behind him. His hackles up again, he whirled about with his fists up, ready to fight, but instead of throwing an immediate punch against the stealthy enemy he figured was creeping up behind him, he froze in place as a confused scowl twisted his features.

The filthy vagrant he'd encountered upon entering the building stood a few feet away, regarding him with surprising sobriety. He looked taller and sturdier now that he was upright and standing in the moonlight directly beneath the hole in the roof. The putrid stench and the grime covering his flesh were still there, but now those things struck Sean as purposeful, as if they were elements of a particularly cunning disguise.

The man approached him, moving with an easy fluidity hinting at uncommon grace and strength. It struck him as the way a panther or a real wolf might move while wading into the thick of a volatile environment. Unconcerned and fearless, but ready to leap into violent, lethal action at the drop of a pin. What made this even more impressive was that he carried no visible weapon, yet the intense fear the Night Wolves experienced at the mere sight of him was undeniable.

A moment of brief but unnerving eye contact occurred as the man moved past Sean. "Get moving, son."

Sean's frown deepened. "But who–"

The man's glare intensified. "*Now.*"

That did it for Sean, something in the man's commanding tone immediately convinced him there was no more room for hesitation.

He backed away from the man, turned, and started running again.

Seconds later, he was outside in the cool evening air.

He hopped on his motorcycle, got it kick-started, and roared off into the night.

SEVEN

THE LAWMAN RETURNED LESS than ten minutes after departing, Krista tensing again at the creaking of the front door as it began to open. She was still on edge in the wake of the hooded assailant's disappearance and kept expecting him to pop up again like one of the unstoppable killers in those old slasher movies.

Then the door came all the way open and she saw Ray Hall. The relief she felt was tempered by the knowledge that Nick was hurt and in need of help, along with the conviction that something wasn't right about this town. The strange behavior of both the sheriff and the patrons of Nowhere Special contributed significantly to this impression. The assault was the biggest part of this equation, but the overall vibe in Beleth Station filled her with unease.

It was just...off. All of it.

She didn't feel safe in this place or in the presence of any of these strangers. Perhaps it was just paranoia, but she had a sense of unspoken conspiracy existing among the silent patrons of the bar. She felt them staring at her out of the corners of their eyes while pretending their attention was elsewhere, all of them thinking silent, private things, things unknowable to her but which they all understood. It made her skin crawl.

It made her want to scream.

Yet when Hall beckoned her to join him outside, she went

without hesitation. The lawman creeped her out too, but she hoped being in the presence of just one strange local instead of an entire bar full of them would be easier to handle. She got up from her stool and moved quickly out of the establishment, stepping out onto the sidewalk as Hall held the door for her.

The white cruiser was parked at the curb. Her understanding was it hadn't been here during his conversation with her earlier. He'd had to go "fetch" it, yet he'd been gone such a short time she could only assume that whatever building or office functioned as this town's nominal sheriff's department was within easy walking distance of Nowhere Special. She thought about all the screaming and crying out for help she'd done while running up Main Street, and found it difficult to believe the man had heard none of that. Maybe she was wrong. Maybe his office was several streets over on the other side of the bar.

She didn't think so though, because, well, call it a hunch. All that screaming, someone in this town must have heard it, probably at least several people, yet they'd all remained silent and hidden behind their closed doors and drawn curtains. Paranoia tinged her thoughts again, but she couldn't help it, because the more she replayed those desperate moments in her head, the stranger it all seemed. It was like there was an understanding among the denizens of Beleth Station, that a woman or other person screaming in terror in the streets was something to be ignored, at least under certain circumstances.

Maybe the time of night had something to do with it. A time when locals knew better than to poke their heads outside, lest they fall victim to some beast or malign force. Something supernatural or perhaps just a man, a deranged killer who roamed the streets with a sack over his head, killing interlopers either for sport or some twisted sense of civic duty, cleansing the town of foreign impurity. Perhaps there was something ritualistic about it. Some sinister institutionalized thing. Whatever, she didn't really know, these were just the confused and frightened thoughts spinning through her head in that handful of tense moments while she waited at the curb and Hall exchanged a few last indistinct parting words with the bartender.

As she waited for Hall to conclude his business, whatever it was, she looked up and down the dark street, still seeing no one out and about. She hugged herself, shivering in the chilly evening air. It was perceptibly colder now than it'd been a mere twenty-some minutes ago. Some more minutes passed. Too many. She caught a fleeting glimpse of a dark figure on the opposite sidewalk two blocks up the street. Whoever it was, they were too far away to see clearly, but the shadowy figure was definitely there, standing at a corner just beyond the edge of a pool of light from a street lamp.

Krista glanced at Hall, still standing at the open door to Nowhere Special. She opened her mouth to shout at him, alerting him to the presence of the lurking figure, but some tingling sense at the back of her brain made her glance down the street again before she could do it.

The figure was gone.

Because of fucking course it was.

Hall at long last came away from the entrance to Nowhere Special, the door swinging shut as he let go of it. He directed a frowning glance at Krista as he moved past her on the sidewalk and opened the cruiser's passenger side door for her. "You okay, ma'am? You look a bit spooked."

She shivered. "I thought I saw something."

Hall smiled and nodded in an indulging way. An infuriatingly patronizing way. "That's your nerves, most likely. Sometimes when folks have had a good scare, they start jumping at shadows, seeing things that aren't there."

Krista grunted, but said nothing.

They got in the cruiser and drove away from the bar.

Hall sat in ruminative silence behind the wheel as he steered them through the quiet and empty streets. He didn't talk and didn't look at her, but she nonetheless believed she could feel his mind working. It was like a signal emanating from his brain, difficult to read and scrambled like an intercepted satellite broadcast, but detectable because there was so much energy behind it. She sensed he was struggling with something, but also sensed that whatever it was, it didn't necessarily portend any positive turn in her fortunes.

He remained silent until they arrived at the gas station after no more than three minutes of driving. Beleth Station wasn't a big place, and what had seemed like a considerable distance while fleeing for her life on foot was revealed to be not very far at all.

Krista's eyes widened in disbelief when they pulled into the parking lot. The gas station's inside and outside lights had been extinguished. There was no sign of the Sentra and Nick was gone.

She shook her head as Hall pulled up in front of the little building and parked. "This isn't right."

Hall's expression took on a stern cast as he nodded. "That's for sure. I see nothing corroborating your story."

Krista scowled. "I don't like the way you're looking at me. I've done nothing wrong. I'm telling you, we were here, my boyfriend and I, no more than thirty minutes ago. This place was open and Nick's Sentra was here. He was attacked and wounded right over there." She pointed to the pumps, her scowl softening into a frown of worry when she spied a wide, wet stain on the asphalt. "What the fuck?'

She opened the door and slipped out of the cruiser, hurrying over to the pumps. Hall also got out and followed at a slower pace, but she barely noticed because that underlying sense of wrongness she'd perceived about the entire town now felt like a lot more than mere paranoia. She moved between the two pumps to the opposite side and saw an even wider stain of wetness, and now it was clear what had happened. Someone had dragged a hose out here and had sprayed away any physical evidence of the attack, erasing every spilled drop of Nick's blood. She recalled how he'd dropped his phone before putting himself between her and the assailant, but that was gone, too, and with the Sentra missing, there was nothing to prove they'd ever been here.

Hall stood between the pumps and watched her scurry about in a hunched-over fashion, meticulously scanning the dark parking lot for even the most miniscule trace of...something. She didn't even know what she was looking for at this point. This wasn't a situation where she was going to find Nick by emulating crime scene investigators from TV.

She stood up straight and turned toward Hall, trying hard not to visibly shake or otherwise show the massive level of fear and worry surging within her. "Someone has covered it all up." She stalked closer to the dubious cop, pointing to the wetness on the ground. "His blood was spilled right there. I saw it go flying when that crazy motherfucker started hacking at him. Now the ground's all wet."

Hall shrugged. "That might only be rain water. We get little pop-up downpours all the time out here that only last a few minutes. If you're inside at the time, you might never notice."

This was so absurd Krista couldn't help laughing, a sound with an edge of mockery to it. "Right. A quick downpour so concentrated it only wet the ground right around the covered gas pumps. That makes total sense."

Hall's brow furrowed. "I don't think I care for your tone."

Krista sneered. "And I don't give a shit. Something is wrong here. Something is wrong about this entire town. I also think you know a lot more about what happened here than you're letting on, and I just need you to know I don't care about whatever weird shit it is you have to keep under wraps whenever strangers are passing through. I'm not going to tell anybody or try to get anyone in trouble. I just really need you to help me find Nick, so we can get the fuck out of here and never bother any of you again."

Hall stared silently at her for what felt like a long time, her unease continuing to deepen as she tried to imagine what might be going on behind the man's flinty eyes. He stepped away from the pumps and approached her, only stopping when he was within touching range. He was taller than she was, so she had to look up at his face. That sense of something unknowable but intense churning within him came through clearer than ever.

When he finally spoke, it was in a low tone barely above a mumble, one that would have been inaudible to anyone else, even if they were standing just a few feet away. "I believe something truly upsetting happened to you tonight, ma'am, but you're letting your imagination run out of control. I'm just a man doing my job, or trying to, at least. I'm not covering up anything. You'll just have to take my word for that."

He said these things in a way outwardly intended to comfort and reassure, but the words also felt threaded with an underpinning of implied menace. A subtle suggestion that she should be careful about anything else she might say, because any further implications regarding conspiracy or wrongdoing on his part might result in a far deeper level of trouble for her.

Tears welled in her eyes as she trembled beneath the weight of the man's penetrating stare. She hated the way he was making her feel small and weak, especially considering male physical intimidation was the primary thing she'd sought to escape by running away with Nick.

She took some deep breaths and managed to compose herself. "I'm worried sick about my boyfriend. He's missing. I feel like his life is on the line and nothing is being done to help him. That's literally the only thing I care about right now. Before leaving the bar earlier, you said you'd put in a call to the hospital. Is there any chance that's where he is now? Would an ambulance have been able to get out here and leave already?"

Hall held her gaze for another tense, silent moment, then a tentative smile began to slowly pull at the edges of his mouth. "As a matter of fact, I did put in that call, and you know what? I bet that's exactly what happened." He started backing away from her, gesturing for her to follow him back to the cruiser. "Come on, let's get moving."

In the wake of so much weirdness, allowing herself to feel anything resembling hope or optimism felt dangerous, like accepting an invitation to almost certain disappointment, but Krista followed the lawman without hesitation. At the moment, she could think of no other viable course forward, at least not without summoning help from outside the town. Outside help would take a significant time to arrive, however, time she felt she couldn't afford to waste.

Once they were back inside the cruiser, Hall steered them out of the gas station's parking lot and drove out of the main part of town. Another silence fraught with things unsaid settled between them as Hall drove fast down a dark and winding back road.

The cruiser went around a bend in the road and then into a straighter stretch of two-lane asphalt, at which point the lights of a building not far up ahead came into view. Krista's heart started beating faster as she leaned forward in her seat, expecting to soon discern the exterior of a hospital as they neared the building. What she saw instead was a tall sign near the edge of the street that read VACANCY in red neon.

Hall steered the cruiser into the parking lot of a place called the Paradise Inn, a dreary-looking lodging establishment with a single row of rooms branching off from a main office. A car was parked near the office and another one, presumably belonging to a guest, was parked in front of one of the rooms. Hall pulled up to the office and cut the cruiser's engine.

Krista looked at him, confusion etched in her features. "This isn't a hospital. What are we doing here?"

Hall's expression was once again impassive, betraying nothing. "Wait right here. I need to see Misty Lee, the lady who runs this place."

He got out of the cruiser and threw his door shut before she could respond, walking fast toward the office and disappearing through its front door an instant later. Upset by the lack of explanation, Krista popped her seat belt loose with the intent of following the lawman into the office, but she hesitated, fearing it might only further delay their eventual arrival at the hospital. Her hope was that this was only a quick pit stop along the way, some unknown minor matter Hall was tending to before resuming their journey, and she relaxed again when he reemerged from the office no more than two minutes later.

Instead of getting in behind the wheel again, however, he moved to the other side of the cruiser and opened the front passenger door. "Out of the vehicle, ma'am."

Krista looked up at him, blinking in confusion. "What? Why? Aren't we going to the hospital?"

Hall backed up a step and waved her out. "Just get out and I'll explain. Follow me."

Nothing happening made any sense to Krista. Once again lamenting the avoidable twist of fate that brought her to this accursed place, she got out of the cruiser and closed the passenger side door with considerably more force than necessary. Slamming it shut made the sheriff wince, but her frustration was such that she was past caring what he thought.

Hall led her along the row of dingy-looking rooms until he stopped at a door and inserted a key in the lock. He opened the

door and waved her into the room. Instead of immediately stepping through the opening, she tilted her head and peered
inside. The interior looked like any average dumpy room in an
out-of-the-way roadside inn. Nothing about it struck her as
ominous. Nothing, that is, beyond Hall's inexplicable desire for
her to enter the room instead of continuing on to the hospital,
but then another possibility occurred to her. One that made her
stomach twist as a sick sense of dread took root inside her.

What if what Hall really had in mind here was rape? She
didn't want to believe someone in his position would do such a
thing, but she knew that was naive. The news lately was rife
with proof to the contrary. People in positions of high authority
abused their power all the time.

She backed away a step, but Hall seized her by a wrist and
pulled her into the room. He gave her a shove and she fell upon
the bed, shrieking in fright as she bounced immediately back up
and tried making a run for the door. This time Hall grabbed her
by the shoulders and gave her a hard shake.

"Ma'am, I don't know what you think is happening here,
but you need to calm down. I'm not trying to hurt you."

Krista glared at him. "Then get your fucking hands off
of me."

Hall relaxed his grip on her shoulders, but did not release
her. "I know you're confused and I'm sorry about that. There's
not much I can tell you yet, but you'll have to trust me if you
ever want to see that man of yours again."

"What the fuck is that supposed to mean?"

Hall grimaced. "I need you to stay here tonight while I look
into some things. You were right about this town. Things here
are...well, they're kind of fucked up. I don't have time to
explain it all now, but you were right to be paranoid. I'm going
to do my best to help you, but it'll be harder if you're tagging
along. You'll be in danger and I might not be able to protect
you."

Krista made a sound of exasperation as he finally let go of
her shoulders. "What the fuck, dude? If what you're saying is
true, why didn't you tell me any of this before?"

Hall started backing toward the door. "Because I have to be
careful. Please try to relax. I'll be back when I can."

Krista ran toward the door, but by the time she got there Hall was already outside. He locked the door from the outside and when she tried the doorknob, she found it wouldn't turn. She pounded her fists against the door, screaming to be let out, but he was already gone. Moments later, she heard the cruiser driving away from the motel.

She further explored the room and found that the thick double-paned windows were sealed shut. There was a phone, but it would only ring to the main office, and accessing an outside line didn't seem possible. No one answered when she tried calling the office.

She was stuck here.

A prisoner.

With only Hall's word that she'd ever get out again.

She sat on the edge of the bed and put her face in her hands.

EIGHT

AT SOME POINT shortly after the display of odd behavior by the blonde woman and her deranged assistant, they composed themselves with startling abruptness and walked out of the room without another word, shutting the door behind them. Left alone in the dank-smelling space, Nick strained once more against the straps binding him to the table, a gesture he already knew was futile, but one he felt compelled to try again anyway.

A bleak hopelessness engulfed him as the straps failed to yield even slightly despite the most concentrated and sustained level of twisting pressure he'd managed to generate thus far. The strong stimulant the blonde had duped him into swallowing powered this effort, allowing him to draw upon reserves of brute strength he hadn't known he was capable of mustering, yet it just wasn't enough. Release from the thick, tightly-drawn straps would require assistance from someone else, which didn't seem likely to happen, at least not yet. His captors might well let him out of the straps at some point, but only when there were additional safeguards in place.

After willing the tense muscles in his arms to relax, his thoughts turned again to Krista. Tears blurred his vision as he was again forced to confront the horrific possibility that she was no longer alive. The sound of her screams ringing out in the empty streets of Beleth Station echoed in his head, the distortion of his memory imbuing the sound with a taunting quality. Guilt lacerated his psyche, filling him with self-hatred for his failure to adequately protect her.

There was at least some small quotient of sexism in that instinct, based on a dated notion of chivalry and male duty, but he couldn't help it. She'd been through so much, years of her life lost, locked into loveless marriage with an asshole who didn't deserve her. What she deserved was a chance at a better and more fulfilling life, even if they didn't wind up together forever. He wanted that brighter future for her more than anything, whatever shape it took, and now it looked like she might not get to have it at all.

All because I fucked up, he thought, *his teeth clenching hard. Because I wasn't good enough or strong enough.*

Nick wanted to scream, to give voice to the bitter fury rising up inside him, but he remained silent, not wanting to give his deranged captors the satisfaction of hearing him surrender to fear and helplessness. There'd already been quite enough of that, and he was done feeding the hungry, ghoulish things living behind their masks of human ordinariness.

An indeterminate amount of time passed. In the silence of the malodorous, gloom-enshrouded room, time felt malleable, illusory. It might have been as much as a full half-hour or it might only have been ten minutes. He heard no voices or other sounds of human activity from the other side of the closed door. After a while he became aware of an increasingly urgent need to piss, and once that awareness existed, it became exponentially worse with each passing minute. He squirmed in discomfort and considered calling out to anyone who might hear him. In the end, however, he relaxed and allowed his bladder the release it needed. What did he care, at this point, about achieving yet another level of humiliation and indignity?

Nick was unsurprised when the door opened again and the blonde woman finally returned within mere seconds of the conclusion of this physical process. It made him wonder if she'd been watching somehow, perhaps via a camera hidden somewhere in the room.

This time she walked in wearing high heels and a short and shimmery red dress better suited to a night of hitting the clubs in the city than whatever was happening here. She strode right past him, not even glancing his way as she briefly disappeared from view, which was unnerving. Twisting his head around, Nick saw her checking the depleted drip bag. The first time he glimpsed the bag it was swollen and heavy, but now it was nearly empty.

She nodded in apparent satisfaction and let the bag slip from her slender fingers, and in the next instant she shifted her gaze, making eye contact with him. "Your strength should be coming back now. Perhaps you already feel it, a powerful tide surging inside you. Embrace it. Revel in that strength. You'll need every ounce of it for what's coming."

Nick grunted. "For the Gauntlet, you mean?"

She smiled. "Yes."

"And what exactly does that mean?"

She moved to the side of the table and examined his wounds, tracing the length of each stitched-up line of divided flesh with a lightly gliding fingertip. "That's as much as I intend to tell you, darling Nick. Anything else would ruin the surprise." The tip of her finger returned to the diagonal slash line across his chest, pressing harder now as it traced the line again. "I must say, I did a superb job of putting you back together. It's something beyond technical skill, almost into a realm of something like artistry. There'll be some seepage later, as you participate in our festivities, but it will not debilitate you."

Nick winced and twisted against his bonds again as she pressed her finger in an even more forceful way against a lacerated spot at the bottom of his rib cage, her mouth curling up on one side in a reflection of sadistic pleasure. He begged her to relent, and when she finally did, it was with a look of profound satisfaction.

He shivered in relief. "You know what I think?"

"This should be good."

Nick grunted. "Go ahead, smirk, you smug bitch. What I think is that a lot of what's happening here is just you fucking with me, because, who knows, because being a smart person in a dead-end hick town gets boring. That's in addition to you just being straight-up sadistically insane, of course."

Her expression sharpened. "What are you really saying?"

"That wasn't pig blood in the bag, was it? Yeah, you wanted me stronger, I believe that, but the over-the-top parts of this are pure theater. You're performing, amusing yourself. I bet you're even recording all this to watch again later."

She stared blankly at him for what felt like a long time before a smile slowly began to curve the edges of her mouth again. "Do you really think I'm smart?"

Nick laughed.

"Yeah. Crazy as a shithouse rat, but smart."

She made a small noise of contemplation as she nodded. "That's really flattering and so sweet. Maybe I shouldn't cut off your cock and balls after all for urinating all over my nice table."

Nick gaped at her.

She laughed. "You should see the look on your face. Priceless. Don't worry, I won't make you a eunuch. Not before the Gauntlet. You wouldn't perform at the required level." She leaned over the table, putting her face closer to his. "Afterward might be another story. If you survive, that is. Anyway, you're wrong about the blood. It really was drained from a pig. It's funny, isn't it? You're a hybrid creature now. An abomination." Her laughter became sharper and shriller, the tittering of a genuine lunatic. "Pig-man."

Nick said nothing, could only continue gaping at her in horror.

She turned away from him at that point and walked back out of the room, but this time she was only gone a few minutes. When she returned, it was in the company of three large men clad all in black. Each man wore an identical cloth sack over his head, the sight of which stirred primal terror within Nick. His assailant earlier in the evening–a man who may have killed the woman he loved–had worn one just like them. For all he knew, the assailant might even be one of these men. In fact, it seemed likely.

He was removed from the leather straps and hauled off the table. After that, his hands were cuffed behind his back and a sack with no eye holes was draped over his head. He stumbled and nearly fell multiple times as he was led out of the dank-smelling little room, but he was jerked to his feet each time and made to keep moving.

Then he was outside, naked and shivering in the cold air. Soon he heard the rising hum of an approaching engine. A vehicle of some kind pulled to a stop several feet away. A door opened and he was roughly guided into the back of the vehicle, which began moving again the instant after the door was thrown shut.

The vehicle's engine roared and then they were on the move. An impulse to break the oppressive silence with a question about where they were going tempted Nick for a moment, but in the end he didn't bother, knowing they wouldn't tell him. He'd have the answer to his question soon enough, and it wasn't likely to be one he liked.

Soon the vehicle stopped again and he was hauled back out into the cold, his bare feet touching freezing pavement. There were sounds of activity from nearby, the chatter of humans gathered in a sizable group. He trembled in fear of what he might see when the sack was removed from his head. The chatter around him grew louder as the cuffs were taken off his hands.

And then off came the sack.

Nick's mouth dropped open and his eyes widened in sheer astonishment as he took a look around.

He'd been returned to the streets of Beleth Station.

But they were no longer empty.

NINE

THE first gently swirling snowflakes began to fall as Sean rode his motorcycle at high speed along winding Crow Road. He hoped the flakes signaled only the onset of brief flurries and not the deceptively mild start of a major storm. His hope was to get out of Beleth Station and drive as far away from the town as he could by sunrise the next day.

An impromptu and unauthorized exit from the place of his birth was a dangerous thing to attempt, a thing he normally would only consider after a large amount of careful advance planning, but after his close call at the mill he'd arrived at a point where staying was no longer a good option either.

His brush with the Night Wolves meant he was now a marked man no matter what. He knew Emma was one of them now, and they would not rest until they were certain this nugget of forbidden knowledge would not be shared with others in the community. Once they had him in their clutches, they might not kill him right away, despite that frenzied chase through the old mill. They'd lost at least one of their number in that encounter and might seek to draw him into their ranks after a lengthy process of torture and brainwashing. There were stories of similar things happening, more of the group's intentionally propagated dark lore.

Sean believed all those stories, and he did not want to become one of them, not even after seeing the girl he desired most join them. He didn't want to hunt and maybe even be forced to maim or kill other citizens of Beleth Station. He'd rather take his chances on the open road beyond the isolated town's border. The Night Wolves would track him relentlessly, but maybe if he drove far enough away fast enough he'd get away. It was unlikely, given the group's notoriously high rate of recapture success, but he had to try.

The advent of snow, however, was a concerning development. He hadn't seen a weather forecast and had no clue what, if anything, the lazily drifting flakes portended. It was the right time of year for a storm, though, and Beleth Station was well past overdue for a big one. A blizzard would drastically hamper his ability to get to any town of significant size. The prospect of wiping out on a suddenly slippery open highway wasn't a pleasant one, but the danger wouldn't sway him. He'd ride away anyway and hope for the best. If he died in an accident on the interstate, at least he'd go to his fate knowing he'd finally made it out of the place he hated so much, even if only for a brief time.

He went around another sharp curve on Crow Road, knowing he was now within a short distance of the highway junction. He'd see it shortly after the road straightened out again. Decelerating slightly as he took the curve, he shifted on the motorcycle's seat, readying himself to rev the engine again and ride faster than ever down this last stretch out of town.

Then the road straightened out and he saw the vehicles blocking his path to the junction. There were two of them, a pickup truck and a battered-looking brown van. They were parked bumper-to-bumper across both lanes of traffic. Men brandishing shotguns stood at the shoulder of the road on each side. Large, bearded men in thick winter coats. Even in the dark, he could read steely determination in their eyes. Each man stood ramrod straight, gripping their weapons like cavemen wielding clubs. One of the men stepped forward, moving into a spot midway between the roadblock and where Sean still sat astride his idling motorcycle, fully prepared to spin about and roar away in the opposite direction at any second.

The only reason he hadn't already done so was because he had a strong hunch he wasn't the reason for their presence here tonight. These men were not Night Wolves, who never conducted business like this without their face coverings. Also, the features of the man who'd stepped forward became clearer in the moonlight as he arrived at that midway point.

He was Virgil Parker, a former good pal of Sean's uncle, the one who'd lived long enough to raise him before checking out of grim reality with one pull of a trigger. Garret Crane once said Virgil was the only man in the world capable of drinking him under the table, a claim Sean was inclined to believe. He'd had ample opportunity to observe both men in action over the years. They treated drinking like an Olympic sport, pounding beers deep into the night in the little yard out front of their townhouse on North Street, often joined by other chronic alcoholic cronies. Night after night for years and years, getting rowdy and howling at the moon. Sean went to bed each night to the sound of their antics, becoming so used to it that the sudden absence of those sounds in the aftermath of Garret's suicide was hard to take.

Sean tried to sound nonchalant as he asked his dead uncle's pal the obvious question. "Hey, Virgil. What's up with the blockade?"

Virgil shrugged. "Some bullshit. What else? Somebody on the council got a wild hair up their ass, decided it'd been too long since some outsider was made to run a gauntlet. So, usual deal, can't risk having *other* outsiders roll into town while that's happening. We were sent out to turn away any potential interlopers." His scowl deepened. "Pain in the ass. More advance fucking notice would be nice, you know?"

Sean nodded. "Yeah, that's rough. Sorry, man."

Virgil grunted. "What can you do? Just how it is when you're on subsistence pay, at the beck and call of the Elders. Lot of downtime for drinking and banging whores, but when duty calls, you've got no choice but to respond. Otherwise that subsistence pay goes away and you gotta get a real job." His laughter had a bitter edge to it. "And good luck with that in fuckin' Beleth Station, you know what I mean?"

Sean did know.

Garret Crane spent the last decade of his life on subsistence pay from the Elders. There wasn't much pride in it, but it was kind of a sweet deal overall for people like his uncle and Virgil. Their time was their own most of the time and the subsistence gig kept them in beer money and all the other bare necessities of life. Where the Elders got the money to fund such an arrangement, no one really knew, but it was one of the two major reasons why the citizens of Beleth Station had never revolted on a mass scale. The other reason, of course, being the Night Wolves' long reign of terror and intimidation.

Virgil frowned. "What are you doing out this way, anyway?" He chuckled. "Not pulling a runner on us, are you?"

Sean forced a laugh.

This was in response to that friendly little chuckle from Virgil and its underlying implications. Sean had no doubt the man harbored suspicions related to his presence here at the outskirts of town, an area locals knew to avoid if they wanted to stay in the council's good graces. A once-in-a-blue-moon quick passage through this stretch of Crow Road on the way to somewhere else on the outer edges of town was okay, but you didn't want to let it happen too often, because then the Elders might start to suspect you were up to something inadvisable, like working up the nerve to shoot down that exit ramp and head out to the highway. There were hidden cameras that allowed them to record and track such things. A couple of runs by the highway junction within a short period of time would earn you a visit from Virgil and his buddies. More than that and the Night Wolves would come for you.

He believed Virgil had enough affection for him to do what he could to protect him within his limited means, but that only went so far. What was required here were some convincing words of reassurance.

"Fuck no. Do I look like a fuckin' idiot?" Sean made his features shift into what he hoped was a scowl of convincing disdain. "Like I wanna be dragged back in by the Wolves. I'm just out clearing my head by riding fast. Been thinking a lot lately, like about how cool it'd be to get on with your crew and never have to get some lame job working at Old Jim's or wherever."

The set of Virgil's features changed, becoming perceptibly warmer, tinged with genuine enthusiasm. "Well, shit. Tell you what, if you're serious about that, I can put your name forward as a candidate at our meeting next week. With a word in from me, that'd just be a formality. What do you think? You want me to do that?"

Sean tried out a deeply thoughtful expression for a few moments before slowly nodding. "Yeah. Yeah, you know what? I think I would like that."

Virgil's warm smile became a big grin. "Fan-fucking-tastic. It's a smart move, kid. Your uncle would be proud."

The mention of his uncle filled Sean with a deep sadness. This was a man who cried a lot in front of his nephew, when he was away from his buddies but still deep in his cups. He'd just cry and moan about how he wished he could escape his dead end fate in Beleth Station. He didn't know precisely what his uncle would've thought of the prospect of him joining the subsistence crew, but it likely wouldn't have involved pride.

He nonetheless plastered an imitation smile of fake enthusiasm across his own mug. "I bet you're right. That's the other reason I want it."

Virgil went on about it in the same jovial way for several more moments before his expression sobered. "I'll drop by your place to talk about this with you soon, but in the meantime, you should probably head back the way you came. This stretch of Crow is officially off-limits until tomorrow."

Sean nodded and began the process of getting his bike turned around. "Look forward to that talk. Bring a sixer of Yuengling."

Virgil snorted laughter. "Fuck a sixer. I'll bring a case."

Sean laughed, too. "Sounds good."

He revved the bike's engine and roared away.

Only when he was back around that sharp bend did he let the fake smile fall away from his face. A slightly thickening swirl of snowflakes made him squint harder against the cold wind buffeting his face, a task rendered even more difficult by the tears falling from his eyes.

TEN

SOMEWHERE AROUND THE half-hour mark of her forced confinement, a sound from outside the motel room roused Krista from a semi-stuporous state. She got up from the creaky old bed and went to the window at the front of the room. Looking out at the parking lot, she saw an old white Buick with a taped up side mirror. The beater's failing exhaust pipe belched out a cloud of black smoke as it pulled up and stopped outside the office. A man got out of the car from the driver's side, leaving the engine running and the door standing open as he ran into the office and disappeared for a few minutes.

Faint music issued from the car's open door, Bob Seger's "Ramblin' Gamblin' Man". There was at least one other person in the car, maybe more. She couldn't make out any of the shapes within from this distance in the dark, but she did see the glowing ember of a lit cigarette moving somewhere behind the windshield. The lean and grizzled-looking driver came back out of the office, got in the Buick, and drove down the line of rooms before pulling into a parking space two spaces down from the one right outside of Krista's room.

The engine cut off and a moment later both doors swung open, the old hinges creaking audibly. The driver got out again and this time he was joined by two women in scanty attire. They had extravagantly teased hair that made them look like refugees from another era. One wobbled on her heels as she moved toward the sidewalk, a cigarette dangling precariously from the corner of her mouth. The other one, a brunette who had legs like sticks and looked strung out, said something that made the man sneer and shake his head.

They were all moving toward the sidewalk when Krista started banging a fist against the window, raising her voice as she called out for help. The women didn't so much as glance her way, but the man shot a quick look in her direction. There was no concern in his expression, only leering contempt. Within a few more seconds, they passed from her view, filing into the room the man had rented.

Krista returned to her previous perch at the edge of the bed, feeling deflated again, robbed of the faint spark of hope she'd felt only moments earlier. She had a strong feeling that any other visitors to the Paradise Inn would be just as indifferent to her plight. This wasn't a place frequented by anyone inclined to help a woman in distress. It was, instead, a haven for various types of lowlife scumbags engaged in a wide range of dubious activities. She suspected it might also function as a staging facility for sex traffickers and that Ray Hall, despite his stated noble intentions, brought her here as the first step in roping her into that world. Tears filled her eyes and she moaned softly as she rocked on the edge of the bed, imagining some future point where she would end up looking like the damaged and strung out women from the Buick.

The phone rang, snapping her out of the reverie. She went to the nightstand, snatched the receiver off the cradle, and put it to her ear. "Hello?"

At first there was only silence, a dead emptiness over the line. It went on long enough to make Krista even more uneasy than she already felt.

"Hello?" she repeated, hearing the aching quality of imploring desperation in her voice. She didn't like sounding that way, like she was weak and helpless, but she couldn't help it. "Is anybody there? Please say something. Please help me."

The line went dead again.

Then the old television atop the dresser popped on.

Krista stood again and moved away from the bed to stand before the television. She frowned at the scrambled image on the slightly curved cathode-ray screen, which shifted and changed colors in a way that allowed her to catch tantalizing glimpses of what might have been a room in the motel before becoming too distorted and washed-out to discern anything revealing.

Instead of a knob for changing stations, the television had a vertical row of channel buttons in front along a panel beside the screen. Examining the buttons, Krista saw that there was a limited range of channels, from two to thirteen. The set was currently tuned to the third channel. She stabbed at the other buttons, but the set seemed locked in its current location on the channel spectrum. Her inability to operate the vintage device frustrated her, but she suspected the problem had little to do with her unfamiliarity with obsolete technology. The set must have been modified in unusual ways, allowing for operation by someone in a remote location. To test the theory, she tried turning it off by hitting the power button. Nothing happened. The scrambled glimpses of things that became almost identifiable for seconds at a time remained on the screen.

She had difficulty imagining why someone would remotely power on the set only to show her these distorted images. At first, that is. After a bit more thought, however, a possible purpose occurred to her. The caller who wouldn't answer when she spoke and the remote operation of the television could be seen as coordinated components in a campaign of psychological manipulation. They might be the first steps in a much longer process of breaking her down by making her feel vulnerable and off-kilter.

Krista sneered.

Fuck that.

She pulled the heavy dresser away from the wall and leaned in behind it to reach for the power cord. Before her outstretched, straining fingers could wrap around the cord and rip it from the wall outlet, a voice spoke from somewhere else within the room, making her yelp in surprise.

What the voice said was, "Do not unplug the set. You will receive an electric shock if you do not comply."

The tip of Krista's straining middle finger had just brushed the wire when the voice spoke, but upon hearing those words she jerked her hand away and retreated from the gap between the wall and dresser. A part of her thought the threat of electric shock might only be yet another element of the strange mental game being played, but she saw no reason to take that risk.

She again took up a position in front of the television, her eyes widening in surprise when she saw that the image on the screen was no longer scrambled. Her heart leapt in her chest at the sight of a naked and shivering Nick. He was standing in the middle of a street in Beleth Station, one that had been part of the route she'd followed while fleeing in terror from the man with the machete, only now it wasn't empty. It was lined on both sides with scores of people, all of whom were wearing face coverings of one sort or another.

She saw people in plague doctor masks and vintage oxygen masks that made the wearers look like trench warfare soldiers from the First World War. Others wore simple bandanas or cheap plastic Halloween masks. The sound was on now and someone was shouting through a megaphone in the street, the words too distorted to hear clearly through the old set's tinny speaker. She belatedly realized the voice she'd heard warning her of electric shock had spoken through the same speaker, only with much less distortion. Nick looked terrified. Someone had stitched up the multiple slash wounds across the front of his torso, which pleased her, but there was nothing else at all reassuring in what she was seeing.

The first thing she felt upon seeing him was elation at knowing he'd survived the attack, but that was quickly obliterated by concern over what might be about to happen. She sensed a sort of ghoulish anticipation in the crowd of masked onlookers, which came through despite their hidden visages. It was something in their body language, the way they all seemed to lean forward just a little. One man in a plague mask was actually rocking back and forth on the heels of his boots, barely able to contain his excitement.

Krista let out an involuntary gasp when the screen went black.

Then the phone rang again.

She ran to it and snatched the receiver off the cradle. "Hello?"

"Tonight you will do something cruel for me," a distorted man's voice told her. It sounded exactly like the voice that had spoken to her through the television's speaker. "Your lover will run the Gauntlet. His chances of survival are slim. You will be allowed a chance to save him, although you will almost certainly fail."

Krista's hand tightened around the receiver. "What do I have to do?"

Distorted laughter chilled her to the bone.

But the words that followed that laughter were even more chilling.

ELEVEN

THE SNOW WAS COMING DOWN FASTER NOW, flakes far fatter than the initial light flurry of little white specks landing in Nick's hair and on his bare shoulders. At the same time, the temperature was dropping fast. His physical discomfort became so pronounced he was scarcely cognizant of the words being barked into a megaphone by a man in a white opera mask that covered just one corner of his face. He was bent over slightly at the waist, shivering uncontrollably with his arms crossed over his chest, hands tucked into his armpits. The soles of his bare feet felt freezing cold, and he feared he wouldn't be able to feel his feet at all if this went on much longer.

His teeth chattered as he glanced around and studied the masked faces of the people lining the sides of the road. Some faces were completely obscured except for the eyes, while numerous other visages were only partially hidden by the various types of face coverings. Each mouth that was visible wore a smile, some broader than others, though everyone appeared to be having a good time. His state of misery was a source of joy to them. He couldn't fathom how other human beings–particularly so large a group of them–could derive so much obvious pleasure from the suffering of another person. He wanted to believe at least a few were here only out of a twisted sense of obligation or as a result of coercion and thus were only feigning pleasure, but he detected little evidence of anything supporting this hopeful theory.

Maybe the ones who didn't support this exercise in extreme cruelty had simply stayed in their homes, unable to protest the event any other way out of fear of retribution. It was clear that whatever was happening here must have been sanctioned by the leaders of the strange town, which was baffling. Yes, they'd detoured into an isolated rural town, one that appeared in an advanced state of decay, but this was still the United States of America. This level of mass civic derangement should not be possible anywhere in the country in the modern age, or so he would have assumed until now.

The man with the megaphone stopped talking.

He heard heels clicking on the pavement and an instant later the blonde woman who'd sutured his wounds was standing before him again in her sparkly red club dress. A thin chain, not present before, was draped around her slender neck. Attached to it was a rusty razor blade. Gripped in her right hand was a metal rod, the tip of which was pointed at the ground. She was the only local not wearing a mask.

She made eye contact with him and smiled. "You're wondering about my lack of a mask, aren't you?"

Nick shivered and said nothing.

She laughed. "Of course you are. The answer is simple. When you are done playing our game, as you lie dead or dying in the street, I'll remove your face with this." She fingered the rusty razor blade attached to the necklace. "And I will wear that as my mask." She laughed again. "How does that make you feel?"

Nick swallowed a lump in his throat and made his teeth stop chattering enough to utter his first words since being expelled from the vehicle. "You...s-sick bitch."

She smiled and raised the metal rod, touching the tip of it to his stomach. He shrieked as a strong jolt of electricity came close to knocking him off his increasingly numb feet. Tears flowed from his eyes and he started blubbering in a pathetic way. She touched the tip of the rod to his scrotum and gave him another jolt. This one did cause him to collapse, though he was immediately returned to his feet as two sets of rough hands seized him by the arms and hauled him upright.

The blonde woman stepped to one side and lifted an arm, pointing down the street. "Now you run."

Nick looked at her through his veil of freezing tears and shook his head. "I...I can't."

The woman rolled her eyes. "Nonsense. Your only miniscule chance of survival is to do precisely as I say. Also, if you don't, I will have you returned to my facility, where I will commence the slow process of flaying every inch of flesh from your body. The choice is yours, pig-boy."

She laughed again and this time so did many of the closest onlookers.

Then she brandished the shock rod again, which provided the only motivation Nick needed to finally get moving. The pace he managed at first was more of a stumbling slow trot than a run. His feet felt colder and number than ever, more like blocks of ice attached to his ankles than actual human appendages, but having no other choice, he continued to force himself forward. He was able to increase his speed slightly after a dozen or so halting strides, but his progress down the lane remained maddeningly slow.

The crowd of people lining each side of the street followed along with him, moving at an easy, comfortable pace that was possible in the weather-appropriate attire worn by all of them except for the deranged blonde. He was initially mystified by the movement of the crowd, but by the time he was halfway up the first block of the street the purpose of it became clear. The crowd was moving because there were not enough people in the town to line the sides of all the streets. Or at least not enough willing to condone or participate in this sadistic madness. They were herding him, in a sense, by blocking off access to various side streets.

Until, that is, they arrived at the corner of Ruin Street.

At that point, the line of pedestrians to his left turned at the corner and began to file down the side street, while at the same time the line of people to his right crossed the street to the opposite side of Ruin. That line halted as soon as it reached the corner of the sidewalk there, blocking the way ahead. A glance behind him confirmed that the road he'd traveled down was also blocked. The sadistic blonde woman was almost directly to his rear, following only a few paces behind, her shock rod raised and pointed at his back, ready to deliver another jolt should she deem it necessary. Or just on a vicious whim. Her team of black-clad assistants were spread out behind her, their faces still hidden beneath the cloth sacks over their heads.

There were large gaps between the members of the rear procession, room enough for a person to run through under optimal conditions. Fully clothed and wearing adequate footwear, he might have been tempted to try it, even given the slim likelihood of escape. The current state of affairs, however, meant it wasn't even an option. He'd be writhing on the street in pain for sure after another jolt from the shock rod if he gave even the slightest hint of trying it.

The blonde woman met his gaze and smirked. "Try it, pig-boy. I dare you."

Nick didn't bother responding.

His focus returned to the way ahead as he allowed himself to be herded in the new direction. Not long after turning down Ruin and continuing forward with the same hobbling gait, he saw that there was something in the middle of the street up ahead, down at the end of the block. Something indistinct at first in the swirling snow.

The blonde woman made snuffling, piggish noises from behind. "Do you see it, pig-boy? What is that? Could it be the means of your salvation? You should hurry up and see before someone takes it away, which could happen if you're not fast enough."

Though he was fully aware he was being manipulated and toyed with, the desperation Nick felt was at such an advanced level he couldn't help but respond to her suggestion. He picked up his stumbling pace as best he could, propelling himself forward on feet he could barely feel now. Through sheer force of raw-edged, desperate will, he was able to manage a pace just shy of a trot.

He was halfway down the block when he was at last able to discern more about the object in the street. Upon first spying it from a greater distance, he'd judged it to be roughly the height of an average man, but now he saw that the object stood a couple feet higher than that. At first he remained mystified, but as he continued to draw closer to it, he detected a hint of light from the nearest street lamp glinting off glass. Thereafter the glimmers of reflected light became easier to see with each additional loping stride forward.

The thing in the street was an old-fashioned enclosed phone booth, the first one Nick could remember ever seeing in real life, his previous familiarity with them deriving exclusively from movies he'd seen. At first he couldn't imagine how the obsolete relic could offer any true possibility of salvation. He figured the blonde woman's teasing hint to the contrary was nothing more than yet another cruel trick.

Then a light snapped on inside the glass enclosure, allowing Nick to see there was no phone inside the booth. There had been once upon a time, obviously, but now it was gone. Inside the booth, at the bottom, was a small rectangular box. A shoe box, Nick realized. Propped against the side of the phone booth was a sledgehammer. The purpose of the tool could not have been more clear–to smash through the glass panes of the enclosure and retrieve the box from the bottom.

A part of Nick wanted to fight against the new flicker of hope rising up inside him. The box *might* contain the implied pair of shoes, but there was an at least equal chance of it containing nothing at all. Or maybe it wasn't empty, but whatever was inside it would prove useless, providing no means of alleviating the misery consuming him. Something like that would precisely align with the other forms of psychological torture he'd endured thus far.

In the end, however, it didn't matter. No other scant possibility of relief was currently available to him.

He willed himself to move faster still and was within ten feet of the booth when another man emerged from an alley to his left and also began hobbling toward the enclosure. This man was also sans clothes and, judging from the many scars and fresher suture lines marring his emaciated torso, had been subjected to tortures beyond even those Nick had endured, and for a much longer period of time. The way his skin looked like thin paper stretched over his rib cage suggested he'd been starved as well. His scrotum was gone, appearing to have been surgically removed. He was the most pitiful wretch imaginable, but he moved with surprising speed and determination. Nick noticed that his bare feet looked like chunks of raw, freezing meat, which made his display of determination all the more amazing.

Nick frowned.

There was just one box inside the phone booth. One box that might contain a pair of feet-preserving footwear.

A new surge of adrenaline made him move much faster than he would have guessed possible under the circumstances. He knew what he had to do if he wished to hold onto even the thinnest hope of survival. There was no need of more instructions blared through a megaphone. He and this other man were being pitted against each other, combatants in a battle with only one grim outcome possible for one of them.

Nick's mind cleared of thought as he began to move faster still, his breath emerging from his mouth in great, fogging gasps as he struggled with all his might to reach the phone booth first. Any hope of survival meant he could have no room in his head for pondering moral dilemmas.

He and the emaciated, castrated man arrived at the phone booth at almost precisely the same moment. The other man got there only a small fraction of a second ahead of him, the bony fingers of one of his hands reaching to grasp the handle of the sledgehammer.

Nick did not reach for the sledgehammer. Not at first.

He raised a fist and drilled it straight into the center of the emaciated man's face, feeling the cartilage in the nose crunch beneath the devastating force of the blow.

TWELEVE

MORE PEOPLE FILTERED into Nowhere Special as the evening lengthened, not all of them part of the usual crowd of regulars. These were all faces bartender and proprietor Glenn Carrow recognized as belonging to citizens of Beleth Station. He spied not a solitary stranger or obvious outsider among them, but some here tonight were people who stopped in only on rare occasions, like the sleazy young couple seated at the end of the bar.

Their names were Jackie and Noelle. Jackie was less than a year out of high school and Noelle was a dropout who was maybe twenty by now. The girl, Noelle, worked as a prostitute out of the Paradise Inn. It was something everyone knew, not that she ever made any attempt to hide the source of her income. Nobody gave a damn about such things in a town clinging to life. In Beleth Station, if you were able to cobble together some form of a meager living, you were considered a success, even if it involved things the law would frown upon elsewhere.

In any other town, they'd be kicked out of a place like Nowhere Special for being underage, but Glenn hadn't bothered enforcing age restrictions for many years now. It was another thing no one local gave a damn about. Life in this place could be hell, and as far as Glenn was concerned, anyone capable of lifting a glass and pouring beer or whiskey down their throat was entitled to the particular form of escape he offered. The only form of escape available to most denizens of this rotting and forgotten speck on the map.

The reason for the small influx of non-regulars wasn't a mystery. This was one of a handful of places where those among the discontented in town gathered whenever an outsider was made to run a gauntlet. They weren't here to plan a revolt or otherwise voice dissent in an organized public fashion. The Elders would sniff out any such behavior and shut it down without mercy. Nowhere Special was nonetheless known as a friendly refuge for those uninterested in participating in the town's occasional ritualistic murder spectacles.

That knowledge was rooted in Glenn's own distant past as a vocal malcontent, a time decades ago when the Elders first began instituting their draconian policies aimed at stemming the steady exodus of citizenry that began in the wake of the old mill's closure. That time ended after he was arrested and made to endure weeks of brutal torture. His flesh still bore the scars beneath his clothes. He'd fallen in line after that, never again voicing disapproval of anything the Elders did. Not in public, anyway. But the way he truly felt about things remained and everybody knew that, even the sleazy couple at the end of the bar, mere kids who hadn't even been alive back then. They knew because the stories from that time were still passed on in private, memories of real things that grew ever bigger through constant retelling, until they became like legends.

The loose atmosphere inside Nowhere Special stiffened considerably as Ray Hall came in through the front entrance and strolled up to the bar. One elderly man seated alone at a small table near the entrance got up and walked out, leaving a nearly untouched pint of beer at the table.

The lawman raised a hand in a friendly wave as he glanced around at the assembled faces. "I come in peace, folks. Ain't here to hassle anybody. Not tonight. Next round's on me."

The prostitute at the end of the bar let out a whoop of approval and slapped a palm against the bar's polished wood surface. Frothy liquid sloshed over the rim of her glass, but she didn't appear to notice. Her scrawny boyfriend leaned over the bar to slurp up the beer she'd spilled.

"Set me up with another Natty Boh, Glennie!" the prostitute called out.

Glenn grabbed another clean-ish glass and filled it with the requested beverage. She was the first of well over a dozen patrons who lined up to avail themselves of the cop's generous gesture.

Hall settled onto a stool at the bar and waited patiently while Glenn tended to business.

Several minutes later, Glenn approached the lawman, regarding him from the opposite side of the bar with a raised eyebrow. "You actually good for that?"

Hall dragged his wallet out of a rear pocket, opened it, and removed some bills. The amount was more than sufficient to cover the round of drinks. As Glenn scooped the bills off the bar, the cop leaned closer and dropped his voice to a lower register. "Keep the change. There's something I'd like to discuss with you. The extra bit is to purchase your discretion. I've got some heavy stuff on my mind and you're about the safest person I can think of to hear me out."

Glenn held the man's gaze for a moment before turning away from him and moving to the register. He opened the till with the punch of a button and began feeding the bills into the appropriate slots. This wasn't merely about taking care of business in expedient fashion. It gave him a much needed opportunity to quickly sort through an array of complicated thoughts while denying the cop a chance to read his expression.

The man's position within the community made him difficult to trust in certain sensitive matters. He served at the pleasure of the Elders, enjoying a degree of power and authority exceeding that of anyone else not actually a sitting member of the council.

Hall was okay in most ways, as far as Glenn had ever been able to tell. He didn't abuse his power, at least not in any truly egregious manner. That counted for something. He enforced the rules that everyone here tonight hated, but he was not an unprincipled person. Baring one's soul to the man wouldn't be advisable under most circumstances, especially if one harbored strong non-conformist views, but he was known for his relative fairness. He cut people slack whenever he could, which was more than could be said for Hall's predecessor as Sheriff, a mean son of a bitch who'd been universally loathed.

These thoughts flashed through Glenn's head in a matter of seconds, just long enough to feed the bills into the slots and close the till again. The bottom line was he'd be willing to hear out whatever the man wanted to tell him, as long as he remained wary of being lured down overly dangerous conversational paths and avoided voicing any thoughts of a provocative or rebellious nature.

He turned away from the register and approached the bar again, leaning over it slightly as he gave the lawman his belated response. "You know me, Ray. The secrets I've kept without ever telling a soul could fill a book. What's on your mind?"

Hall nodded in silent affirmation of something. Then he drew in a big breath and slowly expelled it, glancing around furtively as if searching for eavesdroppers. Something was weighing on him in a big way. That much was obvious just studying his expression, which was twitchy tonight in a way Glenn had never seen before.

The cop's mouth dropped open in preparation of saying something. Before he could get the words out, however, a vulgar phrase rang out from the end of the bar with the clarity of a church bell clanging in the quiet stillness of a rural night. Or how Glenn imagined such a thing would sound, that is. There were no churches in Beleth Station. Never had been as far as he knew. God had abandoned this place long before his birth.

The thought-disrupting phrase that came trilling out of the young whore's mouth, addressed to her boyfriend, was, "What would you do if I needed your cum to live?"

Jackie, the boyfriend, looked briefly flabbergasted by her query, gaping at her as his drink-addled brain struggled to make sense of her words. He began to laugh, softly at first, then with slowly increasing intensity until he was nearly falling off his stool from the force of his mirth. He dropped his head, making his long, greasy hair hang over his face as he pounded a fist against the bar, causing beer to slosh out of his own glass.

His face was bright red as he sat up semi-straight again and turned on his stool to look directly at Noelle. "What the fuck did you just say?"

Noelle smirked and took a big slug of Natty Boh. "You heard me, bitch. What would you do if I needed your cum to live?"

Glenn's head swiveled slowly until he was looking straight at the sloppy young couple, an utterly involuntary gesture matched by Ray in the same moment.

Jackie laughed a little more and then appeared to give the absurd question a level of serious consideration. "Well, shit, that just depends. I mean, what kind of creature are you in this scenario that you'd need my cum to live? Some kind of cum vampire? Would you be able to extract my life-sustaining love juice without biting off my dick?"

Noelle shrugged. "Maybe. Hopefully. As a cum vampire, I'd need to maintain a reliable daily source of nutrition, so biting off your dick wouldn't be smart. But, like, I'd need your cum every single fucking day, at least one load and preferably more, because otherwise I'd shrivel up and turn feral and mean, like a regular blood vampire deprived of the red stuff. So if you had a day where you couldn't get it up or just weren't in the mood, I might go into an uncontrollable frenzy the next time I had your dick in my mouth." She paused long enough to down several more big gulps of Natty Boh, then wiped her mouth with the back of her hand. "And who knows what might happen then?"

Jackie grimaced. "Yikes. But, like, what if..."

The conversation continued in that vein, becoming increasingly twisted and distractingly profane. A look passed between Glenn and Ray Hall, a shared recognition that any form of serious discussion would not be possible so long as they remained in the presence of the drunken youngsters.

After Glenn invited one of the more trustworthy regulars to mind the till in his stead, the bartender and the sheriff went outside. The cruiser was parked at the curb. They got in and sat there in silence for several moments as Ray Hall again worked up the nerve to spit out whatever was weighing on his mind.

Then the lawman sighed heavily and looked at Glenn. "I know you've got no reason to trust any of what I'm about to say, but please just hear me out. That woman who came into your place tonight, the outsider..."

Hall trailed off, lapsing into another lengthy silence.

Glenn cleared his throat as he shifted nervously in the passenger seat. "What about her?"

Hall laughed in a rueful way. "It's funny. Well, maybe that isn't the right word, because I'm thinking it's more tragic than fucking funny. I've spent years training myself to think of outsiders as something less than human. I wouldn't be able to do this job otherwise. Because if I can see them as not being like real people, then it's okay, because it's what's best for the town, according to the Elders." His nostrils flared and his hands clenched tight around the steering wheel. "It's taken a heavy toll." One hand came away from the steering wheel as he thumped a fist against his chest. "In here, Glenn." He jabbed two fingers against his temple, perhaps unconsciously miming the shape of a pistol with his hand. "And fucking in here, man. Especially here." He sniffled. "And I don't think I can take it anymore."

He leaned back in his seat and another long silence unfurled.

Once again, it ended with Glenn clearing his throat. "Okay. I can empathize with all that, but...what exactly are you saying, Ray? And what does it have to do with that outsider lady tonight?"

Ray's head swiveled slowly toward him. "I've done a lot more than train myself not to feel things. I've been observing. Watching and learning. Waiting for the right moment. And brother, I'm saying I think the time has come to burn it all down."

THIRTEEN

AFTER ROARING AWAY from the roadblock, Sean continued in the opposite direction down Crow Road for another few miles, his mind and gut churning with frustration. He screamed into the stiffening wind, feeling the cold air sear his straining lungs. His tears continued to flow and the way ahead turned bleary, but he knew every twist and turn of Crow as intimately as the contours of Emma's body and so he felt no need to pull over until he could bring his raging emotions under control, which was why he didn't see the thing in the road until it was too late.

The tires of his bike blew out as he ran across the nail-studded length of lumber laid across the lane in front of him. He made a valiant effort to maintain control of the machine long enough to safely bring it to a stop at the shoulder, but the attempt was doomed to failure. The bike's rear end fishtailed for a moment before it tilted hard to one side. By that point, Sean had no choice but to lean into the slide as the shredded wheels dug into the gravel at the side of the road. His hands came away from the handlebars and he skidded through gravel as the bike shot into the ditch before crashing into a tree on the other side.

He cried out in pain as he flopped onto his back.

Nothing felt broken, but his jeans were shredded and his bleeding skin was scraped and raw in numerous places. In those first post-crash moments, he felt disoriented, too consumed with pain to allow much room in his brain for pondering the implications of what had happened. There was an image in his head of that nail-studded board, a sight that had come into clear focus only in that last fraction of a second, but he didn't know what it meant yet.

That changed as the Night Wolves came out of the woods.

He lifted his head and felt a deeper level of fear steal into his heart as he saw their dark forms emerge from the gloom. There were several of them, too many to take on in a fight even if he'd been capable of heaving himself off the ground. He tried sitting up, but that only sent many more electric jolts of pain sizzling through his body. The idea of getting to his feet and somehow managing to throw even a single punch was a total joke.

They moved without hurry as they came to him, knowing their quarry was wounded and at their mercy. He looked up and saw a bunch of bandana-covered faces peering down at him, dark eyes inscrutable in the night. One made a growling sound low in their throat, a sinister rumble that made his guts clench. Another one mimicked the sound, but the rest remained quiet, including Emma, whom he was able to recognize despite the covering over the lower part of her face. He perceived nothing resembling compassion in her unswerving gaze.

It broke his heart, and he started crying.

One of them laughed.

Nothing was said, however, as he was then seized by multiple sets of hands and roughly hauled up off the ground. He screeched in pain and someone swatted the back of his head. Someone else drilled a fist into his lower back, making his aching knees buckle. He stumbled and nearly fell several times as they dragged him into the woods, but he was jerked to his feet again and shoved relentlessly forward each time. They followed a narrow but well-worn path through the trees, walking in silence for a significant period of time until Sean began to perceive a source of warmth from somewhere up ahead, strong enough to reduce the frigid bite of the cold night air.

A crackling sound signaled the presence of a bonfire well before they emerged from the path into a large clearing. Then he saw the tall, billowing flames rising up from a pit in the center of the clearing. He also saw the man who'd interceded on his behalf back at the mill. The man sat cross-legged on the ground, his hands tied behind his back as two more Night Wolves stood watch over him. His jacket and filthy shirt were gone, possibly tossed into the fire. His bare torso, far more muscular than Sean might have imagined, was marred by a twisting map of scars. It was clear he'd been tortured extensively at some point in the past, and now some new wounds had been added to the topography of his much-abused flesh, some still freely weeping blood.

Disappointment was etched in the man's features when he looked up and saw Sean stumble into the clearing with his captors. The expression was fleeting, there and gone in the space of maybe a second, but Sean happened to look right at the man's face in the moment of its brief appearance. Seeing it was like a punch in the gut. The man was a stranger, just another old drunk moldering in the ruins of the mill, so he couldn't make any immediate sense of why that look of disappointment should sting so intensely, but it did. Though he'd been grateful in the moment, he hadn't asked the guy to put himself in the path of his pursuers. His sacrificial gesture was noble and all, but ultimately it'd been for nothing, a useless gesture on the brink of resulting in more spilled blood.

That was just the way of things in Beleth Station, where qualities like courage and honor were always in short supply, and often not present at all. This place leached every ounce of nobility from the soul, leaving husks masquerading as regular human beings. Sean had seen it happen to his uncle and friends and many others just like him. Thinking about it stirred bitterness as he was made to move deeper into the clearing. Why wasn't this piss-stinking bum like the rest of them? Why did he rise up and fight, tonight of all nights?

What even was the fucking point?

The hands on his arms clenched tighter, bringing him to a halt several feet shy of where his temporary savior knelt on the ground.

Sean glared at him. "Who are you? Why did you help me?"

The man surprised him with a sad smile. "You wouldn't

know my name because you never properly met me, but I held you in my arms once when you were a baby. I was your father's friend. His *best* friend. We worked together at the mill. Back in the days when things were good here." He craned his head slowly around, eyeing each of the Night Wolves in turn. "Before the Elders seized control. Before the rise of these jackals."

Some of the Night Wolves growled and edged closer. One among them–the tallest and stockiest of the group–stopped them with only a gesture, raising a hand and saying nothing. Once he was satisfied, the tall one turned away from the others and approached the bound man, backhanding him across the face so hard the sound of it was like the crack of a rifle in the clearing. The man's nose bent sideways as blood spewed from his nostrils. He let out a sharp, gasping cry of pain, a sound followed by noises of discomfort, which then morphed into mocking laughter.

He looked up into the partly covered face of the man who'd struck him, blood spilling over his chin as he grinned. It was the look of a man who knew he was staring death in the face and was not afraid. "Go on and hit me again, boy. Stomp me into the fucking ground and piss on my corpse when you're done. I'll still die proud, knowing I never gave in, never let them turn me into a monster. Not like you cowardly maggots."

The tall one huffed and puffed behind his bandana, making it billow in front of his face. His hands clenched into tight fists and his shoulders rose and fell as he fought against a rising tide of volcanic rage. Another second or two later, however, Sean realized that wasn't quite right. He wasn't fighting his rage at all, but reveling in it, soaking it in and feeling it fill every bit of him until rage was all he felt.

Unleashing a howl of primal fury, he grabbed hold of the bound man, yanked him to his feet, spun him about, and hurled him into the bonfire. The clearing immediately filled with screams and the sickly sweet smell of burning meat. Some of the screams belonged to the man thrashing about atop the pile of burning lumber scraps, but others leapt from Sean's own throat. The hands gripping his arms clenched tighter again, a safe-guard against any foolish notions he might have of going to the man's aid.

The burning man thrashed and struggled and at last managed to roll off the pile of lumber and away from the flames. At a gesture from the tall one, some of the other Night Wolves went to the man and beat at the flames with blankets until they were snuffed. That the blankets were even present suggested this especially vicious form of torture wasn't as spontaneous as it'd seemed. They'd planned this evil and sickening thing from the start, intending to let him burn just long enough to induce a state of constant, maximum agony without quite killing him. Not just yet, anyway.

Tears burned in Sean's eyes again as he stared at the man's blackened, smoking flesh and listened to his non-stop wails of brain-frying pain. Never in his life had he heard anything so horrible, not even close. One of the Night Wolves stepped in front of him, partly obscuring his view of the dying man.

It was Emma.

At a nod from her, the ones gripping his arms released him. She grabbed one of his hands and pressed a dagger into his palm. "Finish him."

Sean whimpered. "No. No. I...I can't."

She made him curl his fingers around the dagger's handle and then gripped his hand in both of her own. "You love me, right? Yes, I know you do. Finish him and have a chance to become one of us. A chance to be with me, like you've always wanted."

She stared intently into his eyes a moment longer before releasing him from her grip and moving out of the way.

A constant stream of tears poured down Sean's face as he stared at the man's blackened, writhing form and listened to the ongoing howls of agony, a sound he knew wouldn't stop until the man stopped breathing.

In the end, he did as he was told.

He went to the man who'd saved him a short while ago.

The dagger rose and fell, then rose and fell again, punching through charred flesh multiple times as thick, dark blood poured from the new holes in his flesh. At some point someone grabbed hold of his wrist and pried the dagger from his hand.

The screaming had stopped.

FOURTEEN

THE MAN on the phone fell silent after telling Krista about what he characterized as her only realistic shot at saving Nick. She heard him sigh and after another moment the line went dead. The receiver felt far heavier in her hand than it had moments ago, bending her wrist with the weight of the disturbing information it had been used to convey. It wasn't just a component of a communication device—it was a delivery mechanism for pure evil.

She loosened her grip on the receiver, allowing it to slip from her fingers rather than returning it to the cradle. It dangled over the edge of the nightstand, stretching the twisty cord. She heard a click from the front of the room and did not begin to turn in that direction for almost a full minute. The sound signaled the next stage of a game she didn't want to play, one in which she'd become a participant without even realizing it. She felt used and manipulated, a throwaway pawn in a scheme concocted for the sole purpose of amusing the sadistic monster who ruled this blighted, cancerous town.

A monumental sense of dread consumed her as she at last turned toward the door and began moving slowly in that direction. Her hands trembled and her breath quickened, her features crumpling as her eyes misted with tears. The mere contemplation of this horrendous thing they wanted her to do made her guts clench and twist. She was faced with performing an act of utter debasement, a descent into depravity so profound it made her wonder if killing herself might be the better option. The suicidal impulse was not a vague abstraction. She gave the notion serious consideration as she opened the room's now unlocked door and stepped out onto the sidewalk.

Snowflakes touched her face and landed in her hair, but the icy chill of the wind and snow hardly registered as she stared out at the road beyond the motel's parking lot. Perhaps the most attractive aspect of the suicide option was the relatively passive way she could cause her sudden death to occur. All she'd have to do was to start walking toward that road without following the phone man's instructions. She'd been warned that any attempt to flee the premises without first debasing herself in the required way would result in her being shot dead before she could even get to the road. She supposed it was possible this was an empty threat, nothing more than a scare tactic to get her to fall in line, but she didn't actually believe that.

Causing it to happen was so tempting.

She didn't do it, however, because her desire to help Nick was stronger than the revulsion she felt at what she was being asked to do. The memory of the unhesitating way he'd put himself between her and the madman with the machete would not allow her to do anything else. She loved him. It was crazy, because this intense connection they shared had developed seemingly overnight, but it was true nonetheless. She fucking loved him. The chance of saving him she might earn by committing the sickening acts requested of her might only be a slim one, but in the end the grim choice facing her was no real choice at all.

Sighing in resignation, she turned away from the dark ribbon of asphalt and went to the door of another room. After a final hesitation, she raised a hand and knocked. A moment later, a man opened the door and stepped aside, waving her in. He was the same man who'd arrived at the Paradise Inn in the beat-up old white Buick a short while ago. Krista entered the room. The man closed the door behind her and locked it.

"Take your clothes off."

She obeyed at once, shedding her dress, leggings, and shoes, followed by her undergarments.

The aging prostitutes she'd glimpsed getting out of the car with him were also no longer clothed. One of them, a woman with teased blonde hair and too much inexpertly applied makeup, was tied to a chair. There was a gag in her mouth and a strip of duct tape over her lips. The glassy look in her eyes suggested she'd been drugged. Her head lolled precariously to one side, making her look like a broken doll dredged from the bottom of a pile of discarded old toys. One that should have been thrown away years ago.

The other prostitute was handcuffed to the bed's headboard slats. She also appeared to have been drugged. A voluminous amount of duct tape had been wound around her ankles, presumably a safeguard against thrashing for when she woke up, which Krista already knew would happen soon.

A video camera on a tripod was positioned in a way that would allow a wide-angle shot of what was about to happen. The man would be able to record it all without fussing much with the camera.

He looked Krista in the eye and smirked. "You already know what to do, right?"

She nodded stiffly. "Yes."

The man chuckled. "Relax, sweetie. This is gonna be a good time. So here's what's gonna happen. First I'll wake these gals up with a shot of adrenaline. And then you're gonna take this." He handed her a folded straight razor, chuckling again. "Well, shit, you already know what to do with that."

Another stiff nod. "Yes. Your friend told me. Your boss."

The man scowled. "That motherfucker ain't my friend. Not that it helps you any, but that's a fact. Anyway, we're almost ready. The rest of what you need is in the bathroom. Shouldn't take you more than a couple minutes to get ready."

He was right about that.

During Krista's brief time in the bathroom, she pinned up her hair and donned a scarlet-colored wig of dubious quality. The finishing touch was a black domino mask that concealed the area around her eyes. Anyone who knew her well might still recognize her, but the odds of anyone who'd recognize her seeing this video were quite low. Or so she hoped.

Before leaving the bathroom, she opened the straight razor

and looked at the gleaming six-inch blade. She tested its sharpness with the light touch of a fingertip. A small speck of her blood stained the edge of the blade.

Sharp enough.

She looked at herself in the mirror and thought about all the decisions she'd made–along with all the things that had gone wrong in her life–that had brought her to this bizarre moment. It was impossible to reverse any of it now, of course, but she knew one thing for certain–if she hadn't run off with Nick, none of this would be happening. That was an undeniable fact, but the alternative would have been reconciling herself to more gray years of soul-diminishing misery with Tom, and for better or worse, she simply couldn't fathom that.

She wouldn't change what she'd done. Not even now.

The man whistled in appreciation as she returned from the bathroom. "Baby, you look fine as a redhead. You should think about a dye-job, make it a permanent thing."

Krista said nothing.

On the table by the window was a small black bag. The man opened it and removed two preloaded disposable hypos. Grinning again, he went to the bound prostitutes and injected them with adrenaline. Each woman was jolted out of their stuporous state within seconds. They squirmed and squealed behind their gags, eyes bulging in terrified shock as they tested their bonds and glanced around the room.

The man stepped behind the camera and gave Krista a nod. "Get to it."

She went to the bed and climbed up on it, curling up to the right-hand side of the bound woman. Now that the moment of truth had arrived, she felt no more hesitation. The time for that was over. In truth, it'd ended the moment she knocked on the door here. She was in this now, engaged in the commission of a vile act that would strip away multiple layers of her humanity, but she meant to see it through to the end.

The bound woman tried squirming away from her, but there was nowhere she could go. She placed the edge of the blade against one of the woman's quivering thighs and dragged it lightly up and down the bare flesh. The pressure she was exerting wasn't quite enough to draw blood. Not yet. The man on the phone told her to make it sexy. Make it hot. On one level, she was repelled by the notion of anyone finding what she was about to do "hot", but it'd be a lie to say another part of her didn't fully understand it. The woman whimpered and cried. Krista made soft, breathy sounds meant to simulate arousal.

She turned the blade and drew it along the inner part of the woman's thigh, pressing down just hard enough to draw forth a thin bead of blood as the blade began to open her flesh for the first time. The woman screamed behind her gag. Krista pushed back an impulse to tell her to calm down. This was nothing yet. This was just the beginning. The tease and foreplay phase of what was yet to come.

The man behind the camera made a sound of impatience. "Go faster."

Krista didn't so much as glance at him, keeping her gaze on the anguished facial contortions of the bound woman. She made the blade press deeper as it dragged down the length of her inner thigh again. The way the woman's face changed this time was interesting. Her cheeks turned bright red and her bulging eyes looked on the verge of emerging from their sockets. She experienced another moment of strange, vertigo-inducing duality, feeling empathy for this woman and the terror she was experiencing while also feeling a flicker of desire to make her facial expression change again. There was an intoxicating power in wielding the blade as well as a reflexive urge to fight against the feeling, but in the end she allowed herself to fall into it, to become wanton and dangerous. She told herself it was like playing a role, going outside of herself as a protective coping mechanism, and maybe there was some truth in that.

But it wasn't *all* that.

There was more here, a hint of something monstrous that had lurked dormant in the dark recesses of her mind all along.

She shifted her position on the bed, straddling the bound woman across her midsection. The woman squealed again and bucked beneath her, but she lacked the strength to dislodge Krista, who proceeded to slice her open again, drawing a red line from a spot just beneath her collarbone to down between her breasts before stopping at her sternum. The bound woman screamed again as the blood flowed more freely this time.

Krista put the palm of her free hand against the long incision, feeling the warm blood pulse against her flesh. When she took her hand away, her palm was painted crimson and her fingers were dripping with gore. She began to writhe slowly atop the woman as she rubbed the blood over her own breasts.

Make it sexy. Make it hot.

The bound woman's tears flowed in a constant river.

Krista dragged the edge of the blade across the woman's forehead and soon a sheet of blood flowed into her eyes, staining the river of sorrow red.

The sound of a zipper opening made her tense for a moment, but she'd known this was coming. The man on the phone said it would happen. She continued working with the blade, unzipping the bare flesh in numerous more places. It wasn't long before the bound woman's entire torso was covered in blood. Krista licked some of it from her fingers, moaning, playing for the camera.

Then the man climbed on the bed with her.

He was breathing deeply. She could feel his excitement even before he touched her. The look of surprise on his face as she twisted toward him and opened his throat with a vicious slash of the straight razor made her smile. It felt good to harm a predator, even if she'd turned into something monstrous herself. Blood jetted from a severed big vein in his throat, hitting her across the face before splashing her chest. He made a gagging sound and clutched at his throat, a futile attempt to stem the pulsating red tide. Then he fell away from the bed, got to his feet, and tried stumbling toward the door.

He got about halfway there before collapsing.

Krista stared at him, waiting for his body to go still. When she was certain he was dead, she returned her attention to the bound woman, who was still clinging to life. This lasted until the blade dragged across her throat, pressing deep and opening a big vein for the second time that night.

Not quite finished yet, she climbed off the bed and took up a position behind the blonde tied to the chair. She stood right there, absolutely still for perhaps a full minute as the blonde tried twisting her head around to look at her and plead with her eyes. Then Krista placed a palm against the crown of her skull and forced her to face forward again.

She let out a sigh and slashed her third throat of the night.

The woman squealed and thrashed against her bonds, causing the chair to topple over.

Soon enough, she was dead, just like the others.

None of this was betrayal. None of it was defiance. She'd done it all at the behest of the mystery man on the phone. All this carnage was what the Elders of Beleth Station wanted of her, specifically what the leader of them all wanted, the one she'd talked to on the phone. She had no idea why and, now that it was done, no longer cared.

She glanced around at all the bodies and blood and came to a realization.

I'm different now.

She had no idea what might come next for her and Nick if they managed to beat the odds and survive the night, what might happen if they were allowed to leave this town. But she did know that one thing. She'd undergone a metamorphosis.

Different now. So different.

She went to the camera and pushed a button to stop the recording.

FIFTEEN

THE EMACIATED man's nose collapsed beneath the force of Nick's fist, yielding like an overripe tomato, soft, diseased flesh disappearing in an exploding splatter of blood. He flew backward and landed on his bony ass in the street, an impact that resulted in another audible crunch that signaled the disintegration of his tailbone. Instead of a scream, he could only manage a weak groan of despair as he flopped backward, his scrawny frame stretching out in the street, which by now was covered in a thin layer of snow. Snow fell into his yawning mouth as he continued to steadily moan and whimper.

Nick felt pity for the man as he stood over his defeated opponent and took a few moments to catch his breath. The panic he'd felt as he watched the pitiful wretch move with such speed toward the phone booth already felt absurd. It was clear this poor man had put every remaining drop of energy he had into that fast dash across the street. Never in his life had he seen anyone who looked so frail. His arms were long but thinner than those of a small child. There was no chance he would've been able to lift the sledgehammer off the ground let alone wield it with any effectiveness. His eyes looked glassy as he stared up at the dark sky and blinked slowly, a misty ragged breath emerging from his yawning mouth.

Then came a brief moment of terrible clarity as the emaciated man's eyes were able to focus one last time, his head lifting off the pavement by no more than an inch as he met Nick's gaze and said, "Please."

His head settled on the pavement and he said no more.

The man's weakly uttered final word continued to echo in Nick's head. That it would be his final word was something he'd already decided. The way his weakened and abused body was stubbornly continuing to endure when it was so clearly time to surrender to the inevitable was obscene. Allowing it to continue when it was within Nick's power to bring the man's long period of unrelenting torture to a merciful end was something he couldn't accept.

A chorus of excited murmurs rose up from the crowd of masked onlookers as he grabbed the sledgehammer's handle and moved into position above the broken man's head, the large head of the hammer creating a trail in the snow as he dragged it along with him. Once he was satisfied with the placement of his feet relative to the man's head, he lifted the sledgehammer off the pavement and raised it high overhead. A sudden hush of anticipation fell over the onlookers as they watched the heavy implement stand tall above him for a final second before it came swinging down.

The head of the sledgehammer struck the man's face dead-center, the blow heavy enough to demolish the middle part of his head. A wave of sickness came close to staggering Nick as he lifted the sledgehammer again and saw the large, pulpy crater that now occupied the space formerly belonging to a human being's face. At first he thought that was the end of it, but now something even more awful was happening. Somehow the man was still alive, his withered chest rising and falling almost imperceptibly. A wheezing, barely audible hiss of breath emerged from somewhere within that ruined mass of flesh. The dying man's jaw had come unhinged from the force of the blow, hanging sideways against his neck. A red mist speckled his chin each time the bony chest rose and fell.

An anguished sound escaped Nick's throat.

A sound of mocking laughter, recognizable as belonging to the evil blonde woman, came from behind him. "Nice work, pig-boy. I absolutely approve. Having overseen every stage of that worthless worm's misery for years, seeing his suffering prolonged just a little longer gives me great pleasure."

Her cruel words instilled Nick with just enough resolve to finish what he'd started. He lifted the sledgehammer again, adjusted his aim slightly, and brought it down a second time, pulverizing the top of the man's head and the brain housed within.

The rise and fall of the man's chest ceased.

The masked sadists lining the sides of the street applauded, a sound that made Nick wish he had a machine gun. This first murder he'd ever committed felt like a monumental stain on his soul, the creation of a permanent blackness inside him, but in that moment he knew he wouldn't hesitate to blow them all away.

All he had, however, was this sledgehammer and he was not yet finished with it. He glanced down and saw how blue his feet looked in the swirling snow landing around them. Immediate action was required if he was to have any hope of fending off frostbite. The possibility of hypothermia would remain a concern, of course, but one thing at a time.

He moved away from the dead man and in another moment stood before the phone booth again. Before raising the sledgehammer, he stared at the shoebox at the bottom of the enclosure and spent one last moment contemplating the likelihood of it being empty. He didn't know how he could reasonably expect anything else given how the rest of this had unfolded so far, and he didn't much care for the prospect of becoming an object of even more jeering derision, but there was no other move here. He had to perform as expected, and hope for something good to finally happen.

Turning slightly to one side, he lifted the sledgehammer again and swung it around. A pane of glass at the bottom of the booth's door shattered, causing fragments to rain down inside the booth as others fell into the street. He then dropped the sledgehammer, approached the phone booth, and squatted in front of it, reaching inside. Hooking a finger under the lid of the box, he dragged it closer, feeling the modest weight of something within. Maybe shoes but possibly something else inserted to keep his hopes alive a few moments longer prior to crushing them for good. Once it was close enough, he lifted the box off the bottom of the booth and pulled it through the new opening.

Another murmur of anticipation rippled through the crowd as he set the box on the ground. Nick swallowed a lump in his throat, hesitating a few seconds as he stared at the lid and steeled himself for disappointment. Doubt regarding the actual contents of the box remained high.

The tears that came to his eyes when he saw an apparently brand-new pair of sneakers was accompanied by a sting of shame. He was crying out of gratitude and it infuriated him to feel anything like that. These people deserved only his undying hatred.

Yet the gratitude was there anyway.

He sat back on his ass now, feeling the freezing cold from the street permeating his backside as he lifted his feet off the ground and wiped snow from the almost entirely numb soles. Before inserting his feet in the shoes, he examined the insides to ensure they weren't filled with ground glass or nails, which would not have surprised him in the least, but they seemed safe. The fit was tight. Perhaps half a size too small, but they would suffice.

The blonde woman laughed heartily as he clumsily got to his feet and spent a few moments precariously wobbling about before getting into a safely upright position.

She came closer now, brandishing the shock rod. "Bravo, piggie. I admit I had my doubts about you. Any successful running of the Gauntlet requires a mercilessness I didn't think you possessed, but you have proven me wrong." She came even closer and tapped the end of the shock rod against his chest, making him flinch. Her thumb caressed the button that would send another painful jolt of electricity through his body, but did not press it. "So congratulations, you've survived the first phase, but your ordeal is far from finished. Are you ready to continue and possibly earn a chance to round out your wardrobe?"

Nick let out the breath he'd been holding and nodded tersely. "Yes."

The blonde smiled as her thumb continued to caress the trigger button. "Excellent. The Gauntlet doesn't get any easier from here. Making it all the way through to the end will require several more displays of that merciless quality. What you did right here?" She chuckled. "Darling, this was the easy part."

Her thumb stopped caressing the button and pressed it.

Nick shrieked as another jolt of electricity knocked him off his feet. Because the tip of the rod had been touching his chest, the jolt further inflamed the pain from his sutured slash wounds, temporarily restoring it to a level of throbbing agony.

He looked up and saw the blonde looming above him. This time she put the tip of the shock rod an inch away from his right eye. "Next one goes right there." She moved the tip a half inch closer to his bulging eye. "Can you imagine how bad that will be? The sheer agony of it?"

Nick whimpered.

The blonde smirked. "Your eye will feel like it's liquefying inside the socket. Something to look forward to, piggie. Now get on your feet."

Nick wasted no time obeying this order, getting upright again within seconds. This required a significant amount of determination and energy, something his extreme level of physical discomfort might have rendered impossible if not for his terror of the shock rod.

The blonde came closer again and dragged the bright red nails of her free hand across his chest, triggering more flashes of pain in the slash wounds. It was a less severe pain than that induced by the electric jolt, but it was far from pleasant. Her thumbnail dug into one of the sutures, drawing forth a tiny bead of blood.

"Time for the next phase of the Gauntlet. Put your nice new shoes to work and start walking. You'll probably want to move faster this time." She glanced briefly at the sky and smiled. "The way this stuff is coming down, you'll turn into a human popsicle soon if you don't pick up the pace."

At her prompting, Nick retrieved the sledgehammer. She told him he would need it for what was coming. He then turned away from her and continued down the street in the same direction he'd been going. The masked onlookers at the sides of the street moved along with him, while the blonde sadist and her lackeys again followed behind him.

An intense sense of dread consumed him at the mere contemplation of the next challenge facing him. Whatever it was, he had no doubt it would again require something monstrous of him. Something even worse than pulverizing a pitiful broken man's head with a sledgehammer.

Something that might break him forever mentally, even if he survived the night, but the brutal circumstances of the situation left Nick with no good options. He didn't want to have to kill again, but he wanted to die even less.

The snow kept falling, harder and harder.

And Nick kept walking.

SIXTEEN

THEY WERE in the back of a pickup truck now, one that had been waiting for them at the side of the road as they came filing out of the woods. A few rode in the cab up front, while the rest, including Sean and Emma, piled onto the bed of the truck. Emma huddled with Sean in a back corner, her arm around him and her head on his shoulder while the others sat away from them and didn't so much as glance their way as the truck started rolling down the road. These others said nothing to them or to each other. Now that he was apprehended and his father's old friend was dead, they were calm, the tension and frenzy of earlier vanished without a trace, at least for now.

Sean felt defeated, robbed forever of any realistic hope of ever escaping Beleth Station and making a normal life for himself somewhere else. Now that the Night Wolves had him, he was theirs forever. That was the way it worked. He'd heard the stories a million times. They would turn him into one of them, most likely through a brutal and prolonged program of torture and brainwashing. The process would work because it always worked. If for some reason it didn't, he'd be put down, the way a mama wolf would kill a pup too sickly to survive and thrive in the wild. He'd become one of these almost feral things, growling and howling like some kind of deranged beast while tracking prey.

It made him feel sick.

Made him want to kill himself.

Emma snuggled closer and kissed the side of his neck. She had a hand on the inside of his thigh, up close to his crotch. He felt his breath quicken as she squeezed him there, arousing him despite his revulsion for the Night Wolves as a group. Her warm, soft lips as she kissed his neck again had him trembling. He'd rarely ever felt anything as nice as that. Probably because he'd never desired anyone as intensely as he still desired Emma.

She was manipulating him. Everything she was doing now was all in service to the pack, a method of preparation for what was to come, a softening up before the beginning of the difficult indoctrination period. He couldn't help thinking of the way he'd conned Virgil back at the roadblock, convincingly feigning enthusiasm for a future as part of the subsistence work crew. The irony was that now, after everything he'd endured tonight, he'd welcome the chance to embrace that opportunity for real. If escape from Beleth Station was impossible, a life of hanging out and getting shitfaced drunk every night with the subsistence gang would be preferable to the grim future actually facing him now.

Emma moaned softly against his neck, her mouth open and wet against his skin. She licked him and squeezed his crotch. A shiver went through his body that had little to do with the cold wind buffeting them in the open bed of the truck. His state of arousal intensified as she nipped at his skin, the sting of her teeth painful and pleasant at the same time. He remained fully aware of being manipulated throughout these escalating stages of seduction, but being cognizant of what was actually happening here was rapidly nearing a point of irrelevance. He was like soft clay in her hands, malleable to her touch, a thing slowly being shaped in a way that would harden into something new and permanent.

She squeezed the crotch of his jeans, making him whimper and moan. He gasped as she opened his jeans and took his hardness in his hand. His eyes went to the other Night Wolves. He felt weird about this happening in front of them, but they all remained outwardly oblivious or uninterested in what Emma was doing to him, their gazes directed elsewhere. Maybe that was intentional, some form of respectful stoicism while the newest of them performed a duty the rest of them could not fulfill.

Her breath was warm against his ear. "Look at me, not them."

Sean shivered again and looked at her. He saw snowflakes touch the delicately shaped planes of her lovely and alluring face, specks of white against flesh turned ruddy pink by the cold air. No one out in the regular world could look at a face like that and ever guess it belonged to a member of a ruthless gang, but here in Beleth Station the people knew better. Everyone was potentially something more sinister than what they seemed.

Emma made a growl low in her throat. "That's better. I'm all that matters now. Right?"

Another whimper escaped his trembling lips as she squeezed him again. "Right."

There was a surreal quality to what was happening. He felt like he'd entered an altered state of existence, a place where this improbable act felt like the most natural thing that could happen, a world sheathed in falling stardust. A magic place where all the things that troubled him meant nothing.

Then her hand came away from his cock.

She touched his face and sighed. "Hold onto this feeling, Sean. Think of it as a promise of things to come."

He experienced frustration at the abrupt cessation of a transcendently pleasurable sexual act, but there was no time to dwell on that. The truck had slowed down and was in the process of rolling to a stop as it pulled up to a loading bay at the back of another crumbling building. Becoming self-conscious again, he tugged up his underwear and zipped up.

Having been oblivious to virtually everything else during the most compelling parts of Emma's act of physical manipulation, it took him a moment to realize where they were. The size and decrepit state of the place were the big clues. This was the back of Crockett's, a long-shuttered general store out on Lancer Road.

At first Sean couldn't fathom why the Night Wolves had come here, but then he saw a door open next to the loading bay. A man in dark clothing descended the short flight of steps and approached the truck. He left the door standing partly open, allowing Sean to glimpse a sliver of bright artificial illumination. Because there was no outdoor generator running anywhere in the vicinity, he could only assume the building was still connected to the power grid, which surprised the hell out of him.

Then a spark of intuition came to him.

This was their gathering place. The secret clubhouse of the Night Wolves.

The place where the next phase of his indoctrination would begin, a realization that sent a shiver of dread through his body.

A loud exclamation from within the truck's cab occurred after the man from the building had conversed quietly with the driver. There was a strong undertone of anger in the sound and it was followed by a bit of shouting, which abruptly ceased after the man who'd addressed them raised his voice to a thunderous level, cowing the cab's occupants with threats they seemed to take seriously. Muttered words of meek apology followed.

Emma put her mouth against Sean's ear, dropping her voice to a whisper so low only he could possibly hear it. "His name is Quist. Top alpha wolf. Our leader."

Sean nodded.

He didn't know how else to respond to that information. All it meant to him was that this was the person he needed to fear the most.

Quist moved away from the window and again raised his voice to address the Wolves in the back of the truck. "Listen up. Before you go inside, you need to know we have visitors tonight. People not in the pack."

There was some muttering as the Wolves glanced around at each other. Once again, Quist silenced this by raising the volume of his voice.

"*Enough*! Shut up and listen to me." He sighed as he tugged the standard black bandana down from his face. "Yes, this violates our oldest and strictest rule. No fucking outsiders. That's been drilled into your heads without mercy from day one. I know. I fucking get it. But something has come up, something bigger than us, bigger than the pack. Bigger than anything. In a minute we'll go inside and these outsiders will tell you things that'll shock you. You might get pissed off and be tempted to do something stupid. I'm telling you right now you need to resist that temptation at all costs, because if you don't, I'll fucking put you down. You'll listen and you'll listen fucking good to what the outsiders have to say. It's important. It might change everything about life in this town forever. You hear me?"

Murmurs of reluctant assent arose from those in the truck.

Quist nodded. "Good. See that you behave once you're in the building and see who's in there. Or fucking else. Now... everybody out."

He turned away from them and went back into the building.

A moment of stunned stillness ensued.

Then the Night Wolves began to pile out of the truck and shamble toward the former general store's rear entrance. Sean got out with Emma and she held his hand as they walked into the building together. They passed through a short hallway and then through an open door into a largish room that was once the store's stockroom. There were numerous gasps of shock from those who passed through the door ahead of them.

Sean wondered who in Beleth Station could possibly evoke such a reaction. Then he and Emma passed through the door and he understood. The outsiders stood together in the middle of the room.

There were several of them, but the two who really mattered stood at the front of the group, grim expressions on their faces.

They were Ray Hall and Glenn Carrow.

SEVENTEEN

A SENSE of urgency remained for Krista where Nick was concerned. She wanted to get out there and start looking for him, still wanted to escape this warped and uniquely insular, weird little town with him. In the wake of the murderous deeds she'd been coerced into committing, however, she found herself taking her time departing the blood-spattered motel room.

Prior to killing the man and the old whores he'd duped into performing in a snuff film, her intent regarding what would happen once it was done had seemed clear. She would flee the premises and immediately begin the search for Nick. That clarity of intent still existed, but in an altered form. The strong sense of having been transformed by what she'd done caused her to linger and wallow in the strange feelings engulfing her.

The landscape of her psyche felt permanently changed, in ways both subtle and profound. She sat in a chair she'd positioned for optimal observation purposes and studied the corpses. They were her creations. Things made dead by her actions. What she felt while studying them was nothing like she'd imagined before entering the room. Looking at them didn't bother her. Making them dead felt like an act of personal exposure, the wiping away of a thin veneer created by social conditioning. She was seeing something about herself that had been hidden until now.

That hidden thing was a deep capacity for doing evil things

and not feeling bad about it. It went deeper than that. The real truth was that what surprised her most was a capacity for the enjoyment of doing evil things.

She thought about the way she'd held the razor against the second whore's throat for a moment before killing her, letting her feel how hard and unyielding the steel was against her vulnerable flesh. A rush like nothing she'd ever experienced came over her as she used the blade to open the woman's throat, waves of pleasure that stiffened her nipples and made her body tremble.

It felt *good*.

Like something that could become an addiction.

After spending an indeterminate time lingering in that state of gauzy mental haze, she got up and went into the bathroom, turning on the shower. She stepped under the lukewarm stream and washed all the blood from her body. The process took a while. There was so much blood and it was so sticky. Once it'd finally all sluiced away, she spent some additional time in the shower, pleasuring herself even after the water started to turn cold, bringing herself to orgasm faster than she'd been able to in a long time.

A short time later, she was back out in the room, dried off and back in her clothes. She found the dead man's keys in a pocket of his discarded jeans and finally felt ready to leave. At the door, she paused a moment longer to take in the carnage one more time, seeking to absorb every detail and permanently sear the image in her brain. None of it stirred even a flicker of repulsion. She found her creations beautiful, more beautiful than they'd ever been in life.

She sighed wistfully.

Then she went outside and shivered against the deepening cold. The parking lot was white now and snow was falling in heavy sheets. It was the kind of snow that looked like it wouldn't be letting up for a long time. The town would be blanketed in many inches of the stuff before morning, maybe even a foot of it or more. For the first time, she felt the smallest twinge of regret for lingering in the room so long. The worsening weather could make escaping the town much more complicated.

She got in behind the wheel of the old Buick, her nose crinkling at the thick odor of cigarette smoke that permeated the upholstery. This disgusted her far more than her long postmortem examination of the corpses.

Which hadn't disgusted her at all.

After dropping the straight razor on the passenger seat, she got the car started and backed out of the parking space, turning the wipers on as she turned the car around and headed for the street. The wipers made squeaking noises as they swept back and forth across the windshield. Old and in need of replacing, they'd have trouble keeping up with snow this heavy. She'd need to trade the wretched old junker in for something newer as soon as possible.

The car parked outside the motel's office looked in better shape than the Buick, but she erred on the side of caution, believing it wouldn't be wise to engage in confrontation with anyone who worked at the Paradise Inn. The owner was undoubtedly a close associate of the so-called Elders of Beleth Station, and she didn't wish to cross them.

She had no GPS to guide her, but she remembered the direction the deputy had taken bringing her out here. From what she could recall of that tense and largely silent drive, it was a straight shot back to town. The back road had many looping curves and sharp bends, but there would be no turns to make until arriving at the road that would take her into the middle of town.

Once she was there, she would commence a street by street search for Nick. She knew things might not work out the way she hoped. The last she'd seen of him, he was in a dire situation. Her brief glimpse of him naked and shivering was a while ago. Enough time that Nick might easily have already met his demise while running the Gauntlet, whatever that was. The street might already have emptied of masked spectators, her lover's body hauled away and deposited in some dumping ground. She might never find him, but she would not do the easy, self-serving thing and head straight to the interstate.

"I love you, Nick," she said, still watching the snow fall while letting the Buick idle at the edge of the street. "You saved me, and if I have to, I'll die trying to save you."

She hoped somehow he could feel the strength of feeling behind these words. In her head, she saw him standing in that snowy street and abruptly gasping as a wave of powerful emotional energy swept through him, one imbued with enough of her essence to leave no doubt of its origin. She imagined it fueling him, infusing his will with the grit and drive necessary to keep him alive just long enough for her to reach him.

A fanciful and unlikely notion, no doubt, but one she badly wanted to believe in.

Another moment later, she pulled carefully out onto the street and started heading toward town.

EIGHTEEN

A CAR WAS PARKED sideways across the middle of the snow-blanketed street. The sound of the rumbling engine was audible well before Nick was able to glimpse it through the swirling gusts of snow. It was an ordinary sound, one that would never strike him as sinister under normal circumstances, but hearing it now, in this strange place on this miserable night, it felt ominous.

The shoes he'd won by demolishing his adversary's head earlier protected his feet from further deterioration and made it easier to continue slogging forward, but the physical relief only went so far and would only last so long. His feet still felt like blocks of frozen meat. The shoes weren't appropriate winter weather footwear, and once the snow reached a depth of more than a few inches, the scant protection they offered would be negated.

Any truly meaningful level of relief wouldn't be possible unless he was able to get indoors somewhere, away from the cold and rapidly accumulating snow. The rest of his body wasn't in much better shape. His fingers were starting to feel like icicles. He could barely feel the handle of the sledge-hammer as he dragged the thing along with him, walking hunched over with snow gathering on his shoulders and in his hair. His ears felt raw from the cold wind, as did his face and ass. He couldn't feel his cock and balls at all.

After trudging ahead another block, the car at last came into view. It was a decades-old blue sedan, one of those long things that looked like a boat on wheels. He got to within about twenty feet of it before coming to an abrupt halt at the blonde woman's command.

She stepped forward, putting herself directly in front of him again. At some point during the time between now and his last glimpse of her, she'd donned a brown fur coat that fell to a point just above her knees. The sparkling red party dress was no longer visible. She was still in heels, however, which he couldn't imagine being comfortable for much longer.

"How are you feeling, pig-boy? Is the cold getting to you?"

Nick said nothing.

He just shivered and stared at her, waiting for her to get to the point.

Any illusions he'd harbored about surviving this night were gone. Chances were he'd either succumb to the elements soon or be killed by some unknown adversary awaiting him somewhere along the path of the Gauntlet. He still longed to find Krista and save her, but everything about his current reality suggested this was no longer within the realm of even remote possibility. He was doomed and for all he knew, she was already dead.

The blonde woman laughed. "Nothing to say? Hmm, that's no fun. I could force the issue, hurt you bad enough to make you respond, but I might accidentally kill you and that would be even less fun, because I definitely want you to experience this next stage of the Gauntlet. Would you like to know what it entails?"

Again, Nick only shivered and said nothing.

The blonde woman sighed. "Fine. Be like that. Here's the deal. That car has been running since the start of the Gauntlet, with the heat turned up to full blast. By now it's warm and toasty inside. I'm willing to allow you as much as fifteen full minutes of sitting inside it, contingent on the successful completion of your next task. Imagine how much better you'd feel after that, at least for a while. Also, on the passenger seat you'll find a long-sleeved flannel shirt and a pair of winter boots. You'll of course still become miserably cold again once you're back outside, but these things should lessen your suffering somewhat. So what do you say, pig-boy? Does this interest you?" She placed the tip of the shock rod against his throat. "I'm afraid this time I will require an answer."

Nick sniffled. "Wh-what do I...have to do?"

She smiled. "Go to the other side of the car and see for yourself."

There was a leering quality to her smile that troubled him, a sense of gleeful anticipation. Whatever awaited him on the other side of the old sedan would be something horrific. He also knew gaining access to the car would come at a cost. He'd have to do something terrible again, which he hated, but surrender was his only other option. If he just gave up, he suspected he'd be taken to some other location and held prisoner, perhaps for a long time. He had a feeling the remainder of his days would be spent enduring starvation and unending torture, and one day he'd end up looking like the emaciated man he'd killed.

He turned away from the blonde woman and started moving toward the car. As he drew closer to it, he began to detect a soft, barely audible sound of whimpering from the other side. Within a few seconds of first hearing the sound, he realized it was invested with a feminine quality. He was overcome with the sudden certainty that the woman was Krista, a notion that spurred him to move faster.

His heart was pounding and he was huffing and puffing as he hurried around the front of the car. The relief he felt when he came to an abrupt halt and saw that the woman making those sounds was not Krista was only slightly greater than the sick feeling that gripped him in the next instant.

A nude woman was on her knees several feet away from the driver's side door. Her hands were tied behind her back and her bare feet were wrapped in barbed wire. Her face was bloody and her nose looked broken. She flinched and whimpered more loudly when she looked up and saw Nick looming above her from a few feet away. Her lips were held together by a line of safety pins. A length of razor wire was looped tight around her neck, a bright line of slowly trickling blood visible where the wire cut into her skin. The other end of the length of wire was tied to the car's door handle.

She was positioned at an angle away from the door. The intent was obvious to Nick right away. Opening the door would cause the razor wire to draw taut and sink deeper into her flesh. Deep enough, probably, to sever her jugular.

Fresh tears flowed from her bleary eyes and she tried to speak, but it came out muffled behind the line of safety pins. Nick didn't need to know her exact words. She was either begging for mercy or asking him to put her out of her misery. In the case of the latter, simply opening the car door would take care of that, though it'd be a painful, miserable way to go.

The blonde woman and her lackeys now stood arrayed around him, while the line of spectators to either side of the street edged slightly away from the sidewalks. The latter group was eager for a better view of what they hoped was about to happen. Their palpable thirst for blood repulsed Nick. He again wished he could slaughter them all. They were monsters.

The sound of the blonde woman's laughter made him turn toward her. "I have to kill her to get inside, right? Opening the door does it."

She smirked. "Yes, genius. Your keen observational skills are truly impressive. It's not as simple as that, though. I'm granting you the power to spare the life of this miserable little wench. Give the word and the razor wire will be removed from her neck. She'll be returned to her cage in my dungeon. But mercy comes at a cost. This is where the sledgehammer comes in. If you choose to spare her, you'll be required to smash out the windows of the car. You won't get to sit in the toasty, rejuvenating heat for fifteen minutes and you won't–"

Nick let go of the sledgehammer as she was still speaking and approached the car. The woman's whimpering increased in volume as he gripped the door handle. He tried not to look at her as he pushed in the button beneath the handle and pulled the door open, but the loud squeal and the gurgling sounds that followed drew his gaze helplessly in that direction anyway. He saw the wire sink deep into her flesh with shocking ease, resulting in a fountain-like spray of blood, a line of pulsing red stretching from one side of her neck to the other.

The blonde woman was clapping. It was a slow clap. She was mocking him again. "I like the lack of hesitation, pig-boy.

The way you value self-preservation above all other things is truly inspiring."

Nick grunted.

He got in the car and pulled the door shut.

NINETEEN

IN THE BACK of the truck again, Emma huddled with him in that same back corner once more, the wind gusting and the snow falling fast and heavy. Not ideal driving weather. The town would look like an arctic outpost by sunrise. An argument was made that it might be better to wait for more optimal conditions before attempting to mount a revolution. There was disagreement among the members of the pack, boiling dissent that became palpable within those first few moments in the back room at Crockett's, fueled by their intense distrust of outsiders. They nonetheless listened like Quist told them to, quiet and respectful while Ray Hall and Glenn Carrow made their case.

Sean saw the sense in it all right away. The plan came with a heavy element of risk and danger. There was no attempt to downplay that at all. They'd all be putting their lives on the line should the pack decide to join forces with the outsiders, with no guarantee any of them would survive the night. The sheriff's argument was, in part, that the adverse conditions could actually aid the cause, because the Elders would have their guard down, never suspecting participants in a violent revolt would come for them in the middle of a blizzard.

Another thing the sheriff had said also made sense to Sean. He told the Night Wolves the rule of the Elders had lasted for so long that by now they'd grown complacent, comfortable in the perceived safety of their elevated station within the community. Another contributing factor to their theoretical complacency was the secretiveness that formed the basis of the town's shadow government. The members were all anonymous, unknown to anyone but others within that tight circle. In that way they were similar to the Night Wolves, faceless, dread-invoking phantoms that might be lurking anywhere. The members could have been any of the older citizens of Beleth Station. There was no outward way to discern the difference between a regular older person and an Elder.

Except that was no longer true.

The most shocking of the night's revelations also came courtesy of Ray Hall, who revealed he'd been quietly investigating the matter for years, almost from the start of his tenure as the town's sheriff. The dangerous nature of the investigation required painstaking, methodical slowness, because the Elders had eyes everywhere. One wrong move over the course of those years might have spelled his doom.

He kept at it over all that time, never losing sight of the ultimate goal while simultaneously playing the role of remorseless enforcer, a faithful servant of the Elders who followed every order they ever gave him. All the while he was gathering tiny pieces of information whenever he could, little scraps that over time he was able to piece together, eventually solving a puzzle no one before him ever could.

He knew who the Elders were.

Their names and where they lived.

There was disbelief, initially, in that back room at Crockett's. This was expressed with vehemence. Ray countered by laying it all out again, this time in ever clearer fashion. He named some names. Names that made sense. Names that, when they were spoken, caused things to click into place for some who dissented. Others were reluctant to join the revolt because their identities were so heavily wrapped up in being Night Wolves. That sense of belonging, of being part of something special and exclusive meant everything to them. A few pointed out that the pack was responsible for a lot of things that might land them in trouble in a new vision of Beleth Station as a town open and connected to the world again.

That was when another bombshell was dropped.

Ray made a guarantee of blanket amnesty for all Night Wolves who chose to join the revolt. They would not be held responsible for anything done during the repressive rule of the Elders. If the revolt succeeded and normalcy was restored to Beleth Station, there might be some grumbling among other citizens with a beef against the Wolves. It was also possible there might be unrest and violence, including acts of retribution. Hall vowed he would do his best to defuse any volatility in the community. In the event some members of the pack felt uncomfortable living among those they once terrorized, however, they could avail themselves of a new option, one not available to the citizens of Beleth Station for decades.

They could simply leave town and never return.

If the Elders were vanquished, *anyone* could leave without fear of being hunted down and returned.

That was a point Hall drove home with particular emphasis.

The power inherent in liberation.

The power of *freedom*.

Sean was sold long before that stirring juncture in Hall's impassioned speech. He'd spent his life dreaming of escape. No one needed to convince him of the rightness of rising up against the Elders. It was other members of the pack who needed persuading. At first he was convinced winning over all of them simply wasn't possible, but there was a distinct shift in the mood of the room as the sheriff made his concluding argument. Pack members muttered among themselves amidst an air of growing excitement. There was a palpable yearning among the mostly young Wolves, an openness to embrace something new and reject the old order.

Quist called for a vote.

The result was unanimous.

The revolt would move forward tonight with the full weight and support of the Night Wolves.

Sean felt Emma grip his hands tight and shiver against him in the back of the truck. "We'll leave this place tomorrow," she told him, whispering, her mouth against his ear. "Leave and never fucking come back, but not before we taste their blood. Not before we kill them all."

He nodded.

She was right.

Absolute annihilation of the entire council of Elders was the only way to assure permanent victory. He didn't relish committing acts of bloody violence the way others in the pack did, but it didn't matter. Brutal violence was called for tonight and he would not shrink from it.

The truck began to slow down.

Sean turned his head and saw they were stopping in the middle of the first block on North Street. A second truck filled with Wolves stopped directly behind them. The decrepit townhouses here were where several members of the council lived, a thing he was surprised to learn near the end of the meeting at Crockett's. It was, however, another thing that made sense upon reflection. The Elders survived for so long by remaining anonymous. Most chose to protect that anonymity by living among the regular members of the community, and not, as Sean had previously imagined, in one of the isolated big houses on the outskirts of town. Most, but not all. There was at least one notable exception, and another team of rebels was en route to that location.

The Wolves piled out of the trucks the instant they came to a full halt. They moved quickly down the middle of the street. Emma continued gripping Sean's hand as they moved with them. As the group reached the end of the first block, some Wolves moved to one side of the street while others moved to the opposite side. A few others continued down the middle of the street, their destinations still ahead of them.

Sean and Emma followed their group toward the left side of the street. Soon they arrived at a three-storey townhouse and spread out around it. Some climbed the stairs to the porch in front, while others circled around to the back, Sean and Emma among them. They all scaled a chain-link fence and moved fast to the back doors of the townhouse. Everyone came armed with varying kinds of weapons. Clubs, knives, machetes, axes, a sledgehammer. Two of the bigger Wolves carried a battering ram.

There was no hesitation.

The battering ram did its work and the door crashed open. There were screams from within as the Wolves streamed into the house.

The slaughter of the Elders was underway.

TWENTY

THE TREACHEROUS CONDITIONS on the winding back road forced Krista to drive at a far slower speed than she would have preferred, the Buick's balding tires sending the vehicle into skids on multiple occasions. She'd grown up in Maine and was therefore adept at preventing skids from turning disastrous, even in a car without snow tires, like this one. Driving at such a reduced speed frustrated her, though. The increased travel time could mean the difference between life and death for Nick. Yes, it was possible he'd perished before she even left the motel, and the additional delay had her anxiety racing out of control.

One skid a couple miles into her journey came perilously close to sending her off the road. She managed to bring the Buick to a slow, swerving halt right at the shoulder of the road. Another couple feet and the car would have gone into the ditch beyond the shoulder, and she doubted her ability to get it back onto the road if that happened. She stayed right there for a moment, her heart pounding after the close call.

The last thing she wanted at this juncture was to wind up on foot on a dark back road in the middle of a blizzard. She wasn't dressed for it, for one thing, and things could go bad for her if she had any kind of accident walking the remaining distance into town. It was something she would attempt if left with no other choice. Staying in a stranded car for hours until some form of help arrived would be unbearable. So long as even the slimmest hope of Nick's survival existed, she would try to get to him, whatever the potential cost, even if it killed her.

She took a deep breath and eased the Buick back onto the road, slowly bringing it up to twenty MPH, the highest speed she felt she could safely attempt in this weather on shitty tires. Slow and frustrating as hell, but worlds better than being on foot.

An additional couple miles crept by and the journey began to feel like an eternity spent inside some snowy version of purgatory. She wished she'd paid more attention to the terrain on the way out to Paradise Inn, but she'd been too focused on the sheriff's strange demeanor to pay anything else much mind. Thinking of the sheriff made her think of the straight razor. Remembering the way he'd manhandled her into the motel room made her seethe with anger. His bullshit about working on a way to help especially infuriated her. She'd love nothing more than an opportunity to unzip his throat with the blade.

Just when she began to suspect she might never find her way back into town, she guided the Buick around yet another wide, looping curve and at last glimpsed the lights of Beleth Station. As before, the lighting was sparse, the furthest thing imaginable from a glittering metropolis. It looked even deader through the thick veiling of gusting snow.

She slowed the car and turned down the stretch of road that would take her straight into the heart of town. The same road she'd traveled with Nick not so long ago. She slowed further upon realizing there were lights ahead of her that weren't town lights, grimacing when she saw that two large pickup trucks were parked bumper-to-bumper across the road, blocking the way in. Spotlights mounted to the doors were aimed her way, making her squint as she brought the Buick to a stop ten feet short of the roadblock.

A man clad in a parka and armed with a shotgun approached and knocked on the window before taking a step back. Before he reached the vehicle, Krista retrieved the closed straight razor and held it in her lap, palm down to keep it out of sight. The windows in the Buick had old-fashioned hand cranks to roll them down. She used the one on the driver's side door and was once again forced to squint, this time against the snow that swirled through the opening.

"What's going on, officer?"

The words immediately made her feel stupid. Those trucks were not law enforcement issue. This man perhaps worked in some capacity for the weirdos who ran this strange town, but he was not a cop. The same undoubtedly went for the one other person in the vicinity, another parka-wearing man armed with a shotgun. He was leaning against one of the trucks with his weapon pointed at the ground. Looking bored.

The one who'd approached bent over slightly to peer into the Buick. His eyes flicked to the backseat for an instant before focusing on Krista again. "I recognize this shitheap. This isn't your car."

Krista sighed. "I just bought it from the asshole pimp who had it before me. Like, earlier tonight, before the snow."

The man held her gaze for a moment that stretched out just long enough to make her uncomfortable. She was intensely conscious of the deadly sharp piece of steel gripped in her hand during that moment and found herself wishing the man would lean just a little closer.

The man frowned. "I've seen women in this car before. Always riding in back when the pimp shows up at Nowhere Special on Saturday nights. Never in the front. And never alone. And none of them ever looked like you."

"What's that supposed to mean?"

The man's frown morphed, becoming a deep smirk. "All those whores are used up old hags. You look classy. Too classy to ever buy a car from a pimp. You're not from here at all."

Krista didn't have a retort for that. No easy lie to throw back at him.

He was right.

She wasn't from here. And she was too classy for this entire fucking town.

Faking an emotional sniffle, she bowed her head and muttered some words the man wouldn't be able to make out in the gusting wind. Just as she'd hoped, he stepped closer and lowered his head.

He asked her to repeat what she'd said.

She looked at him and said, "You're a dead man."

The straight razor felt so right and natural in her hand, like an extension of her flesh as she flipped it open and reached through the window with her other hand. She grabbed hold of the parka and pulled him close. Her quick movements caught him off guard, and before he could even attempt to resist or fight back, the exquisitely sharp steel was ripping open his throat. A warm rush of blood coated her hand and she loved it. The shotgun slipped from his grasp, landing in the snow. She held onto him as he gurgled and weakly tried to pull away, and dragged the blade across his throat a second time. The second time was just to savor the feeling of his flesh yielding to steel. More blood poured out over her hand, the eruption like ejaculate at the end of an act of dark passion.

Still holding onto him as he sagged against the door, Krista glanced out the windshield to see whether the man leaning against the truck had taken notice of her impulsive act of murder. His head was lowered and his shotgun was still pointed at the ground. There'd been alcohol on the breath of the man she'd just killed. Maybe his partner had been hitting the bottle even harder.

Whatever the case, the time to act was now.

She shoved the dying man away from the Buick, opened the door, and stepped out into the gusting, howling wind and heavy snow. At first she considered picking up the shotgun and using it to blow away the other man at a distance, but she'd never operated any kind of firearm before and feared the discharge might knock her off her feet.

Steel was what she trusted, so steel she would use.

She moved as fast as she could through the accumulation of snow in her ankle boots, which was just fast enough to bring her within a few feet of the other man before he finally stirred and looked up at her with an expression of boozy surprise. Like his partner, he was too slow to react. His throat was open and gushing wonderfully warm, orgasmic blood before he could even start to raise his shotgun.

Krista dragged him to the snowy ground and sat astride him as she ripped at his throat a few more times. Her thighs quivered as she felt him shudder and go still beneath her.

She touched his face and smiled. "Thank you."

A few moments later she was behind the wheel of one of the heavy duty pickup trucks.

She got it pointed toward town and pushed the pedal down.

TWENTY ONE

AN UNEXPECTED NOISE from elsewhere in the house made Robert Livingston flinch in his recliner. Until then his attention had been glued to the closed-circuit video feed of the evening's running of the Gauntlet. There was no sound, but the 4K video quality itself was superb.

Given the harsh wintry conditions outside, watching the event on the eighty-inch screen mounted on the wall in his den made for a far better experience than being there in person. It beat the hell out of moving down the street with the other spectators, which required constant jostling for a better view of the proceedings. As an unavoidable consequence of his anonymity, the other attendees never knew to afford him the deference he deserved as leader of the council of Elders.

Upon hearing the noise in his otherwise quiet and isolated estate on the outskirts of Beleth Station, he leaned forward in the recliner and twisted his head around for a view of the short set of steps leading out of the den. He was sure he'd heard a creaking of some kind. The hardwood floors of the house made sounds like that when trod upon, but it would happen with each footstep. The house was the grandest in all of Beleth Station, but it was old. Movement of any kind resulted in perceptible noise. The creaking he heard this time, however, happened only once.

His heart started beating a little faster as he spent another few moments staring at the steps and the glimpse of the dining room beyond. An intruder seemed unlikely on a severe weather night, but he remained attentive for a repetition of the sound a bit longer, unable to discount the possibility entirely. There was a remote chance some desperate fool from town might attempt to break in, perhaps in search of valuables that could be exchanged for drugs, but the likelihood of any such idiot breaching his security system was low. A well-compensated guard was on duty in a cabin on the estate's grounds at all times. The guard monitored video feeds from all quadrants of the estate and would have alerted him immediately to any form of trespass.

There'd been no such alert tonight.

After a few minutes elapsed, he dismissed the possibility of an intruder, deciding what he'd heard was a house settling sound. Those weren't common, but they did happen at times, a consequence of the age of the place, which once belonged to the president of the old mill. The town seized it after Medallion declared bankruptcy, with Robert moving in with his wife not long thereafter. She was dead now.

Robert did not miss the stern old harridan. If the benzene-induced cancer hadn't killed her, he would eventually have taken measures to have her eliminated. He was not a sentimental man. The plight of his town's downtrodden citizens didn't concern him in the least. To the contrary, he often reveled in their suffering. As a key architect of the new order that arose in the wake of the mill's closing, he considered the suffering of the common rabble part of the point, a feature rather than a bug.

He was also the original mastermind behind the Gauntlet, but had not participated in running the event in years. A man named Danny Lawson had taken over orchestrating the thing for nearly a decade, but he was killed by a Gauntlet participant four years back, at which point Lawson's beautiful and brilliant daughter, Rebecca, took over for him. Under her guidance, the event became more popular than ever, with a far greater percentage of the town's remaining population turning out to watch in person. She had a genius-level creative mind, with a penchant for extreme sadism. His kind of woman, in other

words. He only regretted that he'd become too old and decrepit
to interest her on a sexual level. Oh, sure, he could take her by
force if he so desired, but he wouldn't want to risk ruining the
Gauntlet by doing anything so drastic.

He leaned back in the recliner as his attention returned to
the video feed. Tonight's participant was still seated behind the
wheel of the heated car. Though there was no sound, he knew
precisely what was happening. Rebecca had provided him with
an outline of her plans for the next running of the Gauntlet
weeks ago. The actual events tended to come up in impromptu
fashion, but the planning that preceded them was extensive and
meticulous, allowing for rapid deployment of all the varied
elements.

The man was being allowed fifteen minutes inside the car.
About half that span had elapsed. Robert was eager to see the
man emerge and proceed to the next stage of the event, which
would be one of the most deliciously staged exercises in grue-
some sadism in the history of the Gauntlet. Rebecca had
outdone herself with this one. It would be a joy to watch,
though perhaps not as much fun as watching the outsider
woman slaughter those whores via the Paradise Inn feed a short
while ago. That'd been transcendent.

He shifted his feet on the human footstool kneeling before
him, making her whimper behind the ball-gag affixed to her
face. The sound pleased him and prompted him to squeeze his
crotch through the fabric of his pajama pants. Later he would
take the footstool to the master bedroom and use her for
another purpose, one that would cause her to scream and plead
rather than merely whimper.

He was still squeezing his crotch when he heard the
creaking sound again.

Louder this time.

He sat forward again and was just turning his head toward
the stairs when the severed head of his security man came
sailing into the den, hit the hardwood floor, and rolled toward
his recliner. A moment of frozen shock ensued, followed by
muffled screams from the human footstool. Robert's heart felt
close to exploding in his chest, a feeling accompanied by heavy
stabs of sharp pain. That pain was more than matched by the

terror he experienced upon seeing the stream of people descending the steps into the den.

One of the intruders was Ray Hall. Another was Glenn Carrow. He knew both men well. Years ago he'd personally overseen the brutal torture of Carrow after the man's failed attempt at insurrection. He'd believed the man permanently cowed by the experience, because otherwise he never would have let him live, but it seemed he was wrong. The others who followed these men into the den had the hard-living look typical of patrons of Carrow's Nowhere Special. He saw now he'd been wrong to tolerate the establishment's existence. He'd thought it a safe way of pacifying the town's malcontents, allowing them a place where they could stew in their terminal alcoholism without causing trouble.

Such a colossal mistake.

He knew he was doomed and made no protestations of outrage as they came toward him and hauled him out of the recliner, nor did he attempt to plead or bargain with them. Anything of that nature would be an affront to his dignity. He would go to whatever grim fate awaited him tonight with that intact, at least.

Or so he thought.

His determination on that front lasted right up to the moment he was forced to march outside with the rebels and told to disrobe. He was shivering already by then, the robe he wore over his pajamas offering scant protection against the gusting wind and heavy snow.

When Robert made no move to remove his clothes, Glenn Carrow stepped forward and delivered a hard punch to the center of his face. The cartilage in his nose snapped and blood gushed from his nostrils. He wailed in pain and flailed weakly against the multiple sets of hands grabbing at his garments and tearing them away from his body. Within a few moments, his pitiful attempt at resistance ended with him standing naked and quivering before the rebels. They laughed and said unkind things about his bony, shriveled frame.

Ray Hall approached with a paper sack in hand. He had a smirk on his face as he took a long necklace of raw meat from the sack and draped it over Robert's head. The pieces of meat looked like fresh cuts from the butcher shop inside Old Jim's General Store. They'd been fed through a length of thin metallic wire. The cold meat hanging against his bare chest added to his discomfort. He had no clue what the purpose of the meat necklace was, but strongly suspected it was something awful.

That was when he started crying.

And begging.

Like the pitiful, pathetic wretch he now was.

Hall slapped him hard across the face, eliciting a yelp.

He sniffled and whimpered some more before meeting the traitorous sheriff's gaze. "How did you find me out? I've always been so careful."

Hall laughed. "Does it matter? Your time is finished. You and your cronies are all going down tonight. Tomorrow will be a new day in Beleth Station. A *better* day."

Robert managed one last display of defiance. He sneered and said, "There is so much I can offer you. Money. Women. Anything you desire. All you have to do is take out your gun and shoot all these people. Then all will be forgotten and forgiven."

Hall didn't bother responding.

He turned partly away from Robert Livingston and pointed to the street at the bottom of the large, sloping lawn. "Tonight you run the Gauntlet. See that car parked at the edge of the street?" He took out his gun as he turned back toward Robert and pointed it at his face. "Soon I'll start counting to five. You need to start running as soon as I start. When I get to five, I'll start trying to shoot you down. The odds aren't in your favor, but if you make it to the car alive, we'll let you go. The keys are in the ignition. You can just drive away. Leave town forever. I don't fucking care, just so long as you're gone."

Robert frowned.

There was so much he didn't understand about this exercise.

"But why–"

Hall cocked the hammer of his revolver and started counting.

Robert ran.

He'd gotten perhaps twenty feet down the hill when Hall fired his gun for the first time. The fresh shock of terror that hit at the sound of the weapon's massively loud report caused him to stumble and pitch forward face-first into the snow. The cold that enveloped him was unbearable. He was quickly becoming numb as he pushed himself up and tried getting back to his feet. The gun boomed again, causing him to stumble and fall again. He wailed in despair but kept trying, eventually managing to regain his footing and resume his plunge down the hill.

More loud reports from the gun echoed in the night. He screamed at each report, expecting bullets to perforate his flesh at any moment, but that never happened. It didn't occur to him that Hall might not actually be firing at him until he reached the car and started pulling the door open.

By then it was too late.

The door was open.

Inside was the largest wolf he'd ever seen.

Not one of the Night Wolves, but a real one. It leapt from the car and slammed into him, driving him to the snow-covered ground. Robert Livingston's final scream was a short one, ending as the wolf tore out his throat.

The leader of the council of Elders was dead.

TWENTY TWO

THE GROUP SEAN and Emma were assigned to was given just one directive before entering the townhouse on North Street, and that was to kill everyone inside without hesitation and without regard to the advanced age or physical fragility of their targets. There was no doubt the tactic would make sacrifices of at least a few innocent people, which was regrettable but unavoidable. Successful elimination of the entire council of Elders hinged on leaving nothing to chance. There could be dire consequences if even one of them slipped away unharmed, and though the Wolves knew the names and locations of all the Elders thanks to information provided by Ray Hall, they would not recognize all of them by sight.

Therefore the only solution was absolute annihilation.

The Wolves conducted their business with bloody abandon, painting the walls and floors red with the blood of their enfeebled targets. There were seven of them living inside the house. Three were council members and four were not. That was all they knew. It didn't matter. All of them had to die.

A few tried to stand and fight but were cut down within moments. Others screamed and made ineffective attempts to elude the determined pursuers. Blood from a severed jugular vein hit Sean in the face as he dashed by a man seconds away from death. He had his eyes on the back of one of those who lacked the courage to fight, a scrawny, limping man with a shawl draped around his bony shoulders. The man was hobbling his way toward an open bathroom door, perhaps with the intent of barricading himself inside. All exits from the house were effectively blocked. The man had no other options.

Taking him down would be no more difficult than stepping on a household pest. He would derive no pleasure from killing a man as frail as this one, but this was a historic night in Beleth Station and he was determined to play an active part in liberating the town. Leaving this place without blood on his hands simply wasn't acceptable.

Perhaps sensing he had no chance to reach the open door in time to get inside and close it before being pounced upon, the old man turned and took a swing at Sean with his cane. The ornate silver handle cracked against the side of Sean's head, staggering him.

Emma rushed past him and launched herself at the old man, hitting him in the midsection and driving him through the open door. She landed atop him on the bathroom floor and unleashed a scream of righteous fury as she stabbed him in the eye with her knife.

Wild strands of blonde hair fell across her face as she twisted about and made eye contact with Sean. "Come on, finish him."

Still wincing from the blow, he staggered into the bathroom and moved around her until he was standing over the fallen man, who was letting out reedy little screeches of pain. Emma extracted the knife from the man's eye and looked up at Sean, proffering the blade.

"Do it."

Sean waved away the offer of the blade.

He moved a little closer, until he was positioned directly above the doomed man's head. Anger surged within him. Maybe this man was an actual Elder and maybe he wasn't, but there was no doubt he was connected to them in some way. He thought of all the suffering these people had caused and raised one of his booted feet off the floor, smashing the heavy heel into the man's face. Teeth shattered and the man's jaw came unhinged. Sean brought his boot down again and again, turning the already dead man's head into a pile of bloody mush.

Emma surged to her feet and turned her head toward the

ceiling, howling in the familiar manner of the Night Wolves.

Sean howled along with her.

A short time later, the Wolves streamed out of the house, the mission assigned to them a resounding success. Only Wolves emerged from that house alive, and now they were moving down the street, howling again, letting those residents of Beleth Station who could hear them know that the revolution was underway.

Nick felt sorrow for the woman he'd killed by opening the sedan's door, but he did not feel guilt. Sacrificing himself so that she might live a little while longer would have accomplished nothing of value. She was doomed already, that much was clear from the moment he set eyes on her, and he still harbored some miniscule hope of getting free and finding Krista. He didn't need anyone to tell him how unlikely that was. He knew it. Nonetheless he had no intention of giving up, not so long as he was still drawing breath.

A Club steering wheel lock was in place, denying him the opportunity to simply drive away. This was frustrating, but not unexpected. The blonde woman who was the apparent architect of the Gauntlet was too smart to allow him an easy means of escape. He turned his head and saw her smirking at him from about six feet away. There was a look of cold calculation on her face, a dark promise of far worse things to come. She was evil and possibly insane but also something of a deranged genius. Recognizing this was the thing that disturbed him most, even more than the acts of murder he'd been coerced into committing. He was not at all confident in his ability to outwit her.

The question of how to even try was, however, something he felt unable to answer given his current state of deep misery. He was still in the grip of a freezing chill that penetrated to his bones and it was several minutes before he could even begin to stop shivering. The one bright side was that the blonde had delivered on her promise of a heated car, with air blowing hot through the wide-open vents on the dash. He figured ten of his allotted fifteen minutes had elapsed by the time he finally started feeling warm. At that point, he snatched the folded flannel shirt off the passenger seat and pulled it on, rapidly buttoning it up with fingers that weren't shaking nearly as much now.

He was reaching for the winter boots when he heard a scream from somewhere outside.

Followed by more screams and a weird howling.

The masked spectators at the sides of the street looked around, clearly confused by whatever was happening. He didn't need to see their faces to know it was something startling and unexpected.

A crashing sound from somewhere up the street sparked more confusion.

Nick pushed the sneakers off his feet and pulled on the boots.

Rebecca Lawson felt a sense of almost delirious anticipation as she stared at the man ensconced behind the wheel of the sedan. Though he would face several more daunting tests before the night was over, she believed he might yet prove to be one of the occasional outsiders with the fortitude to make it all the way through the Gauntlet. It would not pain her to see him fail, of course, but nor would she be sad to see him succeed.

In the event of the latter, she would have him taken to her house, a large estate on the outskirts of town a few miles down the road from the one owned by Robert Livingston. After having him shackled to her bed, she would spend some time torturing and teasing him, arousing him against his will. It was easy to do. They always thought they could resist, after having endured so much pain at her hands, but they were always wrong. She was an expert at eliciting pleasure even from the most abused of her subjects.

This man would be no exception.

At the end of it, she would remove her clothes and plant herself on his face, forcing him to pleasure her with his tongue for as long as she desired, a time that might stretch out for an hour or more. Until he was begging her to let him stop. She wouldn't allow that, of course.

And then, once she was finally satisfied, she would

dismount and go to work on him with her blades, removing the face she'd sat upon. It'd be cured and dried and mounted inside a frame on a wall in her study, allowing her to always remember the fun she'd had with him.

She was so deep in her reverie that she didn't hear the howling from the nearby street until moments after it'd started. When it finally registered, she initially felt only confusion, but that quickly gave way to a burgeoning sense of alarm.

She frowned.

Something's not right.

She turned to one of her assistants with the intention of telling him to investigate, but by then it was too late. Dozens of Night Wolves accompanied by a number of regular citizens came pouring out of the alleys on both sides of the street, wading into the crowd of spectators. All were armed with heavy blades and bludgeons. A few had guns.

Screams rang out.

So did gunshots.

Bodies fell and sprays of blood turned the white snow red. Rebecca gaped in astonishment at the chaos unfolding around her. It was so unlike anything she'd ever seen happen in tightly controlled Beleth Station. Until now, she'd believed her position of power could not be challenged.

She'd felt safe. Protected.

But now…

One of her assistants grabbed her by the wrist, perhaps intending to pull her to a place of safety, but the sudden movement startled her, causing her to twist away from him. The man was screaming something at her from behind the cloth sack over his head, but before she could focus on the words, she heard the roar of a powerful engine approaching from behind.

She was just turning toward the sound when the front of the heavy duty pickup truck slammed into her.

Krista Mabry saw the blonde woman sail through the air and smack against the side of the blue sedan, hitting a rear door hard enough to leave an imprint of crumpled metal as she dropped to the ground and stopped moving. She had no idea who the woman was and didn't care. All she knew was the bitch was in her way.

A man dressed all in black went to the fallen woman's side. He had a sack over his head, one that looked just like the one worn by the man who'd chased her earlier in the evening. Maybe this was him. He tore it away and cast it aside as he attempted to rouse the woman, his efforts quickly turning frantic.

Krista's first impulse was to step on the gas again and plow into the man, plastering him against the side of the sedan. She'd just lifted her foot off the brake when one of the sedan's doors began to open. When she saw that the man emerging from the car was Nick, she screamed and put the truck in park. A moment later, she was out of the truck and rushing toward him. There was a look of stunned amazement on his face as she threw herself against him. Then his arms were around her and he was holding her tight, sobbing in relief and telling her over and over how much he loved her, how happy he was to see her.

A faint perception of movement in her peripheral vision caused her to abruptly break out of the embrace. The straight razor flicked open as the man in black rose to his feet and turned toward them, a gun in his hand. As before, the blade felt like a natural extension of her flesh. She wielded the length of steel with speed and precision. The falling snow never touched the blade as it whipped through the cold air in an arc that was straight and true. The man's jugular opened and once again she was rewarded with a geyser of warm blood that splashed against her neck and chest. He was doomed but made a last-ditch attempt to raise the gun anyway. Her blade flashed again, slicing deep across the back of his hand. He dropped the gun as he gurgled and staggered away from her, his hands going to his throat as he dropped to his knees.

Krista looked at Nick, fearing she'd see judgment in his eyes for the vicious thing she'd done, but instead she saw only reverence and love. They embraced again and she felt him shivering against her.

"You poor baby. Let's get you in the truck where it's warm."

Nick murmured in assent, but then he said, "Hold on. There's something I want to do first."

He went to the blonde woman and knelt at her side, holding a hand over her face to check for breathing. Next he touched her throat with his fingers. The woman stirred, moaning softly in pain. As soon as he heard this, Nick grabbed her under the arms and started dragging her away from the sedan. He kept dragging her until he reached the idling truck, where he angled her body so that it was sticking outward from the truck.

Her head was wedged beneath one of the front tires.

He glanced at Krista. "Trust me, she's got this coming."

Krista smiled. "I believe you. Do what you need to do. I'll watch."

The woman moaned again as Nick hopped up into the truck. She lifted a shaky hand in a vaguely beseeching way but still lacked the strength to move. The truck shifted slightly as Nick worked the gear shifter. Then the engine revved a little as the big, heavy tire rolled forward. At the last possible moment, the blonde woman tried moving her head, but it was too late. The tire first pressed it into the snow before popping it like a melon. There was a satisfying crunch and a bright burst of red.

Krista ran to the other side of the truck and climbed in next to Nick.

All around them, chaos continued to unfold. Unmasked people continued to chase and slaughter the masked ones. She had no clue what was happening or why and cared only to the extent that the confusion might allow them to slip away unimpeded. This was a strange town to start with and now it looked like it was at war with itself.

Nick got the truck turned around and started driving. By the time they'd moved forward no more than another block, the way ahead was empty, devoid of vehicles and people. Krista glanced at the side mirror and saw only vague black shapes struggling against each other through the veil of heavy, swirling snow.

They kept going and soon arrived at the spot on the road out of town where she'd killed the men stationed at the roadblock. Their bodies were already being covered by the falling snow. Nick appeared to take only brief notice of them and did not comment. One side of the truck's tires went up and down for a moment as they rolled over one of the corpses.

Not long after that, they were on the road that would take them to the interstate junction. They held hands as Nick drove with one hand, neither saying anything. A time would come when there would be much to discuss, but that time was not now. For now it was enough that they were together again, and that they were still alive and might still have a long future together. Not everything was certain. She'd discovered something new and enthralling about herself, but it was a dangerous thing, a thing she might not be able to share with him or anyone else. It was something to figure out later.

There was a tense moment as they came upon another apparent roadblock. Their clasped hands squeezed tighter. Krista wondered whether the men at this roadblock were armed and what might happen. She squeezed the razor. Perhaps she'd have to use it one more time on the way out of town. She soon saw it would be unnecessary, though. The vehicles blocking the way ahead were pulling away from each other. One turned back toward town while the other went in the opposite direction. As the truck headed toward town drove slowly past them, the bearded driver waved in a way that was almost friendly.

Then the other truck was gone and they were alone on the road again.

Nick looked at Krista. "That was weird."

She nodded. "Yeah."

Something big was going on in this town. Some kind of major shift. She didn't know what it meant and didn't care. They were alive and freedom was within reach. Nothing else mattered.

Nick started driving again and soon they arrived at the interstate junction. He steered them onto the snow-covered ramp and kept going, proceeding with slow caution until they reached the interstate. He increased their speed slightly at that point, but continued to drive slowly in the treacherous conditions. There was no need for recklessness. No one was coming after them.

Soon they were well beyond the town limits of Beleth Station.

They were free.

EPILOGUE

AN EXODUS of many of Beleth Station's surviving citizens began early the next morning. Following the slaughter of the Elders and the subsequent purge of those loyal to the old regime, they were free to leave and go wherever they wanted. Some emerged from their homes and began loading belongings into their vehicles even before sunrise. Many others followed suit not long thereafter. A few worked with frantic speed, still not fully trusting their newfound freedom. They feared it would be revoked if they lingered even a single moment longer than absolutely necessary.

Ray Hall couldn't blame them.

It was hard to believe or trust in anything after being trapped in this place for so long, let alone something as momentous as what had transpired overnight. A profound degree of paranoia lived deep in the hearts of all these people. They wouldn't believe they were truly free until they were hundreds of miles down the road from Beleth Station.

Ray drove slowly up and down the snow-packed streets, watching as the people preparing to leave regarded him with a still-elevated level of wariness. He acknowledged the expressionless looks they gave him with friendly little nods and waves. By now they all knew he was the instigator of last night's events, but the knowledge made no difference to many who previously had only known him as a dedicated servant of the Elders. That he'd served them only to facilitate eventually bringing them down also made no difference. He bore them no ill will for their mistrust. He'd done much to deserve it, after all.

The heavy snow had stopped only about an hour before sunrise. At Ray's behest, Virgil Parker got to work with one of the town's only two snow plows almost as soon as it ceased falling, clearing the way for anyone who wanted to leave sooner rather than later. As it turned out, that was most of the town, which wasn't surprising. Quist, the former leader of the now disbanded Night Wolves, was out clearing the outlying roads with the other plow. Most of the Wolves were already gone, knowing they likely had no place in whatever remained of Beleth Station once things settled.

The first of the regular citizens to leave started heading out as soon as the streets were clear, with more following by the minute. Before long, a caravan of slow-moving cars formed, the drivers proceeding with caution along the still-icy streets. Among those departing as the sun rose was that kid Sean Crane and his girl Emma. They didn't even glance at Ray as they rolled by his cruiser on the kid's motorcycle. Again, he was okay with the lack of acknowledgment. That those youngsters would get to live out the rest of their hopefully long lives in some better, more prosperous place thanks to the things he'd done was all the validation he needed.

Later in the day, he parked his cruiser at the station and walked over to Nowhere Special just as it was opening.

Glenn Carrow was at his usual spot behind the bar. He gave Ray a nod and started pouring him a beer as soon as he came through the door.

Ray took a seat at the bar and sipped his beer as he took a look around. Several of last night's participants in the rebellion were still sleeping it off on the floor, on the pool tables, or up on the stage, having crashed here after a long night of celebration and revelry.

Carrow sipped from a mug of steaming coffee. "Lot of people leaving today."

Ray nodded. "Yep. Pretty much a mass exodus."

"About how many are left, you think? Rough guess."

Ray shrugged. "Hard to say, but I'm gonna guess we might

have a couple hundred die-hards sticking around after all is said and done."

Carrow sipped more of his coffee and made a contemplative sound. "Out of a population of just over a thousand. That's steep. Town might not survive this."

Ray grunted. "Town might not deserve to survive this."

A lengthy silence ensued as the men thought about things and consumed their beverages.

Carrow set down his empty mug and cleared his throat. "Will you be staying?"

Ray sighed. "Not sure yet." He finished his first beer of the day. The first of many probably. He hadn't been able to participate in last night's revelry and felt ready to embark on a delayed bender. "Think maybe I'll stick around a while and see what happens. Maybe leave later on, I don't know. What about you?"

Rather than answering immediately, Carrow opened a fresh bottle of bourbon and poured two amber inches into a clean-ish glass. "Don't know. Might not be possible to keep this place open with so few people left. But I'm in no hurry to leave just yet, knowing those motherfuckers are gone now. Guess I'll stick around and see what happens, too. For now."

Ray chuckled.

Carrow poured him another beer.

They clinked glasses, raising a toast to their uncertain futures.

Somewhere outside, a lone wolf prowling the largely empty streets of Beleth Station turned its head skyward and howled.

ACKNOWLEDGMENTS

Many thanks to Christoph and Leza, as well as the entire CLASH Books team, for publishing and believing in *Beleth Station*. Additionally, thank you to my co-author Bryan Smith for embarking on this adventure with me. This book would not exist without our storytelling synergy and I'm grateful we were able to create together.

Best,
Samantha Kolesnik

ABOUT THE AUTHOR

Samantha Kolesnik is an award-winning author of horror and transgressive fiction. Her debut novel, *True Crime*, was released in 2020 to much acclaim from within and outside of the horror community, earning praise from *iHorror*, *CrimeReads*, *The Library Journal*, *LitReactor*, and more.

Kolesnik's sophomore work, *Waif*, was featured in the Night Worms February subscription package, and has earned praise from *iHorror*, *Mystery and Suspense Magazine*, *The Line-Up*, and more. Kolesnik is a two-time Splatterpunk Award winner, as well as a Bram Stoker Award nominated editor for her horror anthology, *Worst Laid Plans*, now a motion picture from Genre-Blast Films.

Samantha Kolesnik is represented by literary agent Emmy Nordstrom Higdon at Westwood Creative Artists.

Website: www.samanthakolesnik.com

Twitter: @samkolesnik

Bryan Smith is the Splatterpunk Award-winning author of more than thirty horror and crime books, including *68 Kill*, the cult classic *Depraved* and its sequels, as well as *The Killing Kind*, *Slowly We Rot*, *The Freakshow*, and many more. Bestselling horror author Brian Keene called *Slowly We Rot*, "The best zombie novel I've ever read."

68 Kill was adapted into a motion picture directed by Trent Haaga and starring Matthew Gray Gubler of the long-running CBS series Criminal Minds. 68 Kill won the Midnighters Award at the SXSW film festival in 2017 and was released to wide acclaim, including positive reviews in *The New York Times* and *Bloody Disgusting*.

Bryan also co-scripted an original Harley Quinn story for the

House of Horrors anthology from DC Comics. He has worked with renowned horror publishers in both the mass market and small press spheres, including Leisure Books, Samhain Publishing, Grindhouse Press, Death's Head Press, and more. His works are available wherever books are sold, with select titles also available in German and Italian.

Website: www.bryansmithauthor.com

Twitter: @Bryan_D_Smith

ALSO BY CLASH BOOKS

WE PUT THE LIT IN LITERARY

CLASHBOOKS.COM

FOLLOW US

TWITTER
IG
FB

@clashbooks

CPSIA information can be obtained
at www.ICGtesting.com
Printed in the USA
JSHW080849170423
40353JS00002B/2

9 781955 904834